PRAISE FOR JENNIFER EGAN'S

THE KEEP

"Jennifer Egan is one of the most gifted writers of her generation. . . . The risk-taking writer has created an original, postmodern take on the Gothic thriller."

—*Seattle Post-Intelligencer*

"Egan's third novel . . . is a strange, clever, and always compelling meditation on the relationship between the imagination and the captivities (psychological, metaphysical, and even physical) of modern life." —*The Atlantic Monthly*

"Visionary. . . . At once hyperrealistic and darkly dreamed. . . . With Egan's powers of invention running at full tilt, *The Keep* reads like a twenty-first-century mash-up of Kafka, Calvino, and Poe, in which the absurd meets the surreal meets the unspeakable—to edgy, entertaining effect." —*Elle*

"Remarkable. . . . Egan effectively echoes the works of Gothic writers such as Ann Radcliffe (*The Mysteries of Udolpho*) and Horace Walpole (*The Castle of Otranto*), fusing a seemingly moribund genre with elements borrowed from the metafictions of John Barth, Italo Calvino and others. It's tricky; but it's a trick only a terrifically talented writer could pull off." —*San Francisco Chronicle*

"It's precisely Egan's talent for tapping into the American subconscious—with deeply intuitive forays into the darker aspects of our technology-driven, image-saturated culture—that has established the author and journalist as a prescient literary voice."
—*Vogue*

"Egan's clever scenario presents Danny's mental liberation as both thrilling and dangerous—imagination is the ultimate drug, she suggests—and the novel luxuriates in Wilkie Collins–style atmospherics."
—*The New Yorker*

"If Kafka's Joseph K. and Lewis Carroll's Alice had a son, he would have to be Jennifer Egan's Danny. . . . No matter how many symbols and zany subplots she juggles . . . the novelist keeps the action moving and the irony biting."
—*The Boston Globe*

"Egan is an exceptionally intelligent writer whose joy at appropriating and subverting genres and clichés—from prison memoir to Gothic ghost story—is evident on every dizzyingly inventive page."
—*The Washington Post*

"Intelligent, intense and remarkably intuitive."
—*The New York Observer*

"Egan spins a haunting tale. . . . [Her] brilliance is in balancing the deliciously creepy elements of Gothic-castle novels with the dead-on realism of a prisoner's life, to create a book worth keeping."
—*Vanity Fair*

"Egan gets everything right—from the convolutions of the strung-out male mind to the self-deceptions of a drug addict—and her skill will keep you marveling at the pages that you can't help turning."
—*People*

"Arresting. . . . Insightful and often funny, so fluid that you actually have the sensation of sinking into these lives. . . . Strange and beautifully drawn, a place well worth visiting."
—*USA Today*

"Dazzling. . . . A metafictional tour de force. . . . It draws us in with its compelling realism as surely as anything by Dickens or Balzac—not to mention Henry James, who understood better than anyone how to turn the screw."
—*Chicago Sun-Times*

"Egan breaks the mold from page one. . . . [*The Keep*] maintains a frightening, vertiginous velocity. . . . The immersion in these high-stakes psychological tightrope acts gives *The Keep* a page-turning horror. . . . Outstanding." —*The Onion*

"A hypnotic tale of unexpected connections between isolated people, each concealing secrets that ultimately upend how we see them. . . . Though dark with betrayal and violence (both psychological and literal), *The Keep* ultimately reveals itself to be a love letter to the creative impulse." —*Newsday*

"Egan is a contemporary American storyteller in the vein of Stephen King or *The Sopranos* scriptwriters. Her latest novel, a slightly Gothic tale of love and the (possibly) supernatural, is a pleasure to read." —*Minneapolis Star Tribune*

"A dark and fascinating journey. . . . Egan skillfully builds the tension to a tipping point, culminating in an explosion. . . . The complicated plot comes together seamlessly, marvelously." —*Rocky Mountain News*

JENNIFER EGAN

THE KEEP

Jennifer Egan is the author of *Look at Me*, which was a finalist for the 2001 National Book Award, *The Invisible Circus*, and the story collection *Emerald City*. Her nonfiction appears frequently in *The New York Times Magazine*. She lives with her family in Brooklyn, New York.

ALSO BY JENNIFER EGAN

Look at Me

Emerald City and Other Stories

The Invisible Circus

THE KEEP

[handwritten notes surrounding the printed title]

alto - 6, 117, 219, 250

wom - 14, 155, 164 (qu-How Hand)

1st pers nar in

(section break line on 17?)

20 - Rays sophie's not Dann - someone told

him the story

47 - Castle, imagined

chap 4

(55) - writing group chronicles

61 - on words [+ sect — break]

*62 — an anticipated melody

68 - (good mg for Dann / phone / mouth

connect

83 - partnership

95 - narrative intrus - 130-1, 162

96 - Dann throws phone - now he's nearly

only in one plane

102 - Davis (Ray's cellmate / Chants o

ghosts

*158 - title - The Keep = heart?

Chapter 11 - the climax - is it a dream

jue pool while unconscious - a is

Howard the dream - Ray, mom

*198 - pt of hotel - experience vs technology /

information

*221 - D & M as twins - so maybe

H's 2 parts of one person - author &

character - ghost who whispers the

story

THE KEEP

JENNIFER EGAN

Anchor Books
A Division of Random House, Inc.
New York

FIRST ANCHOR BOOKS EDITION, JULY 2007

Copyright © 2006 by Jennifer Egan

All rights reserved. Published in the United States by Anchor Books,
a division of Random House, Inc., New York, and in Canada
by Random House of Canada Limited, Toronto. Originally published
in hardcover in the United States by Alfred A. Knopf,
a division of Random House, Inc., New York, in 2006.

Anchor Books and colophon are registered trademarks
of Random House, Inc.

The Library of Congress has cataloged the Knopf edition as follows:
Egan, Jennifer.
The keep / by Jennifer Egan.—1st ed.
p. cm.
1. Cousins—Fiction. 2. Prisoners—Fiction. 3. Europe, Eastern—Fiction.
I. Title.
PS3555.G292K44 2006
813'.54—dc22
2006011573

Anchor ISBN: 978-1-4000-7974-2

Book design by Soonyoung Kwon

www.anchorbooks.com

Printed in the United States of America
10 9 8 7 6 5 4 3 2 1

For the little boys,
Manu and Raoul

PART I

CHAPTER ONE

The castle was falling apart, but at 2 a.m. under a useless moon, Danny couldn't see this. What he saw looked solid as hell: two round towers with an arch between them and across that arch was an iron gate that looked like it hadn't moved in three hundred years or maybe ever.

He'd never been to a castle before or even this part of the world, but something about it all was familiar to Danny. He seemed to remember the place from a long time ago, not like he'd been here exactly but from a dream or a book. The towers had those square indentations around the top that little kids put on castles when they draw them. The air was cold with a smoky bite, like fall had already come even though it was mid-August and people in New York were barely dressed. The trees were losing their leaves—Danny felt them landing in his hair and heard them crunching under his boots when he walked. He was looking for a doorbell, a knocker, a light: some way into this place or at least a way to find the way in. He was getting pessimistic.

Danny had waited two hours in a gloomy little valley town for a bus to this castle that never frigging came before he looked up and saw its black shape against the sky. Then he'd started to walk, hauling his Samsonite and satellite dish a couple of miles up this hill, the Samsonite's puny wheels catching on boulders and tree roots and rabbit holes. His limp didn't help. The whole trip had been like that: one hassle after another starting with the red-eye from Kennedy that got towed into a field after a bomb threat, surrounded by trucks with blinky red lights and giant nozzles that were comforting up until you realized their job was to make sure the fireball *only* incinerated those poor suckers who were already on the plane. So Danny had missed his connection to Prague and the train to wherever the hell he was now, some German-sounding town that didn't seem to be in Germany. Or anywhere else—Danny couldn't even find it online, although he hadn't been sure about the spelling. Talking on the phone to his Cousin Howie, who owned this castle and had paid Danny's way to help out with the renovation, he'd tried to nail down some details.

Danny: I'm still trying to get this straight—is your hotel in Austria, Germany, or the Czech Republic?

Howie: Tell you the truth, I'm not even clear on that myself. Those borders are constantly sliding around.

Danny (thinking): *They are?*

Howie: But remember, it's not a hotel yet. Right now it's just an old—

The line went dead. When Danny tried calling back, he couldn't get through.

But his tickets came the next week (blurry postmark)—plane, train, bus—and seeing how he was newly unemployed and had to get out of New York fast because of a misunderstanding at the restaurant where he'd worked, getting paid to go somewhere else—anywhere else, even the fucking moon—was not a thing Danny could say no to.

He was fifteen hours late.

boots

He left his Samsonite and satellite dish by the gate and circled the left tower (Danny made a point of going left when he
had the choice because most people went right). A wall curved
away from the tower into the trees, and Danny followed that
wall until woods closed in around him. He was moving blind.
He heard flapping and scuttling, and as he walked the trees got
closer and closer to the wall until finally he was squeezing in
between them, afraid if he lost contact with the wall he'd get
lost. And then a good thing happened: the trees pushed right
through the wall and split it open and gave Danny a way to
climb inside.

This wasn't easy. The wall was twenty feet high, jagged
and crumbly with tree trunks crushed into the middle, and
Danny had a tricky knee from an injury connected to the
misunderstanding at work. Plus his boots were not exactly
made for climbing—they were city boots, hipster boots, somewhere between square-tipped and pointy—his lucky boots, or so
Danny thought a long time ago, when he bought them. They
needed resoling. The boots were skiddy even on flat city concrete, so the sight of Danny clawing and scrambling his way
up twenty feet of broken wall was not a thing he would've
wanted broadcast. But finally he made it, panting, sweating,
dragging his sore leg, and hoisted himself onto a flat walkway-
type thing that ran on top of the wall. He brushed off his pants
and stood up.

It was one of those views that make you feel like God for
a second. The castle walls looked silver under the moon,
stretched out over the hill in a wobbly oval the size of a football
field. There were round towers every fifty yards or so. Below
Danny, inside the walls, it was black—pure, like a lake or outer
space. He felt the curve of big sky over his head, full of purplish
torn-up clouds. The castle itself was back where Danny had

alto

started out: a clump of buildings and towers jumbled together. But the tallest tower stood off on its own, narrow and square with a red light shining in a window near the top.

Looking down made something go easier in Danny. When he first came to New York, he and his friends tried to find a name for the relationship they craved between themselves and the universe. But the English language came up short: *perspective, vision, knowledge, wisdom*—those words were all too heavy or too light. So Danny and his friends made up a name: *alto.* True alto worked two ways: you saw but also you could *be seen,* you knew and were known. Two-way recognition. Standing on the castle wall, Danny felt alto—the word was still with him after all these years, even though the friends were long gone. Grown up, probably.

Danny wished he'd brought his satellite dish to the top of this wall. He itched to make some calls—the need felt primal, like an urge to laugh or sneeze or eat. It got so distracting that he slithered back down off the wall and backtracked through those same pushy trees, dirt and moss packed under his longish fingernails. But by the time he got back to the gate his alto was gone and all Danny felt was tired. He left the satellite dish in its case and found a flat spot under a tree to lie down. He made a pile out of leaves. Danny had slept outside a few times when things got rough in New York, but this was nothing like that. He took off his velvet coat and turned it inside out and rolled it into a pillow at the foot of the tree. He lay on the leaves faceup and crossed his arms over his chest. More leaves were coming down. Danny watched them spinning, turning against the half-empty branches and purple clouds, and felt his eyes start to roll back into his head. He was trying to come up with some lines to use on Howie—

Like: *Hey man, your welcome mat could use a little work.*

Or else: *You're paying me to be here, but I'm figuring you don't want to pay your guests.*

Or maybe: *Trust me, outdoor lighting is gonna rock your world.*

—just so he'd have some things to say if there was a silence. Danny was nervous about seeing his cousin after so long. The Howie he knew as a kid you couldn't picture grown up—he'd been wrapped in that pear-shaped girl fat you see on certain boys, big love handles bubbling out of the back of his jeans. Sweaty pale skin and a lot of dark hair around his face. At age seven or eight, Danny and Howie invented a game they'd play whenever they saw each other at holidays and family picnics. Terminal Zeus it was called, and there was a hero (Zeus), and there were monsters and missions and runways and airlifts and bad guys and fireballs and high-speed chases. They could play anywhere from a garage to an old canoe to underneath a dining room table, using whatever they found: straws, feathers, paper plates, candy wrappers, yarn, stamps, candles, staples, you name it. Howie thought most of it up. He'd shut his eyes like he was watching a movie on the backs of his eyelids that he wanted Danny to see: Okay, so Zeus shoots Glow-Bullets at the enemy that make their skin light up so now he can see them through the trees and then—*blam!*—he lassos them with Electric Stunner-Ropes!

Sometimes he made Danny do the talking—Okay, you tell it: what does the underwater torture dungeon look like?—and Danny would start making stuff up: rocks, seaweed, baskets of human eyeballs. He got so deep inside the game he forgot who he was, and when his folks said Time to go home the shock of being yanked away made Danny throw himself on the ground in front of them, begging for another half hour, *please!* another twenty minutes, ten, five, *please,* just one more minute, *please-*

pleaseplease? Frantic not to be ripped away from the world he and Howie had made.

The other cousins thought Howie was weird, a loser, plus he was adopted, and they kept their distance: Rafe especially, not the oldest cousin but the one they all listened to. You're so sweet to play with Howie, Danny's mom would say. From what I understand, he doesn't have many friends. But Danny wasn't trying to be nice. He cared what his other cousins thought, but nothing could match the fun of Terminal Zeus.

When they were teenagers, Howie changed—*overnight* was what everyone said. He had a *traumatic experience* and his sweetness drained away and he turned moody, anxious, always wiggling a foot and muttering King Crimson lyrics under his breath. He carried a notebook, even at Thanksgiving it was there in his lap with a napkin on it to catch the gravy drips. Howie made marks in that book with a flat sweaty pencil, looking around at different family members like he was trying to decide when and how they would have to die. But no one had ever paid much attention to Howie. And after the change, the *traumatic incident,* Danny pretended not to.

Of course they talked about Howie when he wasn't there, oh yeah. Howie's troubles were a favorite family topic, and behind the shaking heads and *oh it's so sad*s you could hear the joy pushing right up through because doesn't every family like having one person who's fucked up so fantastically that everyone else feels like a model citizen next to him? If Danny closed his eyes and listened hard he could still pick up some of that long-ago muttering like a radio station you just barely hear: *Howie trouble drugs did you hear he was arrested such an unattractive boy I'm sorry but can't May put him on a diet he's a teenager no it's more than that I have teenagers you have teenagers I blame Norm for pushing adoption you never know what you're getting it all comes down to genes is what they're learning some people* *are just bad or not bad but you know exactly not bad but just exactly that's it: trouble.*

Danny used to get a weird feeling, overhearing this stuff when he came in the house and his mom was talking on the phone to one of his aunts about Howie. Dirt on his cleats after winning a game, his girlfriend Shannon Shank, who had the best tits on the pom squad and maybe the whole school all set to give him a blow job in his bedroom because she always did that when he won, and thank God he won a lot. *Hiya, Mom.* That square of purple blue almost night outside the kitchen window. Shit, it hurt Danny to remember this stuff, the smell of his mom's tuna casserole. He'd liked hearing those things about Howie because it reminded him of who *he* was, Danny King, *suchagoodboy,* that's what everyone said and what they'd always said but still Danny liked hearing it again, knowing it again. He couldn't hear it enough.

That was memory number one. Danny sort of drifted into it lying there under the tree, but pretty soon his whole body was tensed to the point where he couldn't lie still. He got up, swiping twigs off his pants and feeling pissed off because he didn't like remembering things. *Walking backward* was how Danny thought of that and it was a waste of valuable resources anywhere, anytime, but in a place he'd spent twenty-four hours trying to escape to it was fucking ridiculous.

Danny shook out his coat and pulled it back over his arms and started walking again, fast. This time he went right. At first there was just forest around him, but the trees started thinning out and the slant under his feet got steeper until Danny had to walk with his uphill leg bent, which sent splinters of pain from his knee to his groin. And then the hill dropped away like someone had lopped it off with a knife and he was standing on the edge of a cliff with the castle wall pushed right up against it, so the wall and the cliff made one vertical line pointing up at the sky. Danny stopped short and looked over the cliff's edge. Below, a long way down: trees, bushy black with a few lights packed deep inside that must be the town where he'd waited for the bus.

Alto: he was in the middle of frigging nowhere. It was extreme, and Danny liked extremes. They were distracting.

If I were you, I'd get a cash deposit before I started asking people to spelunk.

Danny tilted his head back. Clouds had squeezed out the stars. The wall seemed higher on this side of the castle. It curved in and then back out again toward the top, and every few yards there was a narrow gap a few feet above Danny's head. He stood back and studied one of these openings—vertical and horizontal slits meeting in the shape of a cross—and in the hundreds of years since those slits had been cut, the rain and snow and what have you must have opened up this one a little bit more. Speaking of rain, a light sprinkling was starting that wasn't much more than a mist, but Danny's hair did a weird thing when it got wet that he couldn't fix without his blow dryer and a certain kind of mousse that was packed away in the Samsonite, and he didn't want Howie to see that weird thing. He wanted to get the fuck out of the rain. So Danny took hold of some broken bits of wall and used his big feet and bony fingers to claw his way up to the slot. He jammed his head inside to see if it would fit and it did, with just a little room to spare that was barely enough for his shoulders, the widest part of him, which he turned and slid through like he was sticking a key in a lock. The rest of him was easy. Your average adult male would've needed a shrinking pill to get through this hole, but Danny had a certain kind of body— he was tall but also bendable, adjustable, you could roll him up like a stick of gum and then unroll him. Which is what happened now: he unraveled himself in a sweaty heap on a damp stone floor.

He was in an ancient basementy place that had no light at all worm   Cave

and a smell Danny didn't like: the smell of a cave. A low ceiling
smacked his forehead a couple of times and he tried walking
with his knees bent, but that hurt his bad knee too much. He
held still and straightened up slowly, listening to sounds of little
creatures scuttling, and felt a twist of fear in his gut like someone wringing out a rag. Then he remembered: there was a mini-
flashlight on his key chain left over from his club days—shining
it into somebody's eyes you could tell if they were on E or smack
or Special K. Danny flicked it on and poked the little beam at the
dark: stone walls, slippery stone under his feet. Movement along
the walls. Danny's breath came quick and shallow, so he tried
slowing it down. Fear was dangerous. It let in the *worm:* another
word Danny and his friends had invented all those years ago,
smoking pot or doing lines of coke and wondering what to call
that thing that happened to people when they lost confidence
and got phony, anxious, weird. Was it *paranoia? Low self-
esteem? Insecurity? Panic?* Those words were all too flat. But the
worm, which is the word they finally picked, the worm was
three-dimensional: it crawled inside a person and started to eat
until everything collapsed, their whole lives, and they ended up
getting strung out or going back home to their folks or being
admitted to Bellevue or, in the case of one girl they all knew,
jumping off the Manhattan Bridge.

More walking backward. And it wasn't helping, it was making things worse.

Danny took out his cell phone and flipped it open. He didn't
have international service, but the phone lit up, searching, and
just seeing it do that calmed Danny down, like the phone had
powers—like it was a Forcefield Stabilizer left over from Terminal Zeus. True, he wasn't connected to anyone right at that
second, but in a general way he was so connected that his con-
nectedness carried him through the dry spells in subways or certain deep buildings when he couldn't actually reach anyone. He

had 304 Instant Messaging usernames and a buddy list of 180. Which is why he'd rented a satellite dish for this trip—a drag to carry, an airport security nightmare, but guaranteed to provide not just cell phone service but wireless Internet access anywhere on planet earth. Danny needed this. His brain refused to stay locked up inside the echo chamber of his head—it spilled out, it overflowed and poured across the world until it was touching a thousand people who had nothing to do with him. If his brain wasn't allowed to do this, if Danny kept it locked up inside his skull, a pressure began to build.

He started walking again, holding the phone in one hand, the other hand up in the air so he'd know when to duck. The place felt like a dungeon, except somehow Danny remembered that dungeons in old castles were usually in the tower—maybe that was the tall square thing he'd seen from the wall with the red light on top: the dungeon. More likely this place had been a sewer.

If you ask me, mother earth could use a little mouthwash.

But that wasn't Danny's line, that was Howie's. He was heading into memory number two, I might as well tell you that straight up, because how I'm supposed to get him in and out of all these memories in a smooth way so nobody notices all the coming and going I don't know. Rafe went first with the flashlight, then Howie. Danny came last. They were all pretty punchy, Howie because his cousins had singled him out to sneak away from the picnic, Danny because there was no bigger thrill in the world than being Rafe's partner in crime, and Rafe—well, the beautiful thing about Rafe was you never knew why he did anything.

Let's show Howie the cave.

Rafe had said this softly, looking sideways at Danny through those long lashes he had. And Danny went along, knowing there would be more.

Howie stumbled in the dark. He had a notebook under one elbow. They hadn't played Terminal Zeus in more than a year. The game ended without talking—one Christmas Eve, Danny just avoided Howie and went off with his other cousins instead. Howie tried a couple of times to come near, catch Danny's eye, but he gave up easily.

Danny: That notebook's messing up your balance, Howie.

Howie: Yeah, but I need it.

Need it why?

For when I get an idea.

Rafe turned around and shined the flashlight straight at Howie's face. He shut his eyes.

Rafe: What're you talking about, get an idea?

Howie: For D and D. I'm the dungeon master.

Rafe turned the beam away. Who do you play with?

My friends.

Danny felt a little stunned, hearing that. Dungeons and Dragons. He had a kind of body memory of Terminal Zeus, the feel of dissolving into that game. And it turned out the game hadn't stopped. It had gone on without him.

Rafe: You sure you've got any friends, Howie?

Aren't you my friend, Rafe? And then Howie laughed and they all did. He was making a joke.

Rafe: This kid is actually pretty funny.

Which made Danny wonder if this could be enough—them being in the boarded-up cave where no one was allowed to go. If maybe nothing else would have to happen. Danny wished very hard for this.

Here's how the cave was laid out: first a big round room with a little bit of daylight in it, then an opening where you had to stoop to get through into another room that was dark, and then a hole you crawled through into room three, where the pool was. Danny had no idea what was beyond that.

They all got quiet when they saw the pool: creamy whitish green, catching Rafe's flashlight beam and squiggling its light over the walls. It was maybe six feet wide and clear, deep.

Howie: Shit, you guys. Shit. He opened up his notebook and wrote something down.

Danny: You brought a pencil?

Howie held it up. It was one of those little green pencils they gave you at the country club to sign your check. He said: I used to bring a pen, but it kept leaking on my pants.

Rafe gave a big laugh and Howie laughed too, but then he stopped, like maybe he wasn't supposed to laugh as much as Rafe.

Danny: What did you write?

Howie looked at him: Why?

I don't know. Curious.

I wrote *green pool.*

Rafe: You call that an idea?

They were quiet. Danny felt a pressure building in the cave like someone had asked him a question and was getting sick of waiting for an answer. Rafe. Now wondering why Danny's older cousin had so much power over him is like wondering why the sun shines or why the grass grows. There are people out there who can make other people do things, that's all. Sometimes without asking. Sometimes without even knowing what they want done.

Danny went to the edge of the pool. Howie, he said, there's a shiny thing down there at the bottom. You see it?

Howie came over and looked. Nope.

There, down there.

Danny squatted next to the pool and Howie did, too, wobbling on the balls of his big feet.

Danny put his hand on his cousin's back. He felt the softness of Howie, how warm he was through his shirt. Maybe Danny had never touched his cousin before, or maybe it was just knowing right then that Howie was a person with a brain and a heart, all the stuff Danny had. Howie clutched his notebook against his side. Danny saw the pages shaking and realized his cousin was scared—Howie felt the danger pulling in around him. Maybe he'd known all along. But he turned his face to Danny with a look of total trust, like he knew Danny would protect him. Like they understood each other. It happened faster than I'm making it sound: Howie looked at Danny and Danny shut his eyes and shoved him into the pool. But even that's too slow: Look. Shut. Shove.

Or just *shove.*

There was the weight of Howie tipping, clawing arms and legs, but no sound Danny could remember, not even a splash. Howie must've yelled, but Danny didn't hear a yell, just the sounds of him and Rafe wriggling out of there and running like crazy, Rafe's flashlight beam strobing the walls, bursting out of the cave into a gush of warm wind, down the two big hills and back to the picnic (where no one missed them), Danny feeling that ring around him and Rafe, a glowing ring that held them together. They didn't say a word about what they'd done until a couple hours later when the picnic was winding down.

Danny: Shit. Where the hell is he?

Rafe: Could be right underneath us.

Danny looked down at the grass. What do you mean, underneath us?

Rafe was grinning. I mean we don't know which way he went.

By the time everyone started fanning out, looking for Howie, something had crawled inside Danny's brain and was chewing out a pattern like those tunnels, all the ways Howie could've gone deeper inside the caves, under the hills. The mood was calm. Howie had wandered off somewhere was what everyone seemed to be thinking—he was fat, he was weird, there was no blood tie, and no one was blaming Danny for anything. But his Aunt May looked more scared than Danny had ever seen a grown-up look, a hand on her throat like she knew she'd lost her boy, her one child, and seeing how far things had gone made Danny even more petrified to say what he knew he had to say— *We tricked him, Rafe and me; we left him in the caves*—because that handful of words would change everything: they would all know what he'd done, and Rafe would know he'd told, and beyond that Danny's mind went blank. So he waited one more second before opening his mouth, and then one more, another and another, and every second he waited seemed to drive some sharp thing deeper into Danny. Then it was dark. His pop put a hand on Danny's head *(suchagoodboy)* and said, They've got plenty of people looking, son. You've got a game tomorrow.

Riding back in the car, Danny couldn't get warm. He pulled old blankets over himself and kept the dog in his lap, but his teeth knocked together so hard that his sister complained about the noise and his mom said, You must be coming down with something, honey. I'll run a hot bath when we get home.

Danny went back to the caves by himself a few times after that. He'd walk alone up the hills to the boarded-up mouth, and mixed in with the sounds of dry grass was his cousin's voice howling up from underground: *no* and *please* and *help*. And Danny would think: Okay, now—*now!* and feel a rising up in himself at the idea of finally saying those words he'd been holding inside all this time: *Howie's in the caves; we left him in the caves, Rafe and I,* and just imagining this gave Danny a rush of relief so intense it seemed he would almost pass out, and at the same time he'd feel a shift around him like the sky and earth were changing places, and a different kind of life would open up, light and clear, some future he didn't realize he'd lost until that minute.

But it was too late. Way, way too late for any of that. They'd found Howie in the caves three days later, semiconscious. Every night Danny would expect his pop's sharp knock on his bedroom door and frantically rehearse his excuses—*It was Rafe* and *I'm just a kid*—until they ran together in a loop—*It was Rafe I'm just a kid itwasRafeI'mjustakid*—the loop played even when Danny was doing his homework or watching TV or sitting on the john, *itwasRafeI'mjustakid,* until it seemed like everything in Danny's life was the witness he needed to prove he was still himself, still Danny King exactly like before: *See, I scored a goal! See, I'm hanging with my friends!* But he wasn't one hundred percent there, he was watching, too, hoping everyone would be convinced. And they were.

And after months and months of this faking, Danny started to believe in it again. All the normal things that had happened to him since the cave made a crust over that day, and the crust got thicker and thicker until Danny almost forgot about what was underneath.

And when Howie got better, when he could finally be alone in a room without his mother, when he could sleep with the lights off again, he was different. After the *traumatic incident* his sweetness was gone and he got into drugs and eventually bought a gun and tried to rob a 7-Eleven, and they sent him away to reform school.

After Rafe died three years later (killing two girls from his class at Michigan in his pickup truck), the family picnics stopped. And by the time they started up again, Danny wasn't going home anymore.

That was memory number two.

So now back to Danny, walking with his arms up and his cell phone on through the basement or dungeon or whatever it was in a castle that belonged to Howie. He'd come a long way to meet his cousin here, and his reasons were practical: making money, getting the hell out of New York. But also Danny was curious. Because over the years, news about Howie kept reaching him through that high-speed broadcasting device known as a family:

1. Bond trader
2. Chicago
3. Insane wealth
4. Marriage, kids
5. Retirement at thirty-four

And each time one of those chunks of news got to Danny, he'd think, *See, he's okay. He's fine. He's better than fine!* and feel a bump of relief and then another bump that made him sit down wherever he was and stare into space. Because something hadn't happened that should've happened to Danny. Or maybe the wrong things had happened, or maybe too many little things had happened instead of one big thing, or maybe not enough little things had happened to *combine* into one big thing.

Bottom line: Danny didn't know why he'd come all this way to Howie's castle. Why did I take a writing class? I thought it was to get away from my roommate, Davis, but I'm starting to think there was another reason under that.

You? Who the hell are you? That's what someone must be saying right about now. Well, I'm the guy talking. Someone's always doing the talking, just a lot of times you don't know who it is or what their reasons are. My teacher, Holly, told me that.

I started the class with a bad attitude. For the second meeting I wrote a story about a guy who fucks his writing teacher in a

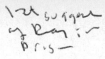

broom closet until the door flies open and all the brooms and mops and buckets come crashing out and their bare asses are shining in the light and they both get busted. It got a lot of laughs while I was reading it, but when I stopped reading the room went quiet.

Okay, Holly says. Reactions?

No one has a reaction.

Come on, folks. Our job is to help Ray do the very best work he can do. Something tells me this may not be it.

More quiet. Finally I say: It was just a joke.

No one's laughing, she says.

They were, I say. They laughed.

Is that what you are, Ray? A joke?

I think: *What the fuck?* She's looking at me but I can't make myself look back.

She says: I bet there are people out there who'd tell me Yes, Ray's a joke. Who'd tell me you're trash. Am I right?

Now there's muttering: *Ow,* and *Shit,* and *What about that, Ray-man?* and I know they expect me to be pissed, and I know I'm supposed to be pissed and I *am* pissed, but not just that. Something else.

There's the door, she tells me, and points. Why don't you just walk out?

I don't move. I can walk out the door, but then I'd have to stand in the hall and wait.

What about that gate? She's pointing out the window now. The gate is lit up at night: razor wire coiled along the top, the tower with a sharpshooter in it. Or what about your cell doors? she asks. Or block gates? Or shower doors? Or the mess hall doors, or the doors to the visitor entrance? How often do you gentlemen touch a doorknob? That's what I'm asking.

I knew the minute I saw Holly that she'd never taught in a prison before. It wasn't her looks—she's not a kid, and you can see she hasn't had it easy. But people who teach in prisons have a hard layer around them that's missing on Holly. I can hear how nervous she is, like she planned every word of that speech about the doors. But the crazy thing is, she's right. The last time I got out, I'd stand in front of doors and wait for them to open up. You forget what it's like to do it yourself.

She says, My job is to show you a door you can open. And she taps the top of her head. It leads wherever you want it to go, she says. That's what I'm here to do, and if that doesn't interest you then please spare us all, because this grant only funds ten students, and we only meet once a week, and I'm not going to waste everyone's time on bullshit power struggles.

She comes right to my desk and looks down. I look back up. I want to say, I've heard some cheesy motivational speeches in my time, but that one's a doozy. A door in our heads, *come on.* But while she was talking I felt something pop in my chest.

You can wait outside, she says. It's only ten more minutes.

I think I'll stay.

We look at each other. Good, she says.

So when Danny finally spotted a light in that castle basement and realized it was a door with light coming in around it, when his heart went pop in his chest and he went over there and gave it a shove and it opened right up into a curved stairwell with a light on, I know what that was like. Not because I'm Danny or he's me or any of that shit—this is all just stuff a guy told me. I know because after Holly mentioned that door in our heads, something happened to me. The door wasn't real, there was no actual door, it was just *figurative language.* Meaning it was a word. A sound. *Door.* But I opened it up and walked out.

CHAPTER TWO

There was a connection between this new Howie and the one Danny remembered as a kid, but it was a distant connection. For starters, this new guy was blond. Was it possible for hair to go from brown to blond? Blond to brown, Danny knew all about— half the girls he'd slept with claimed they were *so blond, you wouldn't believe how blond I was as a kid,* which is why they spent half their paychecks on highlights, trying to recapture their rightful and original state. But brown to blond? Danny had never heard of it. The obvious answer was that Howie bleached his hair, but it didn't look bleached, and this new Howie (except he wasn't Howie anymore, he was *Howard;* he'd told Danny that first thing this morning, before he'd even clamped him in a bear hug) didn't seem like a guy who would bleach his hair.

The new Howie was fit. Built, even. Love handles, girly pear shape—gone. Liposuction? Exercise? Time passing? Who knew. On top of which he was tan. This part really threw Danny, because the old Howie had been white in a way that seemed deeper than not getting sun. He looked like a guy the sun wouldn't touch. And now: tan face and arms, tan legs (he was wearing khaki shorts)—tan hands, even, with blond hair all over them that had to be real, right? Because who the hell would bleach the hair on their *hands*?

The biggest change wasn't physical: Howard had power. And power was something Danny understood—this was one of a slew of skills he'd picked up in New York after years of study and training and practice, skills that combined to make a résumé so specialized it was written out in invisible ink, so that when his pop (for example) took a look, all he saw was a blank sheet of paper. Danny could walk in a room and know who had power the way some people know from the feel of the air that it's going to snow. If the person with power wasn't *in* the room, Danny knew that, too, and when the person turned up Danny could usually spot him (or her) before he opened his mouth—before he was fully in the door, sometimes. It came down to the other people in the room, how they reacted. Here's who was in the room with Howard:

1. Ann, his wife. Shiny dark hair cut in a pageboy, triangular features, big gray eyes. She was pretty, but not the way Danny expected a bond trader's wife to be pretty. She had no makeup, and her jeans and brown sweater were the opposite of sexy. She was lying on her back on the gray stone floor, letting a baby in pink pajamas (which Danny figured meant a girl) pretend to take steps on her stomach.

2. Workers. They were young, they wore dust masks, they were busy doing something, somewhere, and in between whatever they were doing they churned into the kitchen through a couple of swinging doors. Sometimes they carried tools. Howard had told Danny these were graduate students from the MBA program at the University of Illinois and also from Cornell's hotel school. Howard's

renovation was their summer project—in other words, they were doing this for credit. But it looked to Danny like what they were mostly learning was carpentry.

3. Mick, Howard's "old friend." Danny had met this dude last night—he was the one who finally turned up after Danny yelled *Hel-lo-ooo* for God knows how long inside that circular stairwell, where it turned out none of the doors had handles. There was something threatening about Mick. He had a slingshot body, strong but borderline gaunt, just bare muscles soldered together. Mick didn't smile once the whole time he was leading Danny to his room, and when he reached up to pull away a velvet curtain from around the big antique bed, Danny noticed a mess of old track marks on his arms (you couldn't see these now, he was wearing long sleeves). Mick was Howard's number two; Danny figured that out the second he was in the room with both of them. Powerful people either had a number two or needed one or both—meaning they needed a different one from the one they had.

That was everyone in the room.

Except the room is still a blank. These people were in a big medieval kitchen. It had a walk-in brick fireplace with a pot the size of a bathtub hanging from a hook. It had a tapestry on the wall that showed a king spearing someone's idea of a lion. It had a couple of long wood tables with benches where some of the graduate students were starting to take off their dust masks and lounge. It had a state-of-the-art German range where Howard was scrambling a massive pan full of eggs.

A breeze came in through four small windows full of glass in the shape of diamonds. Danny opened one of these wider and leaned outside and a smell of plants rolled up into his face from a few floors down, where that black he'd seen last night from the top of the wall had turned into green so thick he couldn't find the ground underneath it. Rising up out of that green maybe a hundred feet away was the tower Danny had spotted last night. It was square and straight and weirdly majestic.

Howard was telling Danny how he'd bought this castle from a German hotel company.

Howard: They renovated maybe a third, not even, just two levels of rooms in the south wing—which is where we're all sleeping—then this kitchen, the great hall, and two tower stairwells. Then they started having cash-flow problems and the work was stop-and-start for a couple of years, and when they were just about belly-up they flipped the property to us.

Ann (from the floor): For less than two-thirds of what they'd paid, plus all the equity they'd put in!

Howard: It was a deal we couldn't walk away from. But it meant we had to pass on Ann's favorite castle. In Bulgaria.

Ann: God, it was pretty.

They were making conversation, being nice, explaining themselves the way people do when you first meet them. And normally Danny was easy with people. It was another one of his invisible skills: he had radar for how people wanted to be talked to and could switch from one person's way to another person's way without thinking. But right now Danny's radar was down, he was out of range, or maybe he just needed to be reset and programmed in this new place, like his satellite dish. Bottom line: Danny felt uncomfortable around Howard. But *uncomfortable* sounds mild and what Danny felt was not mild, it was miserable. He couldn't define the misery. He couldn't even name the symptoms, except one: he wanted to get away. Now.

This caught Danny by surprise. He'd had multiple phone

calls and e-mails with Howard setting up this castle job, and all that had been fine. But being in the guy's physical presence was different. Something froze in Danny the minute Howard turned up in his room this morning.

Howard: Oh, man, look at you!

Danny: Look at you!

Howard: I don't know if I would've recognized you, buddy. Ditto on this end.

God, it's been a long time. I don't even know how long.

Danny: Scary long.

Howard: I don't want to know—it'll make me feel old.

Danny: Let's just leave it at long.

And that whole time, one sentence was screaming through Danny's brain: *What the fuck am I doing here?*

He wasn't sure where to stand in Howard's medieval kitchen, so he stuck by the window. He felt a prickling on the skin of his arms that gave him hope. Another invisible skill (it was a long résumé): Danny could feel on the surface of his skin when wireless Internet access was available. His biceps, mostly, and the back of his neck. This talent had served Danny fantastically in New York, where he managed to check e-mail all day long without paying for it. And this morning he'd woken up in his big medieval bed and had the feeling right off, like goose bumps or a limb that's been asleep. But it turned out Danny was wrong: when he opened his laptop there was no service, not a flicker. Not even a phone jack in the room. First thing after breakfast he planned to set up his satellite dish—on top of that tower, if possible.

There was a telescope next to the window, and Danny moved it into position and looked through. The tower's pocked sandy stones snapped into view like they were inches away from his face. The corners looked gnawed on. The windows were small and pointed. Danny edged the telescope toward the top window, looking for the red light he'd seen last night, but if it was still on he couldn't see it.

Danny: What kind of tower is that?

Howard didn't hear, but his old friend did—Mick, who was filling up glasses with water at one of the long tables. He came to the window and looked out.

Mick: That's the keep.

Danny: Was it a dungeon?

This question got the first smile out of Mick that Danny had seen. It broke open his grim face and made him handsome, even through the years of junk.

Mick: No, not a dungeon. The keep is the place where everyone holed up if the castle got invaded. Kind of a last stand. The stronghold.

Danny looked back through the telescope. He felt tension coming off Mick, even standing still. Danny had no take on the guy beyond the fact that he was Howard's number two. Although that was something, a big something, because the *randomness* and *chaos* (his pop's words) of Danny's eighteen years in New York disappeared when you looked at them in terms of filling up that number-two slot: he'd scraped into those empty places next to powerful people again and again and again, until by now it was second nature. But Danny was giving that up. For one reason or another it never worked out, and it always seemed to end in violence.

Danny caught something moving in a window of the keep—not the top part but one level down. He tipped the telescope a hair and waited. There it was again, a curtain moving, and then it pulled aside and Danny saw a girl: young, with long blond hair. Just a flash and she was gone. He turned to ask Mick who she was, but Mick had moved away.

A little boy crashed into the kitchen wearing a gray plastic visor and breastplate and carrying a plastic sword. A girl who seemed to be his babysitter came in behind him. Howard introduced her to Danny as Nora. She had white-girl dreadlocks and a pierced tongue—Danny caught the flash and click when she said hello. Her hands were shaking hard. Danny was so relieved to see a fellow style refugee that he had to fight back a grin. Girls with dreads were not into grinning.

Danny: Did I meet you somewhere before?

Nora: Only in your dreams.

She sneaked a smile (not a grin) and peeked at Danny from the sides of her eyes. Here's what Nora saw: a lot of black clothes covering up a lot of white skin Danny made even whiter with Johnson's baby powder. Straight dyed-black hair an inch past his neck. A pewter hoop in one ear with a ruby stuck in it. Today (not always), mud-colored lipstick. That was Danny's style, one of many he'd had over the years. At the beginning he'd thought of his style as being his essence, the perfect expression of who he was inside, but lately the styles had started to feel like disguises, distractions Danny could move around behind without being seen. He looked clearest to himself standing buck naked in front of the mirror so he could see the dregs of the many IDs he'd tried on: an ace of spades tattooed on his ass from his days as a bisexual club promoter, a cigarette burn on his left hand from when the photographer he'd assisted got pissy in the darkroom, a gash on his forehead from jumping into the fin of a wall-mounted sailfish on the day the dotcom he worked for went public, a nut on one temple where the loan shark he'd gone to rather than ask his pop for money whaled on him with a set of keys, a permanent click in his wrist, grease burns on one forearm, a lump on his balls from an infected piercing, a left pinky that wouldn't bend, a torn earlobe . . . you get the picture. And now this limp, which Danny was praying wasn't permanent. Giving Martha Mueller, his ex-girlfriend, the guided tour of these scars made Danny feel macho—his war wounds, he was thinking, so it surprised him when Martha said, You poor boy and kissed his forehead oh so softly, which would be a perfectly normal thing for some girlfriends to do, but not Martha. *You poor boy.* And for no reason, Danny came close to blubbering.

The kid whacked his sword against the table next to Danny and screamed *Hyahhh!* Danny jumped. The kid looked up at him, which meant tipping his head back to a point where it looked like it might snap right off at the neck.

Kid (in a muffled voice): I'm King Arthur.

Danny didn't answer. The kid lifted up his visor and Danny got a lurch in his gut: white skin, soft brown curls. Howie.

Kid: Does he not speak English, Mommy?

That got a laugh from the room.

Ann: Of course he speaks English. This is Daddy's Cousin Danny. Danny, this is Benjy.

Benjy: Why doesn't he talk?

Another laugh. Danny felt the pinch of anger that came when he was supposed to think a kid was cute.

Danny: I guess I don't have anything to say.

Benjy: You could say hello.

Hello, Benjy.

Hello, Danny. I'm four and a quarter.

Danny had no response. He didn't like kids, and parents of kids weren't high on his list, either. It didn't matter how cool you'd been—you had a kid and you were one more sucker spooning goop into an angry little mouth, a guy with pacifiers in his pockets and snot trails on his sleeves and a happy-goofy look Danny could only think was some kind of shock, like those people who sit around cracking jokes after their legs get blown off.

The kid kept peering up at Danny. Danny tried to hold his gaze, but he couldn't. Kids made him nervous.

Benjy: How come you're wearing lipstick?

That got the biggest laugh of all.

Ann: *Benjy!* But she was laughing, too.

Danny: Why does your babysitter have purple dreadlocks?

She likes the way they look.

Well, there you go.

Do you like the way your lipstick looks?

I do.

Benjy: I don't like it.

Ann: Benjy, that's enough. That's rude. She leaned down and spoke into the kid's face. Say you're sorry.

Benjy: No.

Ann: Then you're having a time-out.

Benjy: *No!*

Danny: Hey, don't worry about it. He waved his hand like it was nothing, but he was furious. Benjy glared up at Danny, and Danny glared right back down at him.

Howard: All right, folks. Let's eat while it's hot.

Mick rang a bell outside one of the windows, and the sound rolled through the air. More graduate students poured in, maybe twenty in all. Everyone filled their plates at the stove—eggs scrambled with mushrooms, baked toast, three kinds of melon— and carried them to the long tables. Danny took his plate to the table where the graduate students were sitting, away from Benjy, Ann, Nora, and (he hoped) Howard, who was still at the stove. Danny watched his cousin, searching for some link—in the way this guy moved, the sound of his voice, something—to the Howie he remembered. But he couldn't find one.

The eggs were the tastiest scrambled eggs he'd had in his life.

Danny scanned the graduate students, trying to figure out where he fell in the age spread. He liked being the youngest in a room, but at thirty-six (as of last week) this was getting pretty hard to pull off. Danny was past the point of denying that there were younger people in New York who were technically adults, meaning they had jobs and apartments and boyfriends or girlfriends or even husbands or wives. At first it was just four or five of these adults who were younger than Danny, then all of a sudden it was hundreds, thousands, a whole fucking generation, and this terrified him: the girls especially, with their black bras and purses stocked with multicolored condoms and exact ideas of what they liked in bed. It terrified him because if these were adults then he must be, too. He was some kind of adult, but what kind? Danny's friends were all young—they *stayed* young, because at the point when they got married and started having kids the friendships died off and new ones with people who weren't doing that shit took their place. It was Danny's nature to be new to the game of living in New York—he needed to be young or nothing about him made any sense and he was a failure, a loser, a guy who'd done nothing—all the things his pop said. But Danny avoided those thoughts. They were dangerous.

Someone was speaking to him, a graduate student on his left, one of the older ones (that alone made Danny like him), a little salt and pepper on his temples. Steve. He had a mighty handshake.

Steve: You're part of the team?

Danny: I—I guess so. I'm Howard's cousin.

Steve grinned. So you're joining the revolution? The end of life as we know it?

Danny: You mean . . . the hotel?

Yeah, the hotel. Except—well, obviously that's just the beginning.

Danny: Beginning of what?

Steve went blank, registering the fact that Danny knew

nothing. Then he got careful. He said: Just that Howard has other goals than pure profit. A lot of us are into socially responsible business, so this is a chance to watch that happen from the ground up.

Danny: How long have you been here?

Steve thought a minute, then called down the table: Mick, how many days?

Mick (instantly, not looking up): Thirty-eight.

Danny: And what've you been doing, exactly?

Steve: Uh, it's hard to point to one thing. We've . . . had a lot of meetings, we've talked, we've done some work on the business plan—

Carpentry! Someone else said that, and it got a laugh.

Steve: Yeah, carpentry. Just this and that, wouldn't you agree, Mick?

Mick looked up, still chewing. His eyes were very blue. The other graduate students all seemed to be listening. He said: I would agree.

There was a pause that felt pressurized.

Danny: So you're, like, physically renovating the place.

Another pause. Steve looked at Mick.

Mick: It's been a little diffuse so far. What we're doing.

Howard (from the stove): What's that?

Mick had his back to Howard, but he didn't turn. Instead he answered loudly, in a tone that Danny had a feeling was supposed to be light and flip but landed hard: Your cousin was wondering what we've been doing here all these weeks. I told him things've been a little diffuse.

Howard turned to look at Mick. Diffuse how?

The room went quiet, listening. Mick seemed to struggle. In the sense that we're doing little things, a lot of little things, but nothing really big.

He was breaking a basic rule of dealing with powerful people: you didn't cross them in public. Danny had learned that one a few times.

Howard walked to the table, holding his spatula. His eyes moved over the group in a way that seemed uneasy, and Danny felt a flicker of something—a connection between this Howard and the Howie he remembered.

Howard: What big things would you like to be doing, Mick?

Mick: I can think of fifty. We could start renovating the north wing. We could drain the pool and get to work on the marble around it. We could excavate the chapel—we've done some clearing around the gravestones, but the thing is still half underground. And then there's the keep—

Howard: We can't touch the keep.

I know we can't go *in* it, but we could work on the outside. We could clear around the bottom, we could—

We can't touch the keep, Mick.

Benjy's high, worried voice cut through: Dad, are you having a fight?

Mick: I'm thinking about morale, Howard.

Daddy, are you—

Howard: Whose morale? Yours?

Daddy—

Ann: Shhh. There was pain in her face. Danny felt responsible, like he'd started this thing. He noticed he was sweating.

Howard: Okay, look. Let's get this on the table, everyone. How's your morale?

There was a pause—too long, Danny thought.

Finally Steve, next to Danny, spoke up: It's good.

Good, said someone at the other table, followed by a *very good* and then *great* and *excellent* and pretty soon it was a whole happy chorus, because it felt so good to say these things that they wanted to keep on saying them, especially when it gave Howard such a look of relief.

Howard: I think this is your problem, Mick.

Mick: Okay.

No one moved. Howard stood there like he was waiting.

Finally Ann spoke up: Still, I mean, isn't the goal for everyone to be satisfied?

Howard: Only one person *isn't* satisfied.

Did he really believe it? Danny couldn't tell. Power was lonely—that was a universal rule. Which was why the number two was so important.

Mick stood up. He looked whipped. He carried his dishes to a giant dishwasher, loaded them in and left the room through the swinging door. Some kind of tension went out with him, and people started talking again.

Benjy: Mommy, is he sad? Is Uncle Mick sad?

Ann: I don't know.

Is he angry?

I don't know.

I want to find him.

Ann: Fine. Go.

The kid bolted out of the room, forgetting his sword. His voice echoed down the hall, *Uncle Miiiiiiiiiiiiick,* and then there was some kind of answer.

The graduate students were gathering at the stove with Howard, refilling on eggs. They agreed with Mick, but Howard had the power.

Finally, Howard brought a plate to the table and sat. After all that cooking he knuckled down the food like it had no taste and was nothing but a way to fill up. He kept one arm curled around his plate, as if someone might yank it away. Danny watched his cousin, disturbed. He felt he was seeing an earlier version of Howard, a part that didn't mesh with what he was now. Ann slid along the bench toward Howard and put her arm around him. He finished eating and shoved his plate away.

People were starting to leave. Danny carried his plate to the dishwasher and stood there, wondering if it would be rude to walk out of the room. He didn't want to be alone with Howard, but he had nowhere really to go—wasn't even sure how to find his way back through the halls and doorways and turns to the room where he'd slept.

Howard: Danny, wait.

Danny came back to the table slowly. Ann was still there, and Nora, and four or five graduate students. The baby was using the bench to hold herself in a standing position. The knees of her pink pajamas were dirty.

Danny sat down across from Howard.

Howard: How're your folks, Danny? The argument with Mick had taken something out of him, and his voice was dull and flat.

Danny: They're good, I guess. I don't see a lot of them.

Howard: I always liked your dad.

Danny: Yeah. I'm not too high on his list these days.

Howard looked up: How so?

Shit, why had he even said it? Why try to explain to Howard, of all people, how he'd broken his pop's heart not just one time but again and again, starting when he refused to go to Michigan (Pop's alma mater) and went to NYU instead, which was challenging and thrilling and all that crap but also dangerous, because "self-exploration" is always dangerous for that nice outline you thought was you. And Danny's outline turned out to be fainter than most people's—it looked as pointless in New York City as the Polo shirts he unfolded from his suitcase in a dorm room off Washington Square and never wore again. And when his parents came to visit, his pop had stood in that

Danny dreamnot fallen ky
nat ley
into space anymo

dorm room in his light green sweater, holding Danny's soccer balls in their netted bag, and said: Our hotel's right by Central Park. We could knock these around on Sunday morning.

Danny: Okay. He was pulling on his new boots.

There was a long pause.

Pop: We don't have to.

Danny: Yeah. Maybe not.

Pop: Really?

He turned to Danny, startled, like someone had bumped him hard in the street. Pop's hair was already white, his skin shaved so clean it looked like a five-year-old's. And he stayed like that, in a state of constant surprise through Danny's first years in New York, until Danny dropped out of NYU in his junior year, at which point his pop's surprise turned into deep, sick disappointment. Danny didn't know what it would take to surprise him now.

Howard: It always seemed like you and your dad were close.

Danny: Yeah. We were.

He used to think they'd be close again, but he'd stopped. Because all the things Danny had achieved in his life—the alto, the connections, the access to power, the knowing how to get a cab in a rainstorm, and the mechanics of bribing maître d's, and where to find good shoes in the outer boroughs (it was the equivalent of a PhD, all the stuff Danny knew, on top of which he was *known,* widely known, so when he walked on lower Broadway it wasn't abnormal for him to recognize *every single face*—that's what happened when you'd been a front man for clubs and restaurants as long as Danny had. At times it tired him out, having to nod or say hey all those times, and he'd decide he was only going to greet the people he actually knew, which was practically no one, but Danny couldn't do that, shun people, the sight of a face turning his way was something he couldn't refuse)—all that, so much! everything, it seemed to Danny on a good day, everything in the world you could ever want or need to know, added up to nothing—literally *nothing*—in his pop's eyes. It didn't exist. A blank page. And Danny couldn't be around that. That kind of thinking let in the worm, and the worm ate people alive.

Howard: So look. Obviously last night was a drag for you, and I apologize. We left the gate unlocked, but the problem is there's no light out there and no wiring yet for a light.

Danny: Hey, forget it.

Howard: But I'd—I'd still like to get your impressions. Just, what you saw, coming up here for the first time.

Danny: Sure.

Howard leaned toward Danny across the table and Danny had to fight the urge to move away.

Howard: Just . . . seeing the castle. How did it look?

And right then, for the first time, Danny felt a link between this new guy and the kid he remembered. It was Howard's expression that did it. His eyes weren't closed like they used to be when he'd make Danny tell about an ice castle on Pluto where a band of pirates lived. But wanting to be told a story, entertained, however that looks on a person's face—Danny saw this now and remembered it. It filled him with relief.

So he laid it out for Howard: waiting for the bus in that crummy town, then looking up. Seeing the castle black against the purple sky.

Howard was sucking in every word. And then what? You walked. What did you see?

He'd taken a yellow notebook out of his shorts and started to write. Danny covered it all: Hike. Hill. Gate. Trees. Wall. View. It felt easy, like they'd done it before. They'd done it for years. Which made Danny wonder if this whole castle project was another kind of game for Howard. Maybe you didn't have to make things up when you had this much cash, you just went ahead and bought them.

The last person to leave the kitchen was Nora, holding the baby. Danny felt their going physically. Now he and Howard were alone.

Howard: So you climbed in through an arrow loop—incredible! And what was it like in there?

Danny: Arches, dripping water. I think it might've been a sewer. He left out the part about being afraid.

Howard: Why, did it stink?

Danny: Not especially. It smelled like a cave.

He knew maybe a half second before he said the word that it was the last word he wanted to use. And by then it was out: *cave.*

Danny's face went hot. He made himself look at Howard, but his cousin was watching the window. Light hit his face and brought out deep lines, like someone had scratched them with a pencil. And right then, for the first time, Danny recognized his cousin physically. The eyes gave him away, those same sad brown eyes. It was Howie.

Danny waited. What else could he do?

Howard: What the hell does a cave smell like?

And he looked at Danny and grinned and it was gone, all that. Gone like it never happened. Howard let it go, and Danny felt a rush of relief so intense it was like an oxygen burst to his head. He actually laughed.

Howard: Keep it coming, buddy. I want to hear the rest.

CHAPTER THREE

Danny tried to get away after breakfast to set up his satellite dish. The need to be back in touch was getting uncomfortable, distracting, like a headache or a sore toe or some other low-grade physical thing that after a while starts to blot out everything else. But Howard wanted to give him a tour of the castle, and in the end Danny did what he usually ended up doing when he was dealing with powerful people: he went along.

The first part of the tour looked the way you'd expect a medieval castle to look if you gave that kind of thing any thought. Suits of armor. Burn marks on the walls from old lamps. A little churchy room with a stained-glass window. The great hall made the biggest impression on Danny: it had a long carved table and gold ceiling beams and chandeliers full of bulbs shaped like candle flames. It looked like you'd walked in on another century, but none of it was real—the Germans had renovated these rooms and stuffed them full of antiques. Danny would have known that just from the smells: new carpet, fresh paint. Danny always paid attention to smells because they told the truth even when people were lying.

Howard: This is all what the Germans did. Now we'll see what it looked like before.

From the great hall he led Danny outside onto a short outdoor walkway, plunging views on both sides, and used a key to open up another door. He motioned Danny through, and Danny stepped into a cold dark place where everything seemed to be trashed: broken walls, missing doors, piles of decaying crap everywhere like some kind of violence had happened. And the smells: rust, mold, rot. It looked and felt so different from everything they'd seen that it took Danny a minute to realize the dimensions were identical: windows, arches, halls, doors—it was a mirror image of the hall where Danny's room was, but at a different time.

Danny: Wow.

Howard was grinning, rocking on his feet. No one's touched this part of the castle in eighty-eight years. Amazing, no?

Danny pushed open what doors were still hanging and went into rooms where wind blew through empty window holes and the furniture had been ripped apart by animals. In one room, hundreds of white birds were nesting together with a sound like panting, the air thick with their sulfur smell. Towers of shit everywhere, feathers drifting. They looked like pigeons, but not the ones you saw in New York. These were purple-white, feathers ruffled around their feet.

Howard: We're pretty sure they're descended from carriers. For sending messages during wartime.

Howard's anxious, gloomy mood was gone. More than gone, it was edging into something like a high. The castle had done it. Every sight and sound of the place seemed to excite and thrill Howard: he was in love with it, he couldn't get enough. But the ruined rooms dragged Danny down. He felt it right off, a sort of thud in his gut. There were little things left over from all those years ago: a man's hat still hanging on a stand, a glass jar sitting open by a cloudy mirror, a glove dangling out of a drawer. A bottle of wine on a tray with a glass, brown flakes curling off its insides. Danny could almost hear the worm underneath, devouring all of it.

Danny: Who lived here?

Howard: One family, the von Ausblinkers. They held on to this place for nine hundred years. Think about that for a second, *nine hundred*. It's beyond what the mind can grasp.

Danny: Why did they leave?

Howard: Well, their kids died was the immediate reason. But money was a factor, I'm sure. It's hard to conceive what it costs to run a place this size, but I'm learning fast.

Compared with the medieval antiques of next door, the stuff in these abandoned rooms was actually modern—not modern like today, but in that ballpark. Danny saw a typewriter and a sewing machine, old ones without plugs, but still. It gave him a weird impression that the long-ago past was in perfect shape, but the closer you got to today the more things collapsed into this ruined state.

The hall was practically dark, so Danny didn't see the old phone dangling off a wall until he'd almost passed it. The earpiece was a black cone on a hook—Danny bolted over and grabbed the cone and stuck it next to his ear and listened with his eyes shut. Was that a flicker of life, some echoey spark of connection? Or was it nothing? And that little taste, that flicker that maybe wasn't even a flicker made Danny realize he'd run out of time. He needed to be back in touch *now,* or something terrible would happen: his head would explode, a room would fill up with water, a big spinning blade would start sawing away at his spine. For maybe thirty seconds Danny was frantic—all he wanted was to get away from Howard and set up his dish.

Howard: What's up?

Danny carefully hung up the cone. Nothing. I'm cool. And he forced himself to calm down. Eighteen years in New York had taught him that much.

There were holes in the roof at the end of the hall, which let in some sun and warmed things up. And then a room with no roof, just open sky over a pinkish lump that once upon a time had been a bed. Now it was a fern patch. The room was somewhere between indoors and out: a tree had shoved through a wall, and squirrels dive-bombed across a rotten rug. They wrestled over what looked like a lump of papier-mâché, and little wood bits went flying. One hit Danny's boot, and he picked it up. It was faded red, the board piece from a Parcheesi game.

Danny: What a monster job, trying to get this place into shape.

Howard: Tell me. Although I'll probably leave some of it like this.

Danny turned. Are you serious?

Absolutely. It's evocative. It's . . . history. You know?

Danny didn't know. So when do you start bringing in the construction crews?

Howard laughed. You sound like the kids. Or not kids, but you know, students. My *staff*. They want everything to happen now. I used to be like that, too, but I've become more long haul.

Danny: Meaning what?

Howard: Meaning you bide your time. Wait for the right moment. I spent years doing the most shitty, meaningless work you can imagine, money making money making money into a giant fucking tower of bullshit. I'm not saying there weren't highs—where there's money there are always highs—but a thug can trade bonds. I did it for one reason: to make so much dough I could walk away at thirty-five and do whatever the hell I wanted for the rest of my life.

Danny: Sounds nice.

Howard: And I did it. This (he waved his arm at the dead light fixtures dangling by their wires, the wallpaper coils on the buckled floor), this is what I filled up my head with shit for all those years. And I'm not going to get rushed through it by a bunch of kids.

Danny: This hotel.

Yes.

Danny: But it's more than a hotel.

Howard smiled. I'm glad you picked up on that.

Birds were squabbling in the trees over their heads, knocking twigs and leaves onto the ferny pink lump where someone used to lie down and pull up the covers and shut his eyes.

Howard: Anyway, let's get outside. I want to show you the garden.

Danny was only too happy to get out. He followed Howard back through the dark hall and down a curved staircase like the one he'd been stuck inside last night, except this one had no light and reeked of sooty water. Howard had a flashlight, and they took the steps slowly. Toward the bottom there was graffiti on the walls in a language Danny didn't recognize. Also beer cans, condoms, crud left over from fires.

Danny: Who did all this?

Howard: Local kids, partying over the years. They stripped some of the rooms down here, but I think they were scared to get in too deep. Lucky for us.

At the bottom there was finally some light. The stairs fed into a room that was under construction: scaffolding on the walls, a wood floor partially laid. A pair of old glass doors faced outside.

Howard: Here's where the Germans were when the dough ran out. He wrenched the doors open, glass shards pinging the floor, and Danny went first, stepping into that cool green ocean of leaves he'd been looking down at all morning.

the pool —Mack the
pool once a well
THE KEEP ■ 43

Howard: Back when this was a working castle there was a bakery out here, stables, a garrison where the knights slept. Later on they ripped out the paving and made it all a big garden: landscaping, orchards, fountains, the whole bit. A lot of that is still buried under here if you look.

Buried was right. Danny could feel sun trying to push its way down through the layers of shade but the dirt was cold and black, marked with dregs of paths made out of something white. Broken seashells, it looked like. Danny followed Howard down one of these paths, past fossil trees and broken statues greened with slime, a bench swallowed up by gray flowers.

Howard: Coming up is the thing that just knocked me out. When I saw it I thought, *I have to buy this place.*

They'd reached a sort of wall made out of cypress. It was tall and solid and once upon a time it was probably smooth, but now it looked like a giant cushion with its stuffing popping out. Danny followed Howard through an opening in the cypress that looked like it had been recently cut, and when he squeezed out the other side he felt sun on his face. He was standing in a clearing paved with blotchy marble. In the middle was a round swimming pool maybe forty feet across. Its water was black and thick with scum. At first Danny didn't smell it, but the stink came on fast: a smell of something from deep inside the earth meeting open air, full of metal and protein and blood.

Mick was across the pool on his hands and knees, rubbing at the marble with some kind of long brush. He didn't look up.

Howard: There used to be a tower right where that pool is. Round—see those broken stones around the edges? It had a well, so after the tower collapsed they built a pool in the ruin. Nifty, eh? Anyhow, this is where they drowned.

Danny: Who drowned? The smell was making his nose run.

The von Ausblinker twins. A boy and a girl, ten years old.

No one really knows what happened. He looked Danny over. Allergies?

The smell.

I have a lousy sense of smell. Sometimes I think it's a blessing.

They were drifting toward Mick. The guy was bare-chested, scrubbing so hard his torso ran with sweat. And what a torso. A hundred years of personal training wouldn't have made Danny look like that, or even close. Mick squinted up at them.

Howard: That brush is working better than the liquid.

Mick: Yeah, check this out. He stood up, showing them a patch of glowing spotless white.

Howard: Whoa.

Mick: Picture the whole thing like that.

Howard: Just don't try to do it all yourself. Get some help.

There was no hint of the conflict in the kitchen, not a trace. Danny wondered if his edgy state had made him exaggerate the thing. Or did they do that every day?

Howard: I was telling Danny about the twins.

Mick glanced at Danny—a cold, empty look that unnerved him, like whatever was wrong was his fault. What the fuck? Danny tried to catch the guy's eye and stare him down, but Mick was back to his sanding.

Danny: You know about these twins from the Germans?

Howard: A little. But most of it—Howard took a long breath and looked away—there's a family member still on the property. You could say I inherited her. A baroness. She lives in that tower—the keep, it's called. It's the oldest part of the castle.

Danny followed Howard's eyes and there it was, the keep. Rising over the trees, almost white in the midday sun.

Danny: I'd love to go up there. He was thinking about his satellite dish.

Howard let out a thump of laughter. You catch that, Mick?

Mick nodded.

Howard: I wish I could take you up there, Danny. Unfortunately the baroness is—how should I say this?—not entirely supportive of our project.

Danny: She's young, right? Pretty?

Mick and Howard looked at each other and started to laugh.

Howard: What made you think that?

Danny didn't answer. Their laughing pissed him off.

Howard: She's, uh . . .

Mick: Really really old.

Howard: C'mon, numbers man, cough it up.

Mick: Ninety-eight. We think.

Howard: But she doesn't look a day over ninety. The two of them cracked up over that one. Danny looked at the keep and thought about the girl he'd seen in the window. Obviously Howard and Mick didn't know about her, and he sure as hell wasn't telling them.

Finally Howard pulled himself together and rubbed his wet eyes. I'm sorry, Danny. But if you could see what this broad has put us through—

Mick: And it's not over yet.

Howard: No, it's not. The laughter fizzled in him, and he ran his hands through his hair.

Mick: I still say we should start working on the keep. Just the outside. Why let her call the shots?

Howard: You could be right. Come to think of it.

Mick started scraping again, moving his brush on the marble.

Howard turned to Danny. So. Are you starting to get the idea?

Danny: The idea . . . ?

About this place.

I—I guess I'm just taking it in.

Howard: Not the stuff, not the buildings, the rooms, all that, but the *feel* of it. All this . . . history pushing up from underneath.

He was looking hard at Danny. And what Danny felt wasn't the pushing of history but the feeling he always had when a powerful person's attention was on him alone—like a towel snapping near his face.

Howard: Here's what I mean. Mick, hold off. Here. Listen.

Mick stopped scraping. Howard took hold of Danny's shoulders. The grip of his hands was almost painful, but what amazed Danny was the heat pouring out of them. No wonder the guy wore shorts.

Howard: You hear those sounds? Insects, birds, but not even that. Something behind them, you hear it? It's—what? A hum, almost. But not quite.

The heat from Howard's hands had soaked through Danny's jacket and shirt and was filling up his arms. He hadn't realized he was cold, but it turned out he was—had been ever since they'd gone into the broken-down part of the castle. Danny listened and heard nothing, but it was a different kind of nothing than he was used to. Most quiet was like a pause, a blank spot in the usual noise, but this was thick, like you only heard in New York right after a snowstorm. Even quieter than that.

Howard: I don't want to lose that. I want this place to be *about* that. Not just some resort. He let go of Danny's shoulders. The veins stood out in Howard's arms and neck. Danny knew he'd better understand this or look like he did.

Danny: You want the hotel to be about silence?

In a way, yes. No TVs—that's a given. And more and more I'm thinking no phones.

Ever?

If I can make it work.

So it'll be like a . . . retreat? Where people come and do yoga or whatever?

Not really. No.

Mick: Can I?

Howard: Yeah, go ahead.

Mick started brushing again. He liked to be constantly occupied, that was clear. A perfect number two.

Howard: Think about medieval times, Danny, like when this castle was built. People were constantly seeing ghosts, having visions—they thought Christ was sitting with them at the dinner table, they thought angels and devils were flying around. We don't see those things anymore. Why? Was all that stuff happening before and then it stopped? Unlikely. Was everyone nuts in medieval times? Doubtful. But their *imaginations* were more active. Their inner lives were rich and weird.

(There was no pause in Howard's talking, but I'm taking a pause here to tell you that Danny wasn't listening. The mention of phones, or lack of phones, reminded him that he'd been out of touch too long for maybe an hour by now, and having that much time pass made it easy to imagine how more time could pass, and then more time, and Danny knew from experience that when someone dropped out of the mix it was only a matter of days before it seemed like they'd never been there. Everything shifted and moved and rearranged, no one's place got saved. To Danny, the thought of disappearing like that was worse than dying. If you were dead, fine. But being alive but invisible, unreachable, unfindable—it would be like those nightmares he used to have where he couldn't move, where he seemed to be dead and everyone thought he was dead but he could still feel and hear everything that went on. And right in the middle of thinking this stuff, Danny realized Howard was saying something important. He could tell by the way it rushed out of his cousin like it was breaking free. So Danny started listening.)

Howard: *Imagination!* It saved my life. I was a fat kid, adopted, I didn't have many friends. But I made things up. I had a life in my head that had nothing to do with my life. And what about people in medieval times? They saw one shitty little town their whole lives, their kids caught a cold and dropped dead, they had three teeth left in their heads by the time they hit thirty. People had to do something to shake things up or they would've keeled over from misery and boredom. So Christ came to dinner. Witches and goblins were hiding in corners. People looked at the sky and saw angels. And my idea—my, my . . . plan, my—

Mick: Mission. He didn't pause in his sanding.

My *mission* is to bring some of that back. Let people be tourists of their own imaginations. And please don't say *like Disneyland,* because that's the exact opposite of what I'm talking about.

Danny: I wasn't going to say that.

Howard: People are bored. They're dead! Go to a shopping mall and check out the faces. I did this for years—I'd drive out to the malls on weekends and just sit there watching people, trying to figure it out. What's missing? What do they need? What's the next step? And then I got it: *imagination.* We've lost the ability to make things up. We've farmed out that job to the entertainment industry, and we sit around and drool on ourselves while they do it for us.

Howard was pacing, turning, waving his arms. Mick's soft brushing filled up the background.

Danny: And you think this is something people will pay for?

It came out rude, but Howard seemed to love it. Excellent question! The only question, from a business standpoint. The answer is always the same, Danny: Depends how good a job we do.

Did that *we* include Danny? He wasn't sure. Howard and Mick seemed like brothers.

There you are!

It was Ann, coming through the cypress into the sun. She'd changed into a long green skirt that caught on the branches so she had to stop and unhook it. She wore a sleeveless black top that made her shoulders look very white.

Ann: Husband dear. I thought we were taking Benjy into town.

Howard: Jesus, what time is it? I got caught up in showing Danny—

Mick pulled on his shirt and stood up. I'm gonna head back. Should I tell Benjy you're coming?

Howard: Couple of minutes. Thanks.

Mick picked up his tool bag and headed toward the cypress. Since that first hostile look he hadn't even glanced at Danny. When Mick was gone, Ann shut her eyes and stretched.

Ann: Sun feels nice. Hard to find a place where you can actually feel it on your skin. So Danny. What do you think of our little kingdom? Or duchy. Or fiefdom, whatever it is.

Howard: Barony. He gave an empty laugh.

Ann: Of course.

Danny: It's great. But I—I'm still not clear on the hotel part. I mean, someone books a room and they come. And what, like, *happens*?

No one seemed to have an immediate answer.

Ann: I'll tell you how I picture it, can I?

Howard: Please.

Ann: A woman travels here by herself. She's unhappy, she's—shut down. Maybe her marriage is in trouble; maybe she's alone. Whatever it is, she's become numb, dead to herself. So she checks in and leaves her stuff in her room and then she comes through the garden to this pool—I don't know why, but I always picture this happening at night (Ann was taking steps toward the edge of the pool while she talked, her dark hair shining purple in

the sun)—and the pool's all lit up and the water's clean, obviously, and it's warm, it has to be warm because it's always cold
here at night, even in summer, and she dives in (Ann lifted her
arms in a white V over her head and pulled her body long and
straight, shutting her eyes), and it—it *does* something to her.
Being in that water does something: it wakes her up. And when
she gets back out of the pool, she feels strong again. Like she's
ready to start her life over.

Ann let her arms fall back to her sides and smiled at Danny,
embarrassed. He thought: *That's a lot to ask of a swimming
pool,* but he didn't say it. Didn't really feel it. While Ann was
talking he'd been weirdly caught up.

Howard: You know how I think of this? The Imagination
Pool. You dive in and—*bang*—your imagination is released: it's
yours again, not Hollywood's, not the networks or Lifetime TV
or *Vanity Fair* or whatever crap video game you're addicted to.
You make it up, *you* tell the story, and then you're free. You can
do anything you want. He turned to Danny. The Imagination
Pool. What do you think?

Danny was thinking a few things:

1. That Howard was starting to sound a little nuts. Lots of
   powerful people were nuts, Danny wasn't sure why. But
   was Ann nuts? And what about Mick? Not to mention
   all those graduate students. Could they *all* be nuts?
2. That this hotel sounded like the closest thing to hell
   Danny could imagine.
3. That he needed to set up his satellite dish.

Danny: I guess I'm wondering—
Howard: Tell me.
—what you want me to do. I mean, it's such a . . . grand

scheme, and you've got so many people already working on it. Nothing really seems to be missing.

Howard glanced at his watch. Ann, you want to take Benjy into town and I'll meet you down there?

Ann: Are you asking me what I want or telling me what's going to happen?

Danny: Howard, go, please. My schedule's . . . I mean, obviously I don't have a schedule.

No, I'd rather—I'm sorry, honey.

Ann: Okay. We'll see you when we see you.

She left quickly, quietly, her green skirt disappearing through the cypress. The silence settled like glue in Danny's ears. Howard rubbed his foot over the brushed marble. When he looked back at Danny he was serious.

Howard: I've given you the wrong impression. There is something missing.

Danny: What?

Howard: I don't know. I'm trying to figure that out. Here, let's walk. Let's—you feel like climbing a wall? There's an awesome view from the top.

Danny absolutely felt like climbing it—for the satellite dish. He followed Howard through another cut in the cypress. Maybe thirty feet beyond the trees, there was a broken section of wall like the one Danny climbed last night. Howard ran straight up, scaling it like a billy goat in his shorts and hiking shoes, while Danny huffed behind in his velvet coat and slippery boots, trying not to look too ridiculous. It didn't matter—Howard wasn't watching him. He was taking in his view.

The wall was built like a sandwich, two layers of stone with a lot of concrete rubble in between, but unlike the part where Danny had walked last night, this rubble was collapsing, so you had to grip an outside layer of wall to keep from falling into the

Howard tells some mean :-
his vision   f. 32 ■ JENNIFER EGAN
The key

gap and twisting an ankle. So: no satellite dish. Still, the view
was something. At Danny's back was the cliff he'd looked over
into the valley last night, inside the walls to the left was the block
of castle buildings, straight ahead was the keep. Below, the black
pool looked like a crater, a hole punched into the earth.

Howard: I see all this, Danny, and I'm awed by it, but I'm
still on the outside. There's some way in I can't find. And I don't
know where the fuck to look.

How do you know it exists?

Howard turned to him. I feel it. Right here. He socked a fist
into his own gut with a force that would've made Danny gag.
It's—I don't know what. A map. A clue. A key. It might not even
be a thing. It could be an idea.

Danny: Do . . . other people feel this?

Howard: They feel something. They're restless. They want
me to lead them in some clear direction, and I can't do it. I'm
stuck. He was staring out as he talked, and Danny followed his
eyes to the keep.

Danny: Does it have to do with that old lady in there?

It could. Sometimes I think it's the keep itself. That was
the heart of the castle back in the day, and I can't get my hands
on it. Or it could be something totally different. But I need an
answer—this thing has to work. I've put my marriage on the
line, dragged all these people over here. Everything I've got is
wrapped up in this castle. So it has to work. *It has to work.*

He turned to Danny with a look that was short of desperate
but not by much. A hungry look. Howard needed something.

Danny: This morning, when I was looking through the telescope, I saw someone in there. Inside the keep. But she was
young.

Howard: There's no one young in there.

I *saw* her. Blond, pretty—she was young, Howard. Right in
that window.

He pointed at the keep, but Howard didn't look. He was looking at Danny. And for the first time in a while, he was smiling.

Howard: I'm amazed it's happening so soon.

What're you talking about?

Howard's face was flushed. It happens to everyone who comes here. I felt it the very first time, with Ann—less than an hour in, I noticed my perceptions starting to sway and shift, almost like I was dreaming.

Danny felt himself get cold and still. You're saying I'm hallucinating?

I'm saying the baroness is an ancient hag who looks more dead than alive. I'm saying there's no one else in that keep. And I'm saying that this—what happened to you with the telescope—is the whole fucking point of our hotel. That's it, *bang*! You've got it.

Danny: Okay.

The worm stretched open in him. All it took was the itch of one ugly idea—Howard was fucking with his head—to shake it out of its dormant state. Danny was generally pretty worm-resistant, and he had a knack for slowing down the worm in other people by reminding them that just because you saw four orange cars in an hour didn't mean undercover cops were staking out your apartment for a raid, or that hearing a guy laugh in the window of Starbucks right as you walked past wasn't proof that he'd spent the previous night fucking your girlfriend. But even Danny wasn't completely immune to the worm, no one was.

Howard: I can see you don't believe me, Danny. I don't blame you. Just—stay with me. Keep an open mind.

Okay.

Howard's eyes moved over his property, the high chunky outer walls with their round towers every fifty yards, the wild green inside them, the cluster of castle buildings. So much of it was broken, collapsed or about to collapse, you could almost feel gravity leaning on it, forcing it back into the earth. The whole thing seemed insane to Danny, a doomed venture.

Howard: I spoke to my folks a few weeks ago, Danny, and they mentioned you'd gotten into some kind of trouble in New York.

So now the family was gossiping about *him*. But Danny already knew it.

I had a gut reaction: bring him over. Pure instinct. Danny needs something, I need something—maybe there's a fit. But I'll tell you this: I make all my decisions that way. And you don't make the kind of money I've made unless your instincts are pretty fucking astounding.

Danny: Well, my instincts tend to fuck me up. So we've got your instinct to bring me over here versus my instinct to come.

Howard laughed. It was a big joyful laugh, the kind that makes you glad to be the one who brought it on. Danny felt the worm start to relax.

Howard: So where's the conflict? If I win, you win, too.

CHAPTER FOUR

*writing keep our group
characters*

What I want to know, Tom-Tom says, after I read out my stuff in class, is which one of these clowns is you?

Clowns? I squint up my eyes at him. Clowns are a touchy subject with Tom-Tom. I'm surprised he brought it up.

Okay, he says. Assholes.

Easy there, Holly says. Not because of *assholes*—that's almost polite—but because he's saying it about something I wrote. And on Holly's list of rules, *Respect one another's work* is ahead of *No physical contact*—one more way you can tell she's never taught in a prison before.

Tom-Tom's a guy nobody likes, but that doesn't tell you anything. Tom-Tom's a guy who *likes* the fact that nobody likes him, because it means he must be right about the world being one enormous piece of shit. I guess you could say Tom-Tom likes being right more than he likes being liked.

I already knew who he was because of the geckos. We have a reptile program where inmates keep eggs under lights and then raise the baby lizards or what have you until they're big enough to be sold in a pet store. Tom-Tom's our gecko man. They're medium-sized, the brightest green you ever saw. He takes them

outside on leashes made out of string and lets them run around in the dirt. He rubs their shiny little heads and kisses their lizardy lips.

Maybe a year ago, a horror show named Quince walked up to where Tom-Tom's geckos were playing in the yard and put his boot through one of their heads, just crushed it cold. That was back in the days when all I did was sit—*depression, laziness, despondency, being a goddam snitch spy*, why I did all that sitting depended on who you asked. That day I was on a bench maybe twenty yards away from Tom-Tom, across a chain-link fence. He should've been on his knees thanking God it was only a gecko Quince decided to smash that day, but as soon as Quince was gone Tom-Tom's face did something I've never exactly seen before, it crumpled and collapsed like there was a boot on *his* head crushing it, and his lips drew back so his mouth was a black open hole, but no sound came out. At first I thought he was having a stroke or a heart attack, but then I realized I was seeing pure misery, the kind people only show when they think they're by themselves.

Then Tom-Tom saw me through the fence. For a split second I thought, *I'm dead.* And I would be dead, no questions asked, if he was a real con. But Tom-Tom's not a con, he's a meth freak who loves reptiles and hates everything else.

Who says any of these assholes is me? I ask Tom-Tom now.

Well, you sure as shit didn't make it all up.

I did make it up, I say, because I want Holly to think that. Otherwise it's all just stuff a guy told me, so why not be impressed with that guy instead of me?

No one could make this shit up, Tom-Tom says. It's too ridiculous.

More ridiculous than walking into a bank in a clown suit and shooting three people? Hamsam says, and the room gets snickery. It's funny with Hamsam and me: we're friends, but we almost never speak. Maybe that's why we're friends.

Fuck you, shitbag, Tom-Tom says, but his ears get pink.

I write down *shitbag*.

Hey, Holly warns Hamsam in a sharp voice, our crimes stay out, remember that? But she's looking at Tom-Tom and you can tell she's thinking, *Clown suit?*

Alleged crimes, says Allan Beard, our resident brain.

Our crimes? Tom-Tom's smiling up at Holly and his smile is like a lizard's smile. Is that what you said? *Our* crimes?

Only to be nice, Holly says. I have to admit she's learning fast.

I've tried everything to get her to look at me: clamming up, asking questions, laughing, stretching, knuckle cracking. Every week I bring in something to read, and after I read it out she glances my way because she has to, but her eyes don't connect—they're looking next to me or behind me or even through me. I guess the stuff I wrote about the guy fucking his writing teacher made her nervous. And I feel like telling her, Babe, it wasn't you, okay? *That* writing teacher was an actual blonde, not to mention she was under thirty, no wrinkles around her eyes, and had curves on her like you wouldn't have if you ate Snickers bars around the clock, plus she wore *dresses*—ever heard of those? And she smelled like strawberries. Or mangoes. Or licorice. Hell, I don't know. But being inside changes everything. Stuff you'd call common or even flat-out invisible in the outside world turns precious in here, with magical uses you never thought of. A broken pen is a tattoo gun. A plastic comb is a shank, meaning a knife. A couple of plums and a piece of bread are next week's hooch. A packet of Kool-Aid is dye, an airshaft is a telephone. Two paper clips in a light socket plus a piece of pencil lead will light up your cigarette. And a gal like Holly, who maybe you wouldn't raise your head to look at out in the world—in here she's a princess.

I don't think you're nice, Tom-Tom tells her. I think you're guilty just like the rest of us.

Speak for yourself, Hamsam says, and a few guys bang their desks in agreement.

Holly smiles at Tom-Tom. She has pale eyebrows, bloodshot eyes. Her nose is long and kind of pointy. She has nice lips, I'll give her that; they're pink and have a clear soft shape even without lipstick, which she never wears. No makeup of any kind. I'm watching her carefully, which is something you can do with a person who never looks back, and when Tom-Tom tells her she's guilty a kind of ripple happens in Holly's face, and through the ripple I catch something I haven't noticed before but I realize now that it's been there all the time, right from day one. Pain.

Tell us about your crimes, Holly T. Farrell, Tom-Tom says.

She's still smiling. None of your fucking business, Tom, she says.

That's one day. They run together. All you want is for the weeks and months and years to pass so your time inside can be over like a bad dream and you can get back to your real life, but the longer you're inside the more your old life is what starts to feel like the dream. And of course I want it back, but the problem is, when do you have the same dream twice?

Nothing changes in here: 425 steps to my maintenance job (always walking on the right side of the yellow line that runs down the middle of every corridor), 320 from there to chow, 132 to chow from D-block. Lights out at eleven, on again at five for the first count. Four more counts, with a standing count at 4 p.m. in our cells. Three stints a week in the weight cage. Four packages a year, but for me it's usually less because the only family I've got is distant, so my packages are always things I order for myself.

My cell: six feet by ten, two metal trays nailed to the wall with mattresses on top that look like old taped-up cushions from patio chairs. No one ever wants the top bunk—people cut each other over bottom bunks—but I like the top because it gives me the best view of our window: five inches wide, twenty-four high. It has some kind of special glass that smears up what's outside into murky gray shapes, maybe to keep us from masterminding our grand escape, or maybe because a window you can actually see through would just be too nice. But get this: after that second class with Holly when the door in my head opened up, I sat down on my bunk and looked at the window and all of a sudden I could see through it straight to the yard: concrete, fences, guys sucking in fresh air. I practically yelled. But I stopped myself because sudden movements or noises are not a good idea around my cellie, Davis.

Nowadays I can stay on my tray for hours looking down at those figures moving around in the gray. I watch them like I never could if they knew I was there, and I notice stuff: how Allan Beard pulls out the hair in his beard, how Hamsam walks like a chimp. How Cherry turns to the fence and cries when no one's watching. How Tom-Tom lets the geckos sit behind his ears and climb up his ponytail. It's better than television.

The hell are you looking at all the time? Davis asks me.

Nothing.

Then why are you looking?

Why do you care what I do?

I don't give one blessed goddam what you do.

Good. And I go on looking, and Davis goes on hovering, which in a space this size means taking a step toward the window and then a step away from the window and staring at me.

Davis is a porter, so he's always around. He sweeps, he mops the tier halls, and in return the COs never flip our cell and Davis can stockpile shit underneath his bunk, a space that's officially one half mine. God knows what he's got under there—shanks, contraband, a bomb for all I know. He tucks a red-and-white checked tablecloth under his mattress so it hangs down to the floor and covers up whatever's under there. I've never lifted up the tablecloth (Davis gets rabid if I go near it) but I'm curious.

I have certain reasons for asking, he says.

Asking what?

What you're looking at.

And what reasons are those?

You answer my question, I'll answer yours.

My answer is nothing. I'm looking at nothing.

Bullshit. No one looks at nothing.

No, *you* don't look at nothing, Davis. But I *do* look at nothing.

Well, that's a poor use of your time.

As far as Davis is concerned, all I do in here is waste valuable time. His whole day is organized down to the minute—hell, for all I know he budgeted an extra five to hassle me about the window. When they first put us together he gave me lectures on self-improvement, on building and achieving and dragging myself out of the muck, that kind of thing, and then at some point he decided it was hopeless. But here's the funny part: I signed up for Holly's class to get away from Davis one night a week. And since I started that class, everything feels different—brighter, sharper, a little strange, like I'm starting to get sick.

Davis has a project of his own that drives me pretty nuts, although I try not to give him the satisfaction: he does a daily minimum of seven hundred push-ups in our cell. I have nothing against personal fitness, but come on—*seven hundred*? We're talking a level of grunting and sweating and groaning and (by the last hundred) screaming out for mercy that would be hard to take even in a giant space such as a gym. In this little trap it's a horror show. And I don't even mean the catcalls from everyone else on the tier about what I'm doing to Davis to make him howl like that. I mean the sheer racket of it.

But around the same time that our window glass got straightened out, Davis's workouts started hitting me a different way. It happened when I listened to his words. The more shaky and worn out Davis gets from his push-ups, the more the normal words we all say every day start getting mixed up with old words he must've used at some earlier point in his life: *goon* and *dildo* and *asswipe* and *your mama*—words left over from a life that's long gone. And once I noticed the old words Davis uses I started hearing them everywhere, because this place is a word pit— words get stuck in here, caught from when the clock stopped on our old lives. So now when a fight starts up I don't walk away like I used to, I crowd in and wait for those ghost words to start coming up. I've heard *chump* and *howler* and *groovy,* I've heard *fuzz* and *kike* and *kraut* and *coon* and *square* and *roughhouse* and *lightweight* and *freak show* and *mama's boy* and *cancer stick* and *fairy* and *party hearty* and *flyboy* and *knuckle sand-wich* (don't forget we've got lifers in here with false hips and false teeth who can tell you tales about rolling bums on the Bow-ery if you get them going), and I grab up these expressions, I trap them in my head and I save them. Because every one has the DNA of a whole life in it, a life where those words fit in and made sense because everyone else was saying them, too. I save up those words and later on I open up the notebook where I'm keeping the journal Holly told us all to keep and I write them down one by one. And for some reason that puts me in a good mood, like money in the bank.

————

In the next class I read again and Mel speaks up first, which is surprising because Mel hardly ever talks. Hamsam isn't there.

I've got a reaction, Mel says. Actually, it's a problem, Miss Holly.

Shoot, Holly says.

Mel clears out his throat and says, kind of formally, I would like to know what's going to happen next.

Holly waits, she's expecting more, and when nothing else comes out of Mel and she realizes *this* is the problem he's talking about, she smiles. Mel, she says, that's a good thing; it means the story has engaged you.

No, Mel says, it's not a good thing. He has a soft panting voice, a high-blood-pressure voice that goes along with his body, which looks fatter every week. How he does it on the shit they serve in here I don't know. He says, It's not a good thing because it makes me uncomfortable.

You don't want to make Mel uncomfortable. He's big and dumb and dangerous. The word is he tried to kill his wife by grinding up three hundred vitamin C tablets and sprinkling the powder on her clothes and her pillow because someone told him vitamin C was toxic if you inhaled it.

Define *uncomfortable*, Mel, Holly says.

I mean like I get an uncomfortable feeling inside me that's like an empty feeling, it's a disappointed feeling like I want to know what's going to happen and I feel bad not knowing, like Ray's holding out on me. And then I start to have a pissed-off feeling, pardon my French, Miss Holly.

It sounds like you're describing *anticipation*, Holly says. And that's not a problem, Mel. That's what a writer lives and hopes for.

It's a problem because being uncomfortable is not what I like, Mel says. The quieter he gets, the more he means it. Tell me what happens, Ray.

Mel, Holly says, and she laughs like she doesn't believe it. You can't make that demand. It's not fair.

I say it's not fair of Ray to make me wait.

Tom-Tom's sitting next to me. He picks that desk every week, who the hell knows why. Now he's twisting and flicking around and finally he turns to me and says, C'mon, Ray. Tell us what happens. You were *there, right?*

I look at him and smile. I don't know why I like pissing Tom-Tom off. Maybe because it's so easy.

See, Ray won't tell, Tom-Tom says. He'd rather sit there with a shit-eating grin all over his face.

Pardon his French, Cherry says, and he and Allan Beard start to laugh.

I write in my notebook *shit-eating grin.*

Mel waves away the laughs. You've got no reason not to tell me what happens, Ray, he says, and his voice is butter melting in a pan. The way I feel right now, he says, I'll be personally offended if you don't.

I have no interest in personally offending Mel. He was in the hole for three months after he stabbed a guy named Julian Sanchez with a toothbrush he'd made into a shank by scraping it over the pavement. Luckily for Sanchez, in the heat of the moment Mel accidentally used the brush end.

But when I start talking, it's not to make Mel happy. I do it for Holly, to get her to look at me. Being inside turns us back into infants: guys kill each other over a volleyball call, they throw their food and piss and shit because what else is there? What else have we got? And I need Holly's attention, that's all. I need it.

Well, I say, the next thing is that Danny's going to set up that satellite dish he's brought and call his ex, Martha Mueller.

Okay, Mel says. And say what?

You don't have to do this, Ray, Holly says, eyes to my left.

The main thing is, I tell Mel, Danny wants to get back together with Martha. But she won't.

I need the *words,* Mel says. Right now you're just making noise in my ear.

Holly's waiting, but she's not happy.

Okay, I say to Mel. Here are some words: "Hey, Martha, it's Danny. . . . Yeah, I made it okay and I'm here in this old castle with my cousin and some other people, and I'm thinking about you." I get a heat reaction in my face, but I keep on going. "I was wishing we could . . . I was hoping we could—" Now I'm stumbling, hardly getting the words out, and the guys are laughing like mad. Holly, too, she can't help it. "I was hoping we could start things over again—" Oh, fuck, I groan because I'm having a stroke, I'm dying of shame. I can't do this, Mel.

He's the only one not laughing. That was fine, he says. Up until the *oh, fuck.*

So forget I said, *oh, fuck.* I won't write *oh, fuck.*

Mel pins his blank, mean little eyes on me. Ray, he says, like he's talking to a kitten. Before, you were painting a picture. You had atmosphere and all that. Now you're just going through the motions. Your heart's not in it, man, you're not painting a picture anymore and that shit makes me *uncomfortable.* Excuse the French, Miss Holly.

We're going in circles, Holly says. I say we move on.

No one's going to move on until Mel gives the say-so. He looks at me. Keep it coming, Ray.

I'm done, I say. Better ask the clown. I don't even look at Tom-Tom.

Mel says something, but his voice is like a butterfly wing moving, and I can't hear. Holly takes a step toward the desk, which is where she keeps the pendant with the emergency switch that they all wear around their necks. Holly takes off the pendant as soon as she walks in the room each week. She puts it on the desk, I guess to show that she trusts us. Now she hesitates. If she pushes that button, class is over, and she hates to lose a class. You can tell. Every one is precious to her.

Take your seat, Tom, Holly says, because now he's on his feet.

Just stretching my legs, Tom-Tom says, and grins his hateful lizard grin at Holly, and I think how small she is in those baggy pants she wears and right then I see how the point of that outfit is to make her look and feel like a man or even a boy, to hide the female under there so she won't feel weak. By the time Tom-Tom swings around at me, it's too late. Holly's nowhere near the pendant and Mel's up too, moving fast for a fat guy.

I could stop this thing a hundred different ways. Even now, with everyone in motion. It's that way with violence: a slow quiet opens around it and suddenly there's all this space to move and rearrange things or shut them down. Or maybe that's just how it seems later on, when you wish things had gone a different way. I feel Mel and Tom-Tom watching me, waiting for a sign even while they move, but I'm giving them nothing. Because I want it. Something inside me is pulling this way. I feel the mystery of it as Mel takes my desk in his hands and flips it upside down and my head smacks the floor and I lie there with my eyes shut and those electric sparks flying around against the black: I've made something happen and it's happening, now, and I don't know what it is.

She's scared, I can smell it. She kneels down and puts her hand on my head and I feel her skin, her palm and thin warm fingers on my forehead and attached to those fingers is a body with life pushing out from inside it. Holly Farrell. Her hand on my head. It's the weird and terrible way of this place that a little thing, a hand on a head, can matter so much.

I wait as long as I can. Then I open up my eyes and look at her. She looks back: soft worried bloodshot eyes. Pale blue.

Enough drama, she says. Up. And she goes to meet the COs at the door.

Class ends early that day.

CHAPTER FIVE

Eventually Howard left for town. When he was gone, Danny tracked down the room where he'd slept, gathered up the parts of his satellite dish, and hauled them back through the garden to the round pool. He circled it, trying to figure out which spot would give his dish its straightest shot at that nice blue oval of sky. Now that he was alone, Danny noticed how clear and hot the sunlight was, full of buzzing insects. Also how weeds had squeezed up between the panels of marble around the pool and made them uneven, like they were floating on water. There was a marble bench next to the pool, and facing it from the other side was a sculpted head with a dried-out spigot for a mouth. Danny realized it was Medusa, her angry noggin wrapped up in marble snakes.

The pool stink didn't bother him now, maybe because he was about to get on the phone. How could a satellite phone affect Danny's sense of smell? someone's probably asking. Well, he'd lived a lot of places since moving to New York: nice ones (when it was someone else's place), and shitty ones (when it was his place), but none of them had ever felt like home. For a long time this bothered Danny, until one day two summers ago he was crossing Washington Square talking on his cell phone to his friend Zach, who was in Machu Picchu in the middle of a snow-storm, and it hit him—wham—that he was at home *right at that instant*. Not in Washington Square, where the usual crowd of tourists were yukking it up to some raunchy comedian in the empty fountain, not in Peru, where he'd never been in his life, but *both places at once*. Being somewhere but not completely: that was home for Danny, and it sure as hell was easier to land than a decent apartment. All he needed was a cell phone, or I-access, or both at once, or even just a plan to leave wherever he was and go someplace else really really soon. Being in one place and *thinking* about another place could make him feel at home, which was why knowing he was about to get on that phone made the pool smell seem faint, a thing he'd already left behind.

He picked a spot near Medusa and went to work. Danny was no engineer, but he could follow a manual and get a job done. He set up the physical contraption, a long folded-up umbrella that was the actual dish, plus a tripod, plus a keypad, plus the phone itself, which was heavy and fat like cell phones ten years ago. Then he started in on the programming, backing up after each dead end: wrong country codes, foreign operators, recordings in languages he didn't know. It didn't matter. He was hearing *something,* he was connected to *someone,* and the joy of that after almost seventy-two hours of total isolation got Danny through the snags with a smile.

An hour later he was punching in the password to his New York voice mail, half dizzy from that carbonation he got in his chest whenever a long time had passed since he'd checked it. Each new message starting up made Danny's heart stretch like it was reaching out for something. And each time, once he realized what the message was, he got a shove of disappoint-ment. Mom: Where are you now? in that worn-out voice he'd gotten so used to it barely made him feel guilty anymore. Bill collectors he ID'd in two words or less and deleted. His sister Ingrid, the spy (how else would his parents have figured out that the restaurant where he was maître d'ing was a "total mobster hangout" within twenty-four hours of her last visit?), *Just checking in.* Yeah, right. A dozen friends reporting on bars and parties and clubs, all of which was fine but none of which was *the thing.* Danny had no idea what the thing was. All he knew was that he lived more or less in a constant state of expecting something any day, any hour, that would change everything, knock the world upside down and put Danny's whole life into perspective as a story of complete success, because every twist and turn and snag and fuckup would always have been leading up to this. Unexpected stuff could hit him like the thing at first: a girl he'd forgotten giving his number to suddenly calling up out of the blue, a friend with some genius plan for making money, better yet a person he'd never heard of who *wanted to talk.* Danny got an actual physical head rush from messages like these, but as soon as he called back and found out the details, the calls would turn out to just be about more projects, possibilities, schemes that boiled down to everything staying exactly like it was.

Danny programmed his New York voice mail to route his calls straight into the new phone. Then he set up his new voice mail and started dialing: Zach, Tammy, Koos, Hifi, Donald, Noon, Camilla, Wally. Mostly he left messages—the point was to shoot his new number into as many phones as possible, and getting that done let off a pressure that had been building in Danny for the many hours he'd been out of touch. He reached actual people maybe one-fifth of the time, and the conversations went something like:

Danny: Heywhatsup.
Friend: Danny-boy. You back in town?
Danny: Any day, now. Any day.

Which was false—he didn't even have a return ticket—but Danny knew the best way to stay front and center in people's heads was to act like you'd barely left no matter how far away you were. And while he got caught up on seventy-two hours' worth of gossip, he soaked in the roar of New York that leaked in *around* the gossip, which made a perfect balance against the pool and trees and quiet buzzing. He was at home.

He waited awhile before he dialed Martha Mueller's number at work. He liked to warm up a little first.

Martha: Mr. Jacobson's office. Her landline gave him his best connection yet, Martha's scratchy voice so deep and soft in Danny's ear it was like she was talking from inside his brain.

He said: Martha.

She lowered her voice: Baby, are you out of here?

Way out.

Those guys drove by my place again this morning. In the black Lincoln. I told them you were gone.

Tell me word-for-word what you said.

I said, "He's gone. Now leave me the fuck alone." Something like that.

I wouldn't say *fuck* to those guys.

Too late.

And what did they say?

"Cunt," I think. They were already rolling up the window.

Danny: Were you scared? He liked the idea.

Martha snorted. If I were twenty-two and blond, I'd be scared.

She was forty-five, by far the oldest girl that Danny had ever slept with. He'd met her in an ATM line and followed her to a bus stop. First it was just her perfume, although it turned out Martha didn't wear perfume, she mixed fresh sage in with her underpants. She had red hair with a lot of gray in it. Three weeks ago she'd pulled the plug on Danny, saying the picture they made together was grotesque. They'd hooked up a few more times anyway—she was wild and dirty in bed. From Martha, *Get away, you fucker* was a come-on.

Danny: Martha—

Stop.

She was right, he was going to say it. And he did: I love you. Please.

And you love me.

You're losing it.

He could hear her lighting up. She was a longtime secretary-actress. When the office where she'd worked for fifteen years went smokeless, she kept lighting up until they fired her, then used her unemployment to land a job at Philip Morris.

Martha (exhaling): It's not love, it's some kind of erotic delusion.

Danny: That's what love *is*.

Martha: Admit you're bored, Danny.

With you?

With this conversation.

Normally it led to sex. Danny noticed he was grinding his teeth, and it crossed his mind he could jerk off right here, with her rough voice in his ear. But one look at that rancid pool and the urge dried up.

Danny: I'm the opposite of bored. I could go on forever.

He loved her. She had a sly, proud face and a fuzz of invisible hair over every part of her. She made the girls he'd slept with before—models or might-as-well-be models (would be, could be, wished they were, mistaken for, proud they weren't, etc.), girls with elastic faces who ate a lot of popcorn and green peppers and nodded respectfully whenever he went on about his money-making schemes, whereas Martha said once, You can find out it's bullshit by wasting a chunk of your life or just admit it's bull-shit right now and drop it—made them seem interchangeable.

And some miracle had led Danny through that clutter of identical girls to Martha.

Martha: How's the knee?

Hurts.

You get it looked at?

When would I do that?

It made a funny pop.

I don't remember a pop.

When the fat guy had you in a headlock and the other one was stomping on your—

Okay, okay. But Martha—

I'll hang up.

Don't!

The balance was starting to slip. Being at home meant being in an even mix of locations, like a seesaw with two kids on it that weigh exactly the same. Being *only* where you were was incomplete, but being *not at all* where you were (because you were getting upset by the conversation you were having on your cell phone) was flat-out hazardous. That's when you walked in front of cars. And Danny was getting upset. He'd started to pace.

Martha: I'm forty-five. My tits are sagging—I own cats, for God's sake! And now it turns out *in vitro* doesn't work for women my age, it's all egg donor, if that, which means I'll never have kids or at least not my own kids, and men—young men, especially—basically want to spread their seed. You can't argue with that, Danny, it's a biological fact.

Danny: But you don't want kids! And I don't want kids! I love the fact that you can't have kids because that means I'll never have to have any. From my end, it's a plus!

Martha: You say that now.

Danny: When else can I say it? Now is when we're talking. All I've got is now!

Martha: But you're still a kid yourself.

Danny stood still. These were the words he never got tired of hearing—words he waited for, hoped for. Hearing them from Martha now was like being skewered. Danny started pacing again, but right away his feet caught on something and he lost his balance—shit, he'd forgotten where he was and now that putrid pool was leering up at him; he was falling toward it! Danny flailed wildly the other way and somehow vaulted onto the marble, his left shoulder taking the whole impact of his weight. Pain shot tears into his eyes.

Tiny voice: What happened? Danny? That was Martha, inside the phone, which had landed a few feet away. Danny groped for it with his nonparalyzed arm. The dark cypress and blue sky turned crazily over his head.

Martha: What's going on? Are you okay? She sounded not scared, exactly, but anxious. Danny was in too much pain to enjoy it.

I'm fine. He was wheezing. Sweat pricked him under his arms and around his groin. He hauled himself into a sitting position.

Martha: Talk to me. Is it your knee?

She cared about him, it was obvious. Danny kept discovering this right when he wasn't expecting to, right when he'd given up on Martha, and then as soon as he'd figured it out she would make him forget all over again. Now Danny had one of those clear seconds where everything extra kind of drops away and all you see is what's actually there. He saw himself with Martha. He got a feeling of peace. Then the phone started shorting out and Danny's eyes hooked on something he didn't comprehend at first, but then he did—oh, fuck, he did—the satellite dish in the black pool, sinking.

Danny (bellowing): No!

He jumped up, lunging for the dish. It was already halfway underwater. Somehow he must have kicked it in when he tripped, or could *that* be the thing he'd tripped on? It was too far away from the pool's edge for Danny to grab it and fish it back out, so he flattened himself gut-down on the marble and stuck his torso straight out over the pool as far as it would go and tightened his ass and grabbed the rim of the dish with two fingers of each hand and tried to ease it back out without bending at the waist and dunking his head, and that's when the smell got him—oh God, what a smell: not rot but something after rot, a moldy emptiness, the smell of stale pollen, bad breath, old refrigerators that haven't been opened in years, rotten eggs and certain wool when it got wet, the afterbirth of his cat Polly when Danny was six, his aching tooth when the dentist first drilled it open, the nursing home where Great-aunt Bertie dribbled pureed liver down her chin, that place under the bridge near school where the piles of shit were supposedly human, the wastebasket under his mom's bathroom sink, the school lunchroom when you first walked in—every smell that ever made Danny even a little bit sick gushed up into his face as he leaned over that pool, smells that one time or another got him thinking just for a second (but then he forgot it) that normal life was thin, it was flimsy: a flimsy thing stretched over another thing that was nothing like it, that was big and strange and dark.

Danny shut his eyes and tried to breathe through his mouth. He tensed every muscle in his back to the shaking point, making his torso into a rod so he could use his long fingers like chopsticks to try to lift out the dish, but the pool had settled in around it now and didn't want to give it back—Danny would have to reach underwater with his hand, both hands, his head, all of him, dive in and dredge the thing back out, and he couldn't do that. The smell told him not to: *No,* it said, *stay away, because a thing that smells like this is going to kill you.*

So Danny didn't reach under the water. He didn't touch the water. And then the dish was gone.

He eased himself back onto the marble, shaking and snot-nosed. He found the phone and picked it up, thinking maybe by some fluke or miracle or grace period like they gave before they cut you off for nonpayment, Martha would still be there. Nope. It was dead, and not that tunnelly deadness of an open line—that would've been the sound of angels singing in heaven compared to this, which was the sound of no sound—an object that was just *what it was* and didn't lead to anything or anyplace or anyone.

Danny: Oh my God! No! I can't—*No!* What kind of—*No!*—Give me a—*No!*

He did all that useless stuff people do when they can't accept what's just happened: he crouched, jumped, turned in circles and punched his fists against his head; he stamped weeds under his boots and chucked his phone into the cypress with a throwing arm he hadn't used in years. Each move was Danny's answer to some new thought ripping through his brain: his $1,500 deposit blown to hell; his credit massacred; Martha Mueller out of reach; his New York voice mail routing calls into a dead line; his e-mail untouchable; himself stranded in the middle of fucking nowhere, lopped off from the flow of communication Danny needed the way most of us need to move or breathe, and maybe you're saying, But *why* did he need it so badly? It's not like the guy was running General Motors, which is true: Danny had not much going on and no real prospects on the horizon, but what about all those prospects floating around maybe an inch or two *beyond* the horizon? Those were the ones he was thinking about.

Eventually Danny calmed down enough to start looking for his phone. The longer he groped in the cypress, pulling threads in his jacket and sending fat little birds squawking out into the air, the more precious that clunky plastic thing started to get in his head. Like a relic. Just to have it. And there it was, finally, caught between two branches. Danny felt like sobbing. He couldn't resist holding the phone up to his ear one more time.

A voice said: Give it up. We're off the grid.

It was Nora, the nanny, coming toward the pool through the opening in the cypress wall. Danny wasn't sure if it was actually Nora he was so happy to see or just another human being. He stuck the phone in his pocket.

Nora: Didn't mean to scare you.

I look scared?

You do.

She went to the edge of the pool and sat on the marble bench across from the Medusa head. Danny followed her over, and she offered him a Camel that he turned down. He felt weak, but there was no way Nora could see that. And the fact that Nora couldn't see it made Danny start to feel after a minute or two like he wasn't totally weak, and after another minute or two, feeling not totally weak started to make him feel stronger. I'm saying minutes, but it wasn't minutes, it was seconds. Maybe just one second. Short enough that all Danny noticed was that suddenly he felt a little bit better.

Nora: How's the jet lag?

Danny: In and out.

She took a long drag. She was one of those people who make smoking look like eating. Her hands had stopped shaking—maybe she'd taken her meds. Maybe cigarettes *were* the meds. She wore army pants, black lace-up boots and a frilly white blouse that gave him a decent view of her medium-sized breasts.

Danny: I have to say, you don't look like a nanny.

Nora: Please. Child Care Specialist.

Is that a master's degree?

She laughed: PhD. I wrote my dissertation on Mary Poppins.

Danny: The phallic implications of the umbrella? He had no idea where he got this stuff, it just jumped out of his mouth. And getting a smile out of Nora made Danny feel even a little bit better than he'd already started to feel, to the point where his state of mind touched the very low end of good.

Nora: The feminist implications of the unmarried caregiver.

Danny: I almost believe you.

Don't get carried away.

Why? You're a liar?

She flicked the half-smoked cigarette into the pool. It floated for a second, then sank. She said, I don't like facts.

Danny: I don't like nouns. Or verbs. And adjectives are the worst.

Nora: No, adverbs are the worst. He said brightly. She thought hopefully.

Danny: She moaned helplessly.

Nora: He ran stiffly.

Danny: Is that why you're here? To get away from all the adverbs back in New York?

Who says I'm from New York?

Aren't you?

Nora cocked her head. Short-term memory problems?

Oh, yeah. Facts.

Nora: Anyway, there's no getting away from adverbs. They're rampant.

Danny: She confessed anxiously.

Nora: They're in our heads.

She cried desperately.

Nora: I hope you don't actually write like that.

Danny: I write for shit.

Nora: I'm an excellent writer.

She said smugly.

Nora: Not smugly. Factually.

Danny: Ah. So you'll make an exception to brag.

Nora lit up another cigarette. Danny felt like he'd won. Conversation, banter, whatever you wanted to call this thing he was doing with Nora—to Danny it was like an IV dose of joy. He felt linked to her, which made his problems seem like Nora's problems too, which meant if *she* wasn't freaking out about the fact that his satellite dish had just sunk into a pool full of rotten water, then maybe it wasn't such a big deal. Maybe it *hadn't even happened at all.* Danny didn't think all this out, he just felt better, so if he'd already reached a level one of happiness, now he jumped up to level three. And because he'd recently felt bad— like shit, actually—going from level-one to level-three happiness was like riding in one of those elevators that skip a lot of floors on their way to the top and make your stomach flop against your lungs.

Danny: So. You like working for Howard?

Howard is a genius.

She said . . . ironically?

Howard's beyond irony. That's one of the amazing things about him.

Tell me you're joking.

Nora: I wouldn't joke about Howard. Seriously.

Danny stared at her, still not believing. You buy all his crap about imagination? The Imagination Pool?

How much has he told you?

Danny: Enough to know it's a loser. *No phones?* Come on.

Nora looked at Danny full in the face, maybe for the first time. Have you always been jealous of him?

He was speechless.

Not that I blame you.

Danny: Whoa. Hold on. Let's just . . . back up a second. It was suddenly hard for him to talk. I—I wish you could've seen him in high school.

Nora: *High school?* Wasn't that kind of a long time ago for you?

Danny wanted to tell her to fuck off. Instead he took a slow breath. So is this like a cult? Is Howard your guru or something?

Fuck off.

I wanted to say that to you, but I didn't.

Live dangerously, Danny.

Danny: Fuck off.

Well done.

Is this a fight? Are we having a fight?

Nora: We can't. We don't know each other.

So how would you define this conversation?

Nora stood up. It's an acknowledgment of the chasm between us.

Danny: There's no chasm. We're the same person, almost.

Now you're scaring me.

I feel like I've known you my whole life.

Nora: I know what you mean, but that's an illusion.

She moved toward the cypress like she wanted to leave, and Danny felt a sharp pinch in his gut, like he'd swallowed a staple. He didn't want to be alone.

Danny: That's an illusion, she said coyly?

Nora: She said frankly.

My ass. Ominously.

You're paranoid. Indifferently.

Danny: Coldly?

Not coldly.

Well, not warmly.

Nora: Sympathetically. Actually.

Really?

Nora: I have to go. And then she left.

Within about five minutes of Nora going, the sun went, too. It dropped behind the trees and the second it did the pool and everything around it went dim. The change was huge, like an eclipse. And it wasn't just the light that changed, it was the mood: the mood went gloomy. Not just because everything was suddenly covered up with shadows, not because that oval of blue sky looked small and far away, not because the pool got blacker and the insects went quiet and there was no more warm feeling on Danny's skin or hair—because of the atmosphere of the place, which was . . . *gloomy.* Danny sat on the bench where Nora had just been sitting and put his elbows on his knees and his chin on his fists and looked up. There was the keep above the trees, smeared with orange sun. Danny wished he was up there, looking down from a place that was light.

And in one of the windows—was it? Danny sat up and rubbed his eyes, thinking he saw the girl again. Yes! He could barely make her out at this distance, but there she was, sun on her face, her gold hair shining. Then she moved away.

The jet lag was hitting him hard, or that was how Danny thought of it. But it wasn't just the jet lag, it was the fact that in the last half hour he'd lost:

1. His satellite dish
2. His girlfriend
3. His link to anyone outside this castle
4. His level-three happiness
5. His connection to Nora
6. The chance of ever possibly being at home in this weird place
7. His credit
8. The sun

All of which made Danny feel like his legs had been cut off, to the point where he didn't even have the juice to sit on a bench with no back, or to sit period. He lay belly-down on the marble, head on his arms, and looked at the water. Where it wasn't cov-

ered in scum it had a dark wet picture of trees and sky. Bugs
zinged over it on hair legs. Danny lay there zoning out, drifting
in the direction of a snooze, when the pool rippled like something had fallen into it, and he caught some reflection of movement on the water. He lay there, waiting for the reason to show
itself without his having to move, but when no one came into
view or said hello he scrambled into a sitting position. He looked
across the pool at where the movement had been, by the Medusa
head, but there was no one. Nothing. Danny ran his eyes slowly
over the wall of cypress, watching for someone hiding behind it,
inside it, and when he was looking the other way it happened
again—some quick motion right across the pool from where he
was sitting. And then the water moved, like a big mass had
dropped into it or was coming up from under the surface.

What the fuck?

Somewhere in Danny's gut, the worm stretched awake. Who
was fucking with him? He stood up and turned around very
slowly, three hundred and sixty degrees, looking at the black
ring of cypress around him but even more, listening: for a
crunch, a crack, a step. The wind was picking up, and dry leaves
rattled over the marble and dropped in the pool, resting on the
scum awhile before they started to sink. But there were no
sounds of people.

And then, when his eyes were pointed near the Medusa head
but not directly at it, Danny saw it again, from the corner of his
eye: two shapes that might have been people or shadows of
people, right near the edge of the pool. They started out apart
and then sort of merged into one. Or else one disappeared. They
weren't real people; it was a head trick, an eye trick, like the
trails his fingers made in the air when he was coming on to E.

Danny circled the pool to the Medusa head and stood listening, but he knew that no one was fucking with him. He was
fucking with himself. It always amazed Danny how much sleep

deprivation was like being high, with the one big difference that being tired was never fun. Danny felt like shit, loose in the knees, sweaty, but also cold. And something else, too: prickling. On his arms, the back of his neck, all the way over his scalp so he felt the hair lift up from his head. On the streets of New York, this prickling would make Danny perch on a stoop or lean against a wall and open up his laptop, because nine out of ten times—no, nineteen out of twenty, ninety-nine out of a hundred—wireless Internet service was what he was picking up. It was an awareness in the air, a possibility. Danny felt this now. Very carefully, not wanting to disturb it or move out of range, he took the phone out of his pocket. He dialed Martha's number with some words in his head that were like praying. Danny felt the world out there like one of those phantom limbs—it tingled, it itched, it hurt to be reattached to him. But the phone just searched. It searched and searched and Danny waited, thinking (praying) that maybe all that searching would lead to something, a gap in this blankness. He waited, watching the phone, until his hope dried up. The loss hit Danny all over again, except this time without the release of yelling or kicking—just that feeling of wanting something so badly you can't believe the force of your wanting won't make it be there, won't make it come back.

That's what death is, Danny thought: wanting to talk to someone and not being able to.

He put the phone away. He rubbed his face and rubbed his eyes and ran his fingers through his hair. He wanted to get away—from the dark pool, the prickling, all of it.

Danny climbed out through the cypress back into the garden, which closed over him like a lid. Under there it was like night, and he tripped on a root and barely stopped himself from falling. He let his eyes adjust and kept going, but not in the direction of the castle. He was headed for the keep.

CHAPTER SIX

Baroness

As Danny got close, he saw the girl again. It was getting near sunset, and the light on top of the long stone tower was going pink. She stood in one of the pointy windows, and she was gorgeous the way any blonde is if you look at her from far enough back.

That was the baroness at fifty feet.

Closer in, Danny realized the girl was no girl: she was a woman, which didn't mean someone Danny's own age (those were girls)—it meant someone who looked the way his friends' moms used to look when he was a kid (in other words, his own age). She wore a sleeveless blue-green dress and her arms were long and white and a little soft toward the shoulders, and her blond hair swayed down from her head in a way that seemed styled. And she was waving, that was the best part. Inviting him in.

That was the baroness at thirty feet.

It wasn't obvious how to get inside the keep. There was no door at the bottom—just a narrow stone staircase wrapping the building's outside, no railing, the wind picking up as Danny climbed out of the trees. It happened quickly, like an airplane shooting above cloud cover. And there was the sunset, stewy pink on the horizon.

The stairs kept turning around the outside of the keep, but eventually Danny hit a carved door that opened into a small dark space with narrow stone steps leading up and down. It smelled of dust and standing water. Another door was straight ahead, heavy and thick like it was left over from centuries ago. Danny pushed that open into a square room full of heavy draperies and lighted candles and a lot of the color gold—gold all over the place, so the room looked like some fantastical king's chamber. Walking in there, Danny felt a swell of excitement that half lifted him off his feet.

There were four windows, one in the middle of each wall. In front of one, the woman was standing on a chair. Sunset was all around her, making her hard to see, but Danny could tell she was older than he'd thought—some of what he'd taken to be her features turned out to be makeup arranged in the shapes her features should have had and maybe did have once, a long time ago, when she was one of those ages he'd thought from outside.

She said: I have some troubles with this window. Her voice was like a man's—a man who smoked too much and shouted a lot and came from a foreign country that maybe was Germany, although Danny had never been great with accents.

That was the baroness at fifteen feet.

With every step Danny took, the lady aged—her blond hair whitened out and her skin kind of liquefied and the dress paunched and drooped like a time-lapse picture of a flower dying. By the time he got to her side he couldn't believe she was on her feet. But she was, in high heels, fighting with a curtain rod.

That was the baroness at two feet.

Danny: Hey, watch it! If that window popped open, she'd drop like a flowerpot.

Baroness (chuckling): I'm stronger than you think. You're very tall. I think you can fix this without even the chair.

Danny helped her down. The feel of her hand made him shudder: twigs and wire floating around in the softest pouch of skin he'd ever touched—like a rabbit's ear or a rabbit's belly or some even softer rabbit place. She had angry black eyes and a long full mouth that was unusual for an old lady. She had a high forehead, a chin with a dimple, and some pale yellow still left in her thick white hair. Her way of moving was jerky, impatient, like she was shaking off a person she was sick of. Her sleeves were long, it turned out—all he could see were those hands.

Danny didn't need the chair. He looked at the curtain rod and saw that the brackets holding it up were barely attached to the wall, old screws slipping in and out of their holes. Danny had no talent for home repair, but even he could handle this.

Danny: Have you got a screwdriver? And a hammer?

Baroness: Of course not. You should have brought the tools you needed.

Danny turned to her. *What the fuck?* he almost said.

Baroness: What sort of handyman doesn't carry tools?

Danny was a foot taller than she was, maybe more. He pulled himself very straight and looked down. Her eyes pointed back at him like a pair of darts.

Danny: Do I look like a handyman to you?

Baroness: Everyone looks like a handyman to me. And then she laughed, one of those soupy laughs that could stay a laugh or else turn into a coughing fit. And Danny got it: she was playing herself. A *character*. He liked these types because they pretty much told you what reactions they wanted you to have, and they liked Danny because he went ahead and had them.

Danny: If there's an opposite of a handyman, I'm it.

The baroness reached out her tender, bony hand. Danny was nervous to touch it again. He didn't squeeze it or shake it but more just held it for a second, like it was a fragile thing he'd found that was barely alive. He wondered if all her skin could be this soft. The idea made him a little sick.

Baroness: I am the Baroness von Ausblinker. This castle is mine, and all the land around it in every direction you can see. She glanced out the window, sunset reaching out over miles of black trees.

Danny: Including the town? He was playing along.

Of course including the town. The town and the castle have served each other for hundreds of years. And your name?

Danny. Danny King. Cousin of Howard King, who's got the nutty idea *he* owns this place.

Well, he paid for it. And now he lives in my house. It's the American way.

Danny: What do you know about that?

The baroness narrowed her eyes. I was married to an American for forty-three years: *Al Chandler*—she squawked out the name in a way that made her start to cough, and then she choked around the coughing—he was a champion golfer.

Al Chandler, Al Chandler. . . . Danny muttered the name like he was trying to place it, but this was pure theater. He could tell in under a second if he'd heard a name before. He'd never heard of Al Chandler.

All this time they were standing by the window. Danny could see the edges of the castle buildings to the left, lights coming on in the windows.

Danny: Did you and Al Chandler live in America?

We certainly did. On and off for forty-three years while my husband was alive. My children are there today: Tucson, Gainesville, and Atlanta. They're more American than you are. My sons wear shorts in summertime. You would never see a European man in shorts—never! A man's legs out in the open like that, it's . . . it's miserably low-class.

Danny: I've seen plenty of European guys in shorts.

Not real men, obviously.

What the hell does that mean?

The baroness smiled. Here, sit. She beckoned Danny with a finger toward a pair of soft chairs by a corner fireplace that took up a big chunk of the small room. Two logs were burning in it. Danny sat, and dust and some old body smell leaked up around him. The baroness leaned forward, elbows on her sharp knee-caps, and gored Danny's face with her eyes. She said: You're homosexual. Pronouncing it *homosex-sual.*

I am?

You're wearing makeup.

Oh. He laughed. That's just a style thing.

Don't people assume you're homosexual if you wear makeup?

Some, I guess.

Any normal man wouldn't stand for it.

Any normal man being Al Chandler? For some reason he liked saying that name.

Al disliked homosexuals, but he hid it perfectly. He was a gentleman. Not that you'd know what that means.

You're right, I have no idea.

It doesn't exist in America.

Actually, I think homosexuals *are* the gentlemen in America.

The baroness smiled, that beautiful mouth coming apart in a way that must've knocked people out when she was young. It gave Danny a funny shiver, because imagining that was like seeing it, in a way.

Baroness: You're confident. So you must be successful at something.

Working on it.

Hmmt. Then maybe you're stupid.

You and my pop would have plenty to talk about.

I doubt that.

Danny looked at his watch. He kept having the feeling he should go, but then he'd remember he had no place *to* go except back to the castle, and that made him feel like he'd been kicked. Then it was a relief to see this old lady sitting near him. She sat perfectly straight, her spine like a pole, watching him.

Danny: What do you mean, the castle is yours?

I mean I was born here. I know every cupboard and drawer and stone, every hall and every door. I mean that before my time there were eighty generations of von Ausblinkers whose blood now runs in my veins, and they built this castle and lived and fought and died in it. Now their bodies are dust—they're part of the soil and the trees and even the air we're breathing this very minute, and I *am* all of those people. They're inside me. They *are* me. There is no separation between us.

Danny: You were born here?

I said that clearly, did I not?

You did, I just. . . . He was surprised Howard hadn't mentioned that part. So you know what all this looked like—before.

Not like the miserable wreck it is now, I can tell you that. It was beautiful. It was perfect.

And then you came back after all those years.

Naturally I came back. It was the obvious thing to do after Al Chandler passed away.

You—what—just showed up one day?

With laborers, yes. The castle was abandoned. I spent a pack getting set up in here. And a few years later the Germans came to make their hotel and they asked me to go. And I told them, I will never leave this place. I *am* this place. I am every person who has lived here for nine hundred years. It's beyond ownership. It simply is.

The idea caught in Danny, all those generations. At times he had trouble even believing that one chain of days connected his first day in New York to this day, right now—that so many years could have passed in such a thin stream, day by day by day. And that amount of time was nothing compared to what the baroness was talking about. Centuries! It thrilled him to think about it.

Danny: So what did the Germans do?

Well, of course they tried to make me go. They sent summonses and all this sort of nonsense, they called the police. I stopped letting them in. I was afraid they would drag me into the forest and slit my throat. But I spoke to them from the window, that one right there.

She staggered up from the couch and Danny followed her to another window. The baroness unlatched it and pushed it open.

Look outside, she said, and Danny leaned through. The burned-out sunset had left an orange stain low in the sky. The garden looked like a black ocean tossing around the bottom of the keep. It smelled rotten and sweet, but that smell was mixed with a freshness the wind brought in from somewhere. Next to the window, on the outside wall of the keep, a white rope was looped around a hook. It ran down the length of the tower and disappeared into the trees.

Danny (calling back): What's the rope for?

Baroness: It's attached to a basket. People from the town come and bring me food and things I need. The older ones still remember my family. If I leave a request in the basket, they bring it the next time.

When he pulled himself back inside, Danny felt like he'd washed his face. So you talked to the Germans from up here?

Baroness: They stood in a group underneath those trees. And I said to them—she stuck her head out the window and then her whole torso, and before Danny knew it she was cawing into the night—*I'm still a baroness. This may be meaningless to you, but it's real. The title is real. It survives hundreds of years of history.*

The baroness's feet had no contact with the floor: her legs bent from the effort of shouting and her shoes dangled from her bony heels. Danny moved closer, ready to grab her hips if she started to tip.

Baroness (hoarse): I told them, *You're not dealing with one old lady, you're dealing with all the people who have made me, kings and counts, Charlemagne and William the Conqueror and King Ferdinand and Louis the Fourteenth*—she swiveled to look at Danny and he jumped back, not wanting her to see how close he'd been standing—Of course this means nothing to you. There's no such thing as noble blood in America, you're all mongrels. The oldest thing in your family closet is a tennis racket from 1955, whereas I have a thirteenth-century sarcophagus in my basement. But a European understands these things. My point was simply that I outranked them.

Danny couldn't keep the smile off his face. Not just because the baroness was a kook and he liked kooks but because what she was saying did something to him, filled up his brain with kings and knights and guys fighting battles on horses. That stuff had always seemed unreal to Danny, like it only existed in books or games, but here was a lady who was linked to all of it by one thin chain of years and days and hours and minutes. This excited Danny in a way that felt like hunger. It was *physical*. He had to know more, had to keep her talking.

So what did the Germans do? Just stand down there while you yelled?

The baroness hoisted herself back inside, veins pulsing in her neck. A lady never yells. I spoke clearly and calmly.

Danny: Did it work?

Pah. They began their stupid renovation and hoped I would die before they were done. But I outlasted them. That wet laugh trickled up again from so deep in the baroness that it seemed like it wasn't coming from inside her but below her, from the actual keep. She made her way back to the fireplace and sat. All the shouting had left her shaky. Danny stood by her chair.

Danny: It's amazing they didn't just come in here and remove you.

Remove me? The baroness's face contorted with shock and rage to the point where Danny wondered if she was having a stroke. She tottered back onto her feet. Her throat was raw from all that shouting out the window, so she rasped at him: The keep is the tallest, strongest part of the castle, where everyone fled if the walls were breached. This keep hasn't surrendered in nine hundred years, and you're asking why they didn't *remove me?*

Danny: Okay. Okay.

If they'd been stupid enough to try such a thing, I would have poured boiling oil over their heads as they came up the stairs. I keep a tub of oil on hand for exactly that purpose. And I have the ingredients for Greek fire, too, which burns and maims whomever it touches. Historians are still squabbling about what Greek fire was made of, but I have a recipe left to me by my father, who got it from my great-great-great grandfather, whose great uncle left it to him. And so on.

I get the picture.

I have weapons, too. That goes without saying: swords, a longbow, a crossbow, even a cat, which in layman's terms is a battering ram. And revolvers, naturally. You may tell your cousin that.

My cousin? Danny was thrown—he'd completely forgotten Howard. Then he played dumb. Does he want you out of here too?

He must, mustn't he? She gave a crafty smile. But your cousin is smarter than those Germans. He knows I can be useful. She lowered herself back onto her chair.

Danny: Useful how?

Well, the castle's original dungeon is under this keep. There's a whole room filled with instruments of torture—imagine if he could show his tourists that! But he has no idea of how to find it. And there are a thousand things like that: tunnels, passages—a whole city underneath this castle and around it, things your cousin couldn't find if he spent a hundred years looking. If I go, he loses all that—generations of knowledge, secrets, gone. There's no getting it back.

Her voice had changed. It was reaching, calling out to someone else. She was talking to Howard, not Danny. It made Danny feel like his cousin was in the room, leaning against the shadowy wall by the old paintings and the furniture covered up with cloths.

Danny: It sounds like you and Howard need to have a negotiation.

Isn't that why you came?

Me? No. I—I was just walking past and you were . . .

But already Danny wasn't sure. Why *had* he come to the keep?

The baroness leaned forward so her face was only inches away from his. She was swaying in her heels. He dreaded the smell of her breath, but it turned out to be dry and a little sweet.

She said: Your cousin and I have nothing to negotiate. The cards are entirely mine. You may tell him that.

She smiled at Danny, this ancient crone, alone and weak, nuts if she thought she could operate a battering ram on her own. She was powerless any way you sliced it, but she thought she was strong and that made it true in a way. This astounded Danny. He'd never seen it before.

Danny: You must want something. Everyone does.

Nothing your cousin can give me. Or I would demand it, you can be certain of that. Now, shall we put our work to the side and have a glass of wine?

Absolutely. Danny was enjoying himself. It felt like the first time in a while.

He offered to help the baroness get the wine, but she flapped him away. Danny heard her pointed heels clicking on the stone steps. He added a log to the fire and waited. An idea about Howard and the baroness was taking shape in his head, but it took him awhile to know what it was. And then he got it: Was his job, the reason Howard had brought him all this way, to get the baroness out? As soon as he'd asked, Danny was sure the answer was yes.

The bell for dinner must have rung, but he hadn't heard it. Outside the sky had gone black. The baroness was taking forever. It crossed Danny's mind that she might not ever come back and even this wouldn't seem especially strange.

Restless, he got out of his chair and started peeking under furniture cloths around the edges of the room. An old harpsichord. A bulky thing with about a hundred ivory drawers in it. A mirror with a gold outline. A painting he couldn't really see. Danny snapped on his pocket flashlight and aimed its beam at the canvas: a boy and a girl, pale skin, brown eyes, faces so identical they came off as one kid in two different outfits. Dark hair curled around their earlobes. The boy was leaning against the trunk of the tree in short pants and a purple velvet coat, and the girl stood near him in a dress made out of the same purple velvet. Her arm hung around the boy's neck. The baroness came and stood next to Danny, breathing hard.

Baroness: We thought they'd run away at first. But eventually the pool was drained and they were lying at the bottom. Holding each other, was how the story went.

All this was familiar, but from where? Then Danny remembered: the twins who'd drowned in that pool. We, she'd said. He turned to the baroness and saw that her mouth was like the twins' mouths: long full lips that looked as unexpected on their small faces as they did on her ancient one. Their sister, she had to be.

Danny: Were they older than you?

Baroness: By four years. She seemed tired. She was a fighter, Danny thought, but when there was nothing to fight against she went limp.

Danny watched the picture. The kids' exact positions were hard to pin down, like they were moving slowly—too slowly to see, but enough so when he aimed his beam away from them and then back, they'd shifted.

Baroness: Come. I've poured the wine. There it was, on the enameled table in front of the fireplace, a bottle that looked like it had been dug up from a grave. From Papa's wine cellar, the baroness said. The cellar is still intact, exactly as it was, and only I know where it is.

I'll pass that on.

Do, she said, and laughed.

Danny laughed, too—at the bottle. A Burgundy from 1898! He was no wine expert, but he'd been around enough of them to know that a Burgundy from 1898 was like a steak that had been sitting around since 1960. Putrid would be a distant memory. Nonexistent was more like it.

But there was something in his glass that looked like wine. Danny picked it up and smelled: mold, wet wood. The glass was thin and hand-blown, colored bubbles around its base. Danny sipped. The taste was outright freakish: a reek of decay mixed with some sweet, fresh thing the decay hadn't touched. He drank fast, racing to get that freshness in him before the decay wiped it out. A minute later he was pouring more, for the baroness too. He drank again, thinking the goodness might be gone, but it was still there. Danny had to force himself not to chug.

Danny: So did anyone ever attack this keep, like with weapons?

Baroness: Certainly they did, many times. The most spectacular were the Tartars—historians say they never crossed the Vistula, but that's a fantasy. A band of Tartars surrounded our castle on their white horses, their sappers brought down the east wall with an underground fire, and as the Tartars poured through the walls we locked ourselves inside this keep with enough provisions to last eight months. My ancestor, Batiste von Hagedorn, brought knights from a secret garrison through an underground tunnel that led inside the castle walls, and he cut off the Tartars' supply lines and trapped them inside. They were finished in twenty-four days.

She looked at Danny with glittering eyes. The wine was gone—they'd drunk it all. The baroness leaned back into her soft chair, her gold-white hair spreading out on the velvet upholstery. That's why I feel so very safe inside my keep. Do you see?

I see. And he did see: the baroness was like a magnetic field bending his thoughts her way.

It was only when Danny stood up that the wine walloped him. He felt weird. And see, I have a problem here, because I keep saying, *Danny felt weird*. And *Danny felt weird*. So how is this weird any different from all the other weird ways he's felt? Well, here's how: Those other weirds were the opposite of calm and fine, but this weird *was* calm and fine. Danny felt calm and fine, but also like he was asleep. Or at least not awake. His brain was cut off from his body, which had gotten out of its chair and was following the baroness to the door.

Danny: Where are we going? He heard his voice, but didn't know he'd said the words.

Baroness: You asked to see the roof, did you not?

Danny had wanted to go on that roof ever since he'd spotted

it at night from the castle walls. Had he told the baroness that? He trailed her back out the heavy door. She started climbing the narrow flight of stairs he'd seen when he first came into the keep, and Danny followed. They passed door after door, to the point where it seemed they'd gone higher than the keep could possibly be. The higher they went, the narrower the stairs got, until Danny's shoulders were touching the walls on either side. Eventually he had to turn sideways just to get through. It was like squeezing between muscle and skin. The baroness kept stopping to breathe, and Danny heard air rattling through the wet caves in her chest.

Finally they climbed through a trapdoor onto the keep's roof: a stone platform the same size and shape as the room they'd been sitting in. Around its edges were those square indentations Danny had seen on top of the castle walls. Everywhere else there was sky, a giant sky crammed with more stars than he'd ever seen—a splattery mess of them, a garbage dump. It was almost obscene.

Danny stared at the sky. He felt something in one of his pockets and pulled it out. His phone. He'd forgotten it. He stared at the thing, amazed to think he'd ever pushed those buttons and talked to people in countries thousands of miles away. It seemed like a miracle, like calling out to one of those trillions of stars and having a voice answer back.

Danny held the phone and knew it was over, all that. He was somewhere else.

He threw the phone hard, so his shoulder and elbow snapped. It shot straight out into the dark. He didn't hear it land.

Baroness: Did you make a wish?

She was standing across the keep, watching him. Her voice was the same raspy man's voice, but when Danny turned to look at her she'd dropped thirty years, maybe more, her tits tight inside her dress, those pale arms visible again. Danny realized he'd been waiting for this, to see her this way again. Knowing it would come.

She got younger every step he took, until her hair was heavy and gold around her long white neck. Danny took hold of her hands, feeling the sharp bones inside that soft, soft skin. He pushed himself against her, easing her backward onto the stones, which were smooth and flat from hundreds of years of people stepping over them. When they kissed, the taste of her mouth was like that wine. It made him drink wildly, chasing after that sweet last thing.

CHAPTER SEVEN

I ᴠᴀᴜɴᴛ

I have a dream I'm stuck inside a burning tower. When I open up my eyes, there's a flashlight so close to my face I can feel the heat from its puny bulb. It's got me too blind to see who's behind it, but when I hear the voice I remember where I am. It's Davis.

I've got your number, pal, he tells me. Oh yeah, I've got it now.

He's used that one before, *I've got your number*. I already wrote it down.

You've had my number since day one, I tell him.

Davis moves the flashlight back a little, but it's still in my eyes. He's looking at me like there's something hidden behind my skin that he wants to see.

Nope, I didn't have it on day one, he says. Didn't have it yesterday. But now that I do, this camouflage act of pretending you're brain dead is officially out-of-date.

I've got no idea what Davis is talking about, but I'm used to that. I say, What happened since yesterday?

He ducks, and the light is finally off me. It leaves a big green patch in front of my eyes. I look over the edge of my tray and see Davis hunched over, rummaging under the tablecloth that covers whatever's underneath his bed. When he stands back up he's got a bunch of typed pages in his hand. They start sliding and drifting down to the floor and I jerk on one elbow and shoot a hand under my mattress to see if my manuscript is still where I put it. A mistake. Davis drops his flashlight and grabs me in a headlock.

Are those mine? I manage to croak out.

They've got your name on them, he says. Already he's easing up. The headlocks are a reflex with Davis, it's nothing personal. As soon as I can move I push my hand under my mattress right below my head. No pages. I get a gnawing feeling, but I don't let it show.

You read it all? I ask him.

Don't act so surprised. I read up whole books on my bunk while you snooze away the night. I *use* my time. And I'm amazed—I'm in a state of shock, brother, that's God's truth—to find you've been using yours, too.

Brother?

He lets me go and I yank in some breath. Davis's sweating hands have wetted up my hair.

That shit isn't mine, I tell him, for two reasons: one because I don't want Davis to know I give a damn about the pages, two because I want him to take that look he's pointing my way and move it someplace else.

Don't try to back off now, Davis says. Take responsibility for your actions! But Davis can't say *responsibility* in a normal voice: he has to shout it.

Shut the fuck up! Luis yells from next door.

I'm saying I didn't make it up, I tell him softly. *pun?*

Davis snorts. Obviously you didn't make it up.

My pages are all over the floor, and my computer time's shot until next week. If anything is missing from the new stuff I've typed, I can't give it to Holly tomorrow. This started the week after the fight: Allan Beard ate up a whole class reading a long thing about climate change, and when class was done and Holly was leaving, she stopped by my desk and said, Ray. She wasn't looking at me—she still won't even since the fight, but it's different now. Now it's like we've agreed not to look, because our eyes meeting up seems too private. I only want that to happen if we're alone in a room, which in this place is pretty much impossible. In the break, when the other guys swarm around Holly all wanting their little piece, I go out to the hall.

Holly looked at my pages and said, Give me that.

I handed them up. She slipped them in her bag, and the next week she gave them back to me (still not looking) with these beautiful green marks on the edges of every single page, *Nice!* and *Cut?* and *More of this?* and *Careful* and *Heavy-handed?* and *Strange* and *Good tension* and *More?* and *More?* and *More of this?* and *Yes* and *Wow!* and *Yes* and *Very nice!* and this is as close to sex talk as it gets for me in here, so you bet I enjoy it. I never look at my part, the stuff she's talking about—who cares? What I want is more, and the only way to get more is to write more, and every week I try harder so I can rake in all those yeses and nices and wows. Not just blabbing stuff down but really trying to make something out of it.

What I want—I actually have dreams about this—is to hold her hand. I remember how it felt on my forehead right after the fight, those dry cool fingers, and when I think hard enough I can still feel them there, like they left a mark. When Holly gives back my pages I try taking them from her in a way that my fingers will slide against her fingers or even just brush them for a second and I'll feel her body there the way I did when she touched my head. No luck. I think holding her hand in here would be equal to fucking her on the outside.

I get off my bunk slowly, trying to avoid another headlock

from Davis. I crouch down and start picking my pages up from the floor. Our leaky head has gotten one of them wet, smearing up Holly's green ink. I blot it with toilet paper. All this while I'm down by Davis's bunk, which he usually guards like a dog because of whatever the hell he's got under there. But he watches me now like I'm a magician setting up a trick.

Look at you, he says. And here you've been acting all these months like you don't give a shit about anything.

When I've got all the pages I can find, I put them in order and count. My heart kicks up, because if the numbers aren't right I know I'll have to fix it, I'll have to solve it, or I can't do anything else.

I'm missing forty-five, I tell him.

Davis acts like he doesn't hear me, so I get in his face. Four-five, Davis. Page forty-five. I need it.

Look at you, he says. It's like he's fallen in love. His wild face looks soft as a puppy dog's, and he keeps tilting his head and shining his eyes my way.

Stop looking at me, I tell him, because Davis in love is not a sight you want to see.

Relax, he says. We'll put your ghost story back together just like it was.

Ghost story? I say. The fuck are you talking about?

Don't play possum with me, he says, and I hear it, *play possum,* but the missing page has me too rattled to care.

I leave what pages I've got on my tray and crouch on the floor and start looking for forty-five. There aren't a lot of places a piece of paper can go in a room this size, but I feel around behind the head and under the sink and over near the window. There are no ghosts in this story, I say to Davis.

Oh yeah? Then show me where the people are.

I look up at him. What people?

Davis waves the pages I've left on my tray so they flap in the air. *These* people, he says. I can see them, I can hear them, I *know* them, but they're not in this room. They're not on this block. They're not in this prison or this town or this country or even this same world as you and me. They're in some other place.

I think: If one more page falls out of that bunch I'll squeeze Davis's head between my hands until it pops. But all I say is, C'mon, man. It's just words.

Davis holds the flashlight under his face: angles, sweat, eyes, and the sight of him lit that way gives me a shake from my ass to my neck. They're ghosts, brother, he says. Not alive, not dead. An in-between thing.

I can't look at him that way on hands and knees. I stand back up. You could say that about any story there is, I tell him.

Now you're singing my song, brother.

What's all this brother stuff? Since when are you and me brothers?

More than brothers, Davis says. We're one mind.

It's the highest compliment he has to give. I'm going to show you a top-secret thing, he says. Brother that you are. I keep it just here.

He leans down and lifts up the red-and-white checked table-cloth that covers up the space below his tray. Davis points his flashlight under there and I get a pretty good view of a whole lot of crap: Cups. Plastic forks. A shower head. Mustard packs. Newspapers, nail brush, bottle caps, rubber bands, plastic bags, a beat-up phone book, soda cans. It looks like one of those nests a hamster makes, except Davis is 6'2" and can bench-press 350 and he's been in this cell a year plus and the nest is more like what ten thousand hamsters would make. Right on top is a sheet of white paper. I pluck it out: forty-five.

Things settle down in my head. I stand up and put forty-five back in its spot and knock the pages against my mattress until the edges line up and slide it all underneath where my head goes.

Davis is rooting around in the nest. Out come two skateboard wheels and some paper party hats for little kids and a bunch of prison forms: work orders, permission slips—all contraband. I see cotton balls and some kind of birdwatching guide. Finally he pulls out a cardboard box painted orange. It's about the size of a shoebox—in fact it *is* a shoebox, I can see the Adidas logo right through the paint. He lifts off the top and I look inside the box and see dust. Lint, hair, fur. Dust of every color and thickness. A lot of dust balls all clumped into one big clump. Davis holds the box right under my face.

Listen, he whispers.

I think I'm waiting for Davis to tell me something, but he closes his eyes like he's listening, too. Right now is as quiet as the castle ever gets. I hear the quiet, but the more I listen the more the quiet starts to dissolve and I hear all the little noises of 412 men breathing on metal trays. And there's a background noise, too, a ringing sound you almost can't hear but it's there, maybe a leftover vibration from so many gates and locks clanging shut through the day.

It's not an ordinary radio, Davis tells me softly.

I look at him. Radio?

Gaze at the face of a revolution, Davis says.

There are dials on one side of the box. As in: Davis has collected broken dials off other machines and punched them through the cardboard. Now he starts twisting those dials with his eyes narrowed up like he's concentrating. There, he whispers. Wait—that! You hear that? Okay, let me tune it . . . now she's coming through. Listen to that—clear as day. You hear? And he's so goddam believable I have to keep looking at the nubs of those broken dials he's turning to remember that what we're dealing with here is a shoebox full of dust.

What are we hearing on this radio of yours? I ask.

Davis glances at me. You know it, brother. Don't start pretending on me now.

Okay, I know. But say it anyway.

It's the voices of the dead, Davis says. He looks gentle, like the idea hurts him somehow. He says: All that love, all that pain, all the stuff people feel—not just me and you, brother, but everyone, everyone who's ever walked this beautiful green planet—how can all that disappear when somebody dies? It can't disappear, it's too big. Too strong, too . . . permanent. So it moves to another frequency, where the human ear can't pick it up. And in all these thousands of years, no man has found the technology to tune in to that frequency except once in a while— you know, by mistake. Blips and blops here and there, but nothing steady, nothing regular.

Until you.

Until this, he says, and he holds up his box full of dust. Here's what I've been doing all this time, brother: developing this machine! Making the design, tracking down the necessary parts. Assembling and testing and revising and testing some more, until finally I've got myself a prototype that lo-and-behold actually works!

His eyes shine like a little boy's. I've been calling Davis crazy from day one, but in all that time I missed out on the fact that he's actually *crazy*, as in nuts. A genuine bug. A bug who thinks he's built a machine that can talk to ghosts.

I see that look, Davis says. You're thinking, What's old Davis playing at? Is he trying to pass himself off as some kind of sorcerer? But think about it, brother: new technology always looks like magic. When Tom Edison turned on that tin phonograph of his back in 1877, you think people believed that was for real? Hell no. Ventriloquism, they said. Voodoo. They thought no machine could do such a thing. Or Marconi with his radio: voices floating around from one place to another place—you think people believed that shit? Well, this is no different. It looks mysterious when you don't understand the *technology*. But if you're the engineer, if you built the thing from the ground up, there's no mystery to it.

He holds out the box and I open the lid and look inside again. After all his talk I don't know what I'm expecting—something different. But there it is exactly like before, except now I can pick out stuff inside the dust: A burnt match. A piece of wrapper from a straw. A dead spider. Half a blue button. A piece of maybe scrambled egg. A tile chip, a pin. Chunks of cigarette filter. A ton of hair: head, chest, pubic, most of it dark but some light. Some gray. And between all that, around it, *dust*: grit, sand, powder, debris, some of it glittery like sand or glass, some in chunks like plaster, some in little fibers thinner than threads. Someone told me once that ninety percent of dust is dead skin cells. It looks like you could put together a whole human being from what Davis has got in that box.

With all the people out there who are dead, I say—still playing along because why not, what have I got to lose?—how can you tell which ones you're hearing?

Now that's an excellent question, Davis says, and he actually gives me a pat on the back. The fact is, he says, right now I've got no control whatsoever. It's like an old CB radio, picks up whatever happens to be out there at any particular time. It needs years of refinement like any new invention—hell, when Alexander Graham Bell first put in his telephones, every line was a party line. You couldn't even have a private conversation! What we've got right here is just a start, but it's a big start. Eventually other inventors will get involved too, they'll make their own improvements and modifications. And a hundred years from now, a bunch of kids on one of those school trips? They'll look at this old prototype through some museum window and laugh about how crude this old thing was.

I had no idea you were an engineer, I tell Davis. I mean it to be mocking, but it comes out absolutely serious.

Davis gives a cackle. We fooled each other good! Here we've been thinking we had nothing in common beyond where we happen to be, and all this time we've been doing the same thing: picking up ghosts. We're in lockstep, brother. We're like twins.

Don't get carried away.

And we're just getting started. You won't believe the stuff we can pick up with this machine. You're gonna hear shit that'll make your eyes jump in their sockets.

He smiles at me, and damned if his teeth aren't the whitest teeth I've ever seen in a human head. We. *We:* it's an offer, an invitation to believe in his nonsense. I watch Davis put his ear against his "radio" and nod with his eyes closed, and all of a sudden I think: How do I know it's not real? Okay, it's a shoebox full of dust with knobs pushed through the cardboard, but what if it works? What if it actually does what Davis says? And in that split second I go from pretending straight into believing—it's like all the pretending *made* me believe, except that doesn't make sense, because pretending and believing are opposites. I don't know what happens. Maybe it's this place. Maybe if old fruit can be next week's wine and a toothbrush can slit a throat and holding a girl's hand is the same as fucking her, maybe a box of hair is a radio. Maybe in here it's true.

Or maybe it all comes back to Holly. Maybe if you believe that a word—*door*—is a thing you can walk through, and then you walk on through it like I did, there's nothing out there you won't swallow.

You gonna teach me how to make one of these things, Davis?

Oh, Ray, no, he says, apologizing. I'm waiting on my patent, and until that comes through the blueprint is a state secret. But you don't need one, brother! You've got the use of mine any time you want.

Thanks, I say.

The main thing is, let's get to work! Let's put our time to some use!

Work! Time! Use! He shouts them all. Guys on the block are starting to bang and yell. I don't think Davis even hears.

What kind of work do you have in mind? I ask him.

Davis looks at me awhile. It's that same look he's been giving me all night, like I'm blocking his view of another thing he's been waiting to see. I'm starting to get used to it.

How long you got left in here, Ray? he asks me.

This is just the beginning, I say. The fun part. When I'm done in here I go on trial someplace else.

By the time I get out, Davis says, rapping on his radio, you're gonna need one of these to get in touch with me. But I can't wait, Ray. *I can't wait.*

He clutches his box full of dust. His crazy worn-out face is full of life.

I'm in, I say. And I don't even know what it means.

You were already in, Davis says. Right from the start. That's the whole reason we had this conversation.

CHAPTER EIGHT

When Danny woke up, he had no idea where he was. The room looked abandoned, piles of old broken stuff around, cobwebs, like an attic no one had been inside for fifty years. He was in a bed, between sheets that were maybe the softest sheets he'd ever felt because they were old, we're talking *old,* to the point where they were coming apart around his feet. He was naked. And his clothes were nowhere in sight.

Danny felt like shit. In fact he felt shitty in so many different ways that saying *he had a headache* or *he had a stomachache* would be wrong, because it would give the idea that the shitty feeling came *only* from his head or his stomach when actually it came from every part of him at once: head, stomach, chest, hands, neck, face, knees, eyes, feet. *Hangover* doesn't get near it. Every part of him hurt or felt bad in whatever way it could, to the point where he couldn't do what he normally would do within ten seconds of waking up naked in an unknown bed in an unknown room (and it had happened to Danny before, more than once): get the fuck up. He felt too shitty to get up.

The room was dim, but the sun looked bright outside its little windows. Birds were chattering and screeching, all of which gave Danny a feeling like he'd missed something, he was late—there was someplace he needed to be, people he needed to call, an event he'd forgotten about where he was expected. Normally that kind of feeling would make Danny jump out of bed and try to get things under control, but the shitty feeling had him paralyzed. And then he remembered the satellite dish: no people, no events. And none on the horizon.

All that was the good part. Or at least it seemed pretty good compared to the bad part, which was the scenes flashing through Danny's head: the feel of the baroness's hands, her wet laugh, her mouth, the twins looking down from the painting, none of which was so horrible or even horrible at all, but it seemed very horrible now because of what it led up to. When Danny thought about that part—what it led up to—it was like thinking about a food that has poisoned you. Had he really fucked the baroness? Based on the scenes in his head, it seemed like the answer was yes. At the time he'd thought he was dreaming—a layer of fuzz was in between Danny and everything that was happening. But now the fuzz had burned off and the scenes in his head were brutally real, sickeningly real. And they included *him*. He was remembering things he'd never gone through in the first place!

Danny shut his eyes. He held still and listened with both ears, with his whole head, trying to figure out if he was alone in this room and especially in this bed. When he didn't hear sounds or even feel vibrations of anyone else, Danny cracked his eyes and made the turn to look at the other side . . . slowly, so slowly . . . ready if he hit a point where he saw or felt a person there to stop before he had to face them.

He was alone in the bed. Danny got a rush of relief when he realized this. No one was there, thank God! He managed to raise himself onto an elbow. But someone had been. There was a dent on the old yellow pillow and the sheets were torn up on that side, shredded like ancient cloths you'd see in a museum. Along the edges were sewn flowers with long green stems that came apart when Danny touched them. There was a cover of faded green velvet, and something made Danny push back that cover and the sheet underneath it to look at the spot next to him. He found a kind of residue on the bottom sheet: a trail maybe five inches long of coarse gray powder like dust or ashes or crushed-up bodies of moths.

That got Danny out of bed—boom—despite feeling like shit. *Because* he felt like shit. He needed to puke is what got him up, and he did it out the pointy window that was closest to the bed. There wasn't much in him; his last solid meal was yesterday's lunch. When he pulled back inside the room he was shaking.

He badly needed to piss, but the logistics of trying to do that out a chest-high window with all his limbs jerking spastically made Danny pretty desperate for other choices. There was a narrow door to his right, and behind it was a hole cut in a slab of stone with an unmistakable smell coming up from below it. Jackpot. There was even a crude stone sink that turned out to have running water. Danny pissed and washed his hands and his head in the sink, where the water was one or two degrees warmer than ice, and that made him feel the best he'd felt so far that morning, meaning toward the upper spectrum of very very very bad, so he went ahead and splashed his whole naked body until he was shivering on top of the shaking.

When he came back out, limping on his damaged knee, Danny spotted his pants dangling over the side of an old Chinese screen. They looked like they'd been thrown there, which made Danny actually say out loud, Don't think about it, meaning the exact scene or moment that had sent his pants flying six or seven feet into the air. *Don't think about it. Just get the pants on.* Danny tugged them over his wet legs. He found his shirt and jacket and underwear and socks in different parts of the same general area—all thrown, it seemed. *Don't think about it. Just get the stuff on* (except the underpants, which he stuffed in his jacket pocket). Danny had advanced skills when it came to not thinking: he would picture himself deleting things, disconnecting them from his brain so they disappeared the way digital stuff disappears—without a memory. But sometimes he still felt them, the disappeared things, hanging around him like shadows.

Within minutes Danny was dressed except for his boots. He couldn't find them around the bed, and when he moved beyond it, looking under furniture, thinking maybe the boots had gotten shoved or rolled or thrown (don't think about it), he found nothing but dustballs the size of grapefruits. The more he looked, the more his heart clenched up. These were Danny's lucky boots, the only boots he owned, although he'd shelled out enough repairing and resoling them over the years to buy five or six new pairs, easy. He'd bought the boots right after he got to New York, when he'd just figured out who he was *not* (Danny King, *suchagoodboy*) and was burning up with excitement to find out who he was instead. He'd come across the boots on Lower Broadway, he couldn't remember what store, probably long gone by now. They were way beyond his price range, but those were the days when he could still count on his pop to fill in the gaps. The store had a big rubbery dance beat coming over the sound system, a beat Danny had been listening to ever since, for eighteen years, in stores, clubs, restaurants—he barely noticed it now. But that day in the shoestore, Danny felt like he'd tapped into the world's secret pulse. He'd pulled the boots over his feet and stood in front of a long mirror, watching himself move to that beat, and got a sudden flash of how his life would be—his new life. Wild, mysterious. Danny gritted his teeth from excitement. He thought: *I'm a guy who wears boots like this.* It was the first thing he knew about himself.

A part of Danny wanted out: to get away now from the keep

and the baroness and all the shit he wasn't thinking about, with or without his lucky boots. But he knew that if he ran outside barefoot it would only be a matter of time before he missed his boots and wanted them back, especially since the only other shoes he'd brought to the castle were sandals. And that would mean coming back in here—an even worse idea than staying to look for the boots now. So Danny stayed and looked, first haphazardly, lifting up dropcloths and finding upside-down chairs, a desk on skinny legs crammed with papers and ledgers and letters tied up in shredded yellow ribbons. Eventually he got organized, searching one section of junk before he moved on to the next. He searched with a sick cringing feeling inside because every once in a while he got a jab of the baroness: two jeweled rings on a silver stand. An ivory comb full of yellow-white hair. Teeth in a glass of water. And every time, Danny would feel a wave of nausea and an urge to run, and when he didn't run he'd get a pressure in his head from all the stuff he wasn't thinking about.

After the teeth, Danny left the room. A dust headache was coming on him. The narrow stairwell was right outside the door, a window at its turn, and Danny pushed the window open and stuck out his head. He was high up in the tower; the trees looked a long way down. This side of the keep faced away from the castle, so all Danny saw was the outer wall and then a slope of green that must be the one he'd slogged up with his suitcase that first night. At the bottom of the hill he made out part of the town where he'd waited for the bus. Danny was surprised by how nice it looked—red roofs, a church steeple—because the town where he'd waited for the bus had been ugly and dark. Maybe daylight made the difference.

Danny heard sounds from the town, shouts, maybe kids, that churning noise of people you heard so constantly in New York that it seemed like silence. It worked on him like suction, pulling him out toward the world, this bit of it he could reach. There had to be an Internet café down there, or at least a cell phone store, and thinking of those things was like a caffeine rush hitting Danny's brain—he had to go, had to get down there, had to find his goddamned boots so he could escape from this weird despair he felt around him—not *on* him, not completely. But too close.

When Danny turned to go back in the room he saw his boots lined up neatly outside the door. He must have taken them off last night after coming down from the roof (don't think about it). Danny's eyes filled up, seeing the boots; that's how strung out he was. He actually pushed them against his face for a second. Then he pulled them on his feet and headed downstairs.

One floor down there was another window. Danny couldn't see the town anymore, but the voices—it was voices he was hearing—were louder. So the sounds weren't coming from the town after all, there were people outside the keep. Which meant Danny couldn't leave, because there was no way in hell he'd risk having somebody see him. He'd face the baroness again before he'd take a chance of Howard finding out he'd fucked her.

He followed the stairs another level down but didn't stop because it was the point where he'd first come in, which meant the baroness was probably in the next room where they'd drunk the wine (don't think about it). A level below there was one last window, and after that the stairs twisted into blackness. Danny flicked on his flashlight and pointed it down, but the dark swallowed up his beam. He had an urge to keep going into that dark, a push from inside as deep and strong as wanting to reach the town, but different. Opposite.

There were foot-sized indentations in the steps. Danny set his feet in the grooves and started down. The air smelled like clay and his chest felt heavy and cool, like the clay was inside him, pressing him deeper into the keep. He was right at the turn in the stairs when he heard the voices again, clearer now, floating in through the window above him. They broke Danny's concentration, and he climbed back up to see who it was.

The window was maybe fifteen feet above the tops of the trees, close enough that Danny could see between the branches in some places. Mick and two graduate students were down there, dust masks hanging around their necks. Bits of talk floated up to Danny.

Mick: . . . could start over here . . .

Girl Student: . . . blocking the . . .

Boy Student: . . . not that there's much . . .

They all laughed. Mick kept looking at the keep, not up where Danny was but the part below him, under the trees. Someone else must be there: Howard? Danny yanked his head back inside. But then the person moved into the light and he saw it was Ann. With the baby girl in some kind of pouch on her chest.

They were all laughing again.

Ann: Why not just put up an awning?

She had one of those voices you could hear, high and clear and a little sharp, like kids' voices are. Danny leaned back out the window.

Mick: . . . hire a sharpshooter.

More laughter. Mick was turning into some kind of comedian. Even in the warm weather he wore long sleeves. His dark hair was pulled back in a thong, and there was sweat on his face. On the ground lay a pile of planks. The graduate students seemed to be leaving.

Girl: . . . until lunch?

Ann: Forty-five minutes.

Boy: So we'll . . .

Mick: Don't let . . .

More laughing. Now Danny knew the time: 12:15. No wonder the sun was drilling a hole through his head. He wished they would get the hell out so *he* could get the hell out in time for lunch. He was light-headed for a lot of reasons, but starvation was definitely on the list.

Mick: Wait.

That came up clear. He was talking to Ann, who'd started to walk away, following the graduate students. The baby was asleep, head lolling to the side. Ann turned around. She had on a yellow short-sleeved blouse. Her cheeks looked sunburned, or maybe just hot. Her dark hair must soak up that sun.

Ann: What?

Mick: . . . talk to you . . .

They stood there. No one seemed to be talking.

Mick: . . . never get to . . .

Ann laughed. Whose fault is that? You disappear every time I show up.

Mick said something Danny couldn't hear. His smile was gone. Ann was serious, too.

Ann: You seem so unhappy.

Mick: . . . keep having . . .

Ann: Yeah, I guess I knew that.

Mick: . . . wondering . . . driving me . . .

Ann took a small step back. Mick, you've got to get this under control. You know that, right?

Something in Danny locked in for the first time. He'd been half listening, waiting for Mick and Ann to go away, expecting any minute to hear the baroness staggering down the stairwell behind him. Now he thought: *Wait, what am I hearing?* It wasn't even the words so much as what he *saw:* How close together they were standing. How Ann didn't walk away. The misery in Mick's face.

Ann: I mean it. You've got to get past this. Or we're headed for trouble.

Mick: . . . still think about it?

Ann: I don't! I make a conscious effort not to!

Mick: (inaudible).

Ann: Okay, but it *wasn't* yesterday. Six years is a long time out here in the real world. I didn't even have a kid yet!

Mick: . . . exactly . . . every single . . .

Ann: I don't want to hear this.

Mick put his hands in his pockets and looked down. Danny thought Ann would walk away, but she didn't. She cupped her baby's skull and shut her eyes. Danny knew what was in her head like he was intercepting her thoughts: she wanted to bolt but she couldn't bolt, she had to fix this thing, get it under control, because if she didn't it was going to explode. And then Howard would know—well, he'd know that Mick and Ann had fucked each other six years ago, was how it was starting to look.

Ann moved close to Mick. She looked up into his face over the head of her sleeping kid and said: Let's just tell him.

It took Mick a second to react. Then he said: What are you talking about? It was the first full sentence Danny had been able to hear from the guy. Mick's lips were white.

Ann: He's strong, he can take it. It'll be rough for a while but in the end I think it'll be okay.

Mick: No. No. No. No. No. Do you hear me?

Okay!

Mick was pacing, frantic: . . . Cut my own throat . . . think I'm kidding . . . ?

Ann: All right, relax. It was just an idea.

Mick: Never . . . the last thing I . . . can't believe you'd . . .

Oh, fuck you, Mick.

Mick went quiet and looked at her.

Ann: *You* tell me what to do. What do you want me to do? If you keep acting like you're acting and making scenes, he's going to figure it out. And I promise you, that'll be worse.

Mick: Don't tell him.

You think I want to tell him? Come on! It's the last thing I want to do. Look, I've got a baby asleep on my chest and I'm having this conversation with you. Jesus Christ!

Mick: . . . your voice down.

Ann started to cry. Danny watched in a state of shock. He couldn't believe what he was seeing and hearing—couldn't believe he was *able* to see and hear it. It kicked up a mess of reactions in Danny that he couldn't separate out. He felt:

1. Sorry for Howard, who had no idea he'd been fucked over by his wife and best friend.
2. Glad Howard's perfect life wasn't quite as perfect as he'd thought.
3. Even sorrier for Howard, because it's easier to feel sorry for someone when their life isn't perfect.
4. Excited to be the one who was seeing and hearing and knowing all this stuff.

And this last feeling—this thrill of being in the know—kicked something back to life in Danny that had been on ice since he'd gotten to the castle: the thinking, active part of him that spent its time figuring out what was going on around him so he'd know where he fit. The part that had kept Danny alive all these years. The world moved and rearranged itself around him and Danny was himself again, which meant not just knowing things but knowing *more* things than other people, seeing all the links when everyone else could see only a few. *Information.* This had worked for Danny, it had! For years and years it had worked. Not because he used the information—that would be dangerous, more likely to blow up in the face of the person who tried it than anyone else's. But there was power in just having it, in knowing where everyone stood. And Danny had a word that could say all that. One word: *alto.*

Mick took hold of Ann's hand. Here we go, Danny thought.

Mick: (inaudible).

Ann (sobbing): It's just . . . I looked forward to coming here for such a long time and now it's . . . I can hardly sleep.

She stood there crying, Mick holding her hand, and then Ann stopped crying and wiped her face. She kissed her baby's head and checked her watch.

Mick: . . . easier if I . . .

Ann: Yeah, but you can't leave, so there's no point talking about it.

Whoa, Danny thought. *You can't leave?*

Mick: (inaudible).

Ann: I agree. Given what's going on now, it was a horrible idea. But you're here and there's no going back.

Danny's mind was churning. Why couldn't Mick leave? What possible reason could there be?

Mick: (inaudible).

Ann: Forget the apologies. I'm a big girl, I got myself into this. I just—I can't find a way out.

She'd let go of Mick's hand.

The sun moved, and Danny lost their faces. Mick was trying to explain something to Ann, but he'd lowered his voice to a mumble. Danny couldn't hear a thing. Ann was quiet, listening. Danny slid a little farther out the window, at which point he caught *inside* and *time to think* and *patterns* but he couldn't make sense out of it. The meaning was one step beyond him. Danny's feet were off the ground and he was balancing on his abdomen, arms and legs floating ahead of him and behind. He shoved himself out a few more inches. And that was too far.

Danny knew it instantly: he'd ignored that grandmaster of the physical world, gravity, and tipped the bulk of his weight outside the window. Now gravity was pushing him down, so only the friction of his pants against the stone window frame held him in place. Danny almost screamed, but he managed to choke it back. He dug and scrabbled his hands around that window looking for a fingerhold, and wiggled and shimmied his ass, trying to jostle enough of himself back over that stone frame that gravity would be on his side again. For a second or two it seemed like this might work, he was starting to ease himself back, but the friction messed him up—the stone resisted his pants and then sweat started running down his legs and soaking into the fabric, which made it slippery. Or maybe it was *him* getting slippery inside the pants. Anyway, Danny dropped—boom, it was out of his hands—he was sliding, falling, bellowing, because who the hell wouldn't bellow when they fell head first out a window?

He caught himself with his feet, flexed them hard so his toes hooked over the window frame and stopped his fall—and held him there, at least for now. Mick and Ann were yelling.

Mick: Who the hell is that?

Ann: I don't know. I think—is it Howard's cousin? Danny, is that you?

Danny tried to answer, but tensing the muscles of his gut to say even one word would siphon vital energy away from his feet.

Mick: Jesus, he's—wow. Okay, I'm going up. Hold on, Danny, I'll be there in just a . . . His voice faded around the side of the keep.

Ann: Hold on, Danny! He'll be there in a second. Just hang in there.

Every bit of Danny's energy was pouring into his feet. His whole body shook from the effort of flexing them, but he could keep it up, no question, he could flex his feet with this intensity for an hour if he had to. The problem was his boots, which couldn't seem to *hold* his feet. In agonizing little slips his feet were coming out, meaning the boots were too big. Maybe they'd stretched in all the years he'd been wearing them, or maybe Danny had shrunk, or maybe his socks were too thin, or maybe the boots had always been this big and he'd never noticed until now. But Danny didn't think so. When he'd bought the boots they fit perfectly. That was one of the reasons he'd bought them, because it felt like fate: he would meet his future in these boots, which seemed like they were made especially for him. Now Danny's head was a dead weight pulling the rest of him down and his feet were coming out, first in sweaty jerks and then in one last awful slide that separated him from his boots for good.

PART II

CHAPTER NINE

Nora: So. Is it a death wish, or are you just really, really accident-prone?

She was sitting near Danny, who opened his eyes to find he was flat on his back in a place he didn't recognize. It was getting to be a habit.

Danny: Where the hell am I?

Nora: Your room.

That threw him. His room? Danny's cloudy eyes made it hard to look around, but after a couple of seconds he recognized the wood canopy on the antique bed where he'd slept when he first got to the castle. And the high stone walls and the fireplace, an orange blur beyond his feet. And the window—black, so it must be night. Unless his eyes weren't working.

But it wasn't his eyes, it was his brain. The melting, liquidy way things looked reminded Danny of painkillers he'd popped over the years. But why would he be on one now? And right when he asked that question, Danny noticed a thing that had been there ever since he'd opened his eyes but muffled, so it took a while to push through into his thoughts: pain. Not headache pain—headache pain was a hand job compared to this. This was head *injury* pain. When Danny touched his head, where the pain started out from, he found a mess of bandages.

And then it all came back, a mudslide of remembering that felt a lot like slipping out of his boots had felt in the first place. Fuck, he was high.

Danny: What kind of shit have they got me on?

Nora shrugged. Some kind of injections.

Each little thing she said had to travel down a long curled-up tube before it got to Danny's brain. And then his answer had to travel down another long tube out of his brain before it could get to his mouth. When the word *injections* finally got all the way down the tube, Danny jumped. He said (after another long gap): What injections?

Nora: Not sure. The doctor speaks that bizarro language they all speak around here.

Danny: Does Howard understand him?

Nope. No one can.

Somehow, Danny managed to heave himself onto his elbows. You're telling me some dude no one understands is giving me injections?

Relax. That old lady who lives in the tower, the baroness. She's translating.

Here? In this room? The idea made him frantic.

No, no, she won't leave that tower—won't even open the door. So Howard and the doctor stand outside, and the doctor yells stuff up at the window, and then the baroness yells the meaning back down to Howard.

Danny lay back and shut his eyes. It was too much to figure out. Suddenly Nora was hopping around, plucking at his blanket.

Nora: Nodon'tgotosleep! Don'tgotosleep! Are you going back to sleep? Don'tgotosleep!

Danny opened his eyes. What the hell is wrong with you?

Nora looked at her watch. Her hands were shaking again.

She unhooked something from her belt and Danny heard a staticky noise.

Nora (into the machine): He's awake. Over.

Crackly voice: How long? Over.

Nora: Ten minutes. Over.

Crackly voice: . . . on my way.

Nora smiled. It was the smile Danny had been waiting for,
the smile that cut through her attitude and dreadlocks and bad
eye contact and hating of facts and turned her straight back into
the pretty suburban girl she'd started out as. But Danny didn't
see the smile. His eyes were—I want to say glued, but it was
more than glued: his eyes were *laminated* onto that walkie-talkie
in Nora's hands. How can I explain what Danny felt, seeing it?
Like a guy on a hunger strike who sees a roast beef go by on a
tray. Like a con doing life without, watching a *Hustler* center-
fold hump a pole. But those examples aren't enough, so instead
I'll tell you what happened *inside* Danny: his mouth watered, his
gut rumbled, his throat got a lump, his nose prickled, his eyes
filled with tears, and he let out a long groan.

Nora: What? What? Her dreads shook as she fluttered over
him.

Is that a . . . what is that? His head was starting to pound.

It's a walkie-talkie. Should I—I think Howard's already on
his . . .

Inside Danny's head a maniac had started clubbing at a door
that wasn't strong enough to hold him back.

Danny: How did you get it? He was having a memory or
maybe a dream: holding that machine, talking into it, having a
voice answer back. His whole gut went watery at the thought.

And then the force of how much Danny wanted the machine
ground against the fact that he didn't have it.

Nora: We've all got them. It's the only way we can find each
other in this . . .

The maniac pounded harder, drowning her out.

Nora: I'm surprised Howard didn't give you—

Wham, wham, wham. The door popped, and Danny passed out.

Can you hear me? Danny. Danny?

Danny opened his eyes. First he saw the ceiling: very high, with black beams running across it. Then he saw Howard by the bed.

Howard: Great, fantastic, you're awake. He checked his watch. Okay, nine forty-eight. And how long was the last one? He was talking to someone who turned out to be Nora. She was standing behind him.

Nora: Thirteen minutes.

You still with me, buddy?

Danny: I'm here.

Howard looked different, but whatever the difference was made him seem more familiar to Danny, more like he'd been before. Or maybe Danny was finally getting used to this new face.

Howard (to Nora): You tried to engage him?

Nora: Yes. I mean, we talked.

Howard: But you didn't stress him.

Nora: I don't think so. She gave these answers absolutely straight—no irony, no sarcasm, no doubletalk. It was like watching a color picture go to black-and-white.

Danny: What the fuck is going on?

Howard: Good question. Excellent question, Danny. You remember you fell out a window?

Danny nodded.

Howard: Well, a tree broke your fall. Thank God, buddy. No point in dwelling on it, but Jesus Christ, you know what I mean? Still, you hit the tree pretty hard, and you've got some cuts on top of your head that had to be stitched. As far as internal damage goes, meaning inside your head, the doc's pretty sure it's just a bad concussion.

Danny: This is the doctor who doesn't speak English?

Howard grimaced. Yeah. He's the best, supposedly, trained in Paris and all that, but the language thing is a nightmare, no question. Anyway, we're getting through it. He's given you some injections to keep your brain from swelling up, which I guess is important for the first twenty-four hours. And meanwhile we've been waking you up every thirty minutes to keep you from slipping into something called a "gripping sleep" or a "grabbing sleep"—there may be a translation issue there, but I'm ninety percent sure he's not talking about a coma, just some kind of deep sleep that's hard to get out of.

Nora: Remember the dreams.

Howard: Yes. Thanks. The doctor wanted me to ask if you've been having a lot of dreams.

Danny: I don't think so.

Howard: See, that's really good. Because apparently this gripping sleep or grabbing sleep has a lot of very weird dreams associated with it, lifelike dreams where you can't tell if you're asleep or awake. So I'm—I'm just incredibly glad to hear you haven't been dreaming.

He leaned close again, his eyes scooping at Danny's face. His breath had a strong mint smell, like he'd just brushed his teeth. Danny noticed sweat beading up on Howard's hairline and realized that the new thing he saw in his cousin's face was fear. Howard was scared.

Howard: Anyway, when you've stayed awake continuously for two hours, we can stop the thirty-minute checks. And as long as you get there within fifteen hours of the injury, which was— he checked his watch—about nine hours ago, we don't have to go any further.

Danny: Further with what?

Howard: Well, the next step would be to airlift you to a hospital for a brain scan.

He said this casually, like it was basically nothing, and that gave him away. Howard was scared Danny was seriously fucked up—fucked up enough to die. But Danny didn't feel scared, seeing this. The opposite, almost. Like Howard's fear would protect him—like the job of being scared was all taken care of. Or maybe he was just too high.

Howard: But I'm not expecting that, and neither is the doctor. I mean, you've already been awake—another watch check— almost ten minutes. And you look pretty alert.

Danny: I feel pretty alert.

Howard: Good, good.

There was a pause. Danny felt exhaustion moving back in around him like a tide. He tried not to close his eyes.

Howard: So, ah—look. There's something I want to ask you, Danny. It's kind of delicate. He glanced at Nora and she moved away, over to the window. Howard leaned close, elbows right on Danny's mattress, minty breath filling Danny's nostrils to the point where they tingled on the inside.

Howard: I—I wouldn't even bring this up yet, but the doctor says we're supposed to keep you engaged as long as we don't stress you. So you've got to speak up if you start to feel stressed. Will you do that, Danny?

Sure.

You don't feel stressed right now?

Danny thought about it. He felt like someone had hacked open his skull with a hatchet, but that wasn't exactly the same as being stressed. No.

Howard: So here's my question. As far as your fall goes, it was . . . I'm assuming it was an accident?

The tube in Danny's brain seemed especially long on that

one. He looked at Nora leaning out the window and wondered if she was smoking. He noticed she had a decent ass. When Howard's question finally hit his brain, Danny laughed.

Danny: If I wanted to off myself, don't you think I would've walked up a couple more flights? Or better yet, jumped off a roof in New York and saved myself the jet lag?

Good. Good. Glad to hear it. Although . . . that's not exactly what I meant.

Danny shook his head.

Well, I guess you've basically answered it. But you weren't— no one helped you out that window at any point along the way?

You mean *pushed me*?

Or even, you know, nudged you.

Danny: The baroness?

It sounds farfetched, I know, but—you've met her, right?

The question caught Danny off-guard. He looked at the shape of his knees through the bedspread, purple velvet, similar to the baroness's green bedspread except new. He felt like something hot had been tossed in his face. Howard seemed to take this as a yes.

So you know. She's berserk. I have no sense of what her limits are.

Danny started to laugh, a jittery laugh that fluttered up from his chest like it might not stop. Then it did. It stopped when he asked himself if the baroness *had* pushed him out. Could she have done it so gently he'd hardly felt anything—tipped him just enough with those spidery hands to turn gravity against him? Had he even maybe felt it, a soft, soft pressure on his feet?

It was goofy. The drugs were messing him up.

Danny: She'd do this . . . because you're trying to get her out of the keep?

Howard: Trying, yeah. She won't leave it, we're talking not for five minutes. Says she's afraid I'll lock her out and slit her throat—tells me this straight to my face. But I don't get the feeling she's really scared. It's all part of a strategy: she wants me to do something so she can do something. But I don't know what those things are.

Danny: She's got weapons in there.

Howard had been looking at the fire. Now his head snapped around to Danny. Weapons?

Danny: A longbow, a crossbow. A battering ram. Oil to pour on people's heads. He'd meant to keep this stuff to himself, save it for a time when he could use it somehow, but the bump of surprise on Howard's face was tough to resist. And the fact that his cousin hadn't already guessed about the baroness and Danny made him realize that he wouldn't guess; it would never cross his mind. And being one foot away from someone who couldn't imagine such a thing as Danny fucking the baroness made Danny feel like maybe he hadn't really done it.

Howard: You've seen these weapons?

Danny: No. But I drank some very weird wine from her cellar.

Howard leaned back in his chair and looked at Danny in a new way, a way Danny had a feeling came from his business life. I'm amazed, Danny. Seriously, you've been here less than forty-eight hours, and you're telling me stuff I didn't know. It's . . . impressive. Nora, how are we on time?

Nora was still at the window. She looked at her watch. Almost forty-five minutes.

Howard pounded out of his chair: That's fantastic! This is huge, Danny, the best you've done yet. Let's try to keep it going, okay? Let's stay with this as long as we can.

Now wait a minute, someone's got to be saying. Three pages ago Danny had been awake almost ten minutes, and now you're telling us it's forty-five? Are you kidding me? I could repeat everything they said on those three pages in five minutes tops,

which means Danny should be awake seventeen minutes maxi-
mum. But hold on, bud, you're forgetting two things: (1) Everything anyone said had to travel down a long tube to Danny's
brain, and so did his answers before they got to his mouth and
(2) there were other things going on in the room that I didn't
write down because I would've needed pages and pages, which I
don't have, not to mention it would be boring as hell. Such as:
Howard got up and poked at the fire. Nora shut the window.
Howard scratched his head and blew his nose in a white hand-
kerchief. Nora went into the hall to talk to someone and then
came back. Howard's walkie-talkie made a staticky noise so he
had to fiddle with it to shut it up. Every one of those things adds
time, to the point where if I'd told you an hour instead of forty-
five minutes, even *that* would be realistic.

Howard: Danny? Are you with me?

Danny shut his eyes. The tiredness was pouring in around
him, warm and sweet and sick, a thing you know is bad for you
and that just makes you want it more.

A blast of mint—Howard was hovering over him. Don't.
Don't close your eyes, Danny. For your sake—Nora, could you
throw another log on that fire? Danny, open up.

Danny heard static on Howard's walkie-talkie. He wanted
to hold it. He tried to open his eyes. Can I hold the . . .

Howard: Danny? Fuck! He's out again.

Danny: Can I . . .

The next time Danny woke up, his eyes stayed shut. But he heard
voices and other sounds, too, like when someone speed-dials you
accidentally and you get a crunchy sound of them walking and
hear gurgly voices you might even recognize, and you yell out
their name a few times before you get bored and hang up. But
Danny couldn't hang up. So he lay there hearing stuff like *her-
balloo* and *shudding* and *scramshie,* and then he felt a stab in his

neck, right below his ear. His eyes popped open. Everything was blurry, but Danny caught a gray-bearded guy with a syringe moving away.

Then it got quiet. Danny thought he was alone, but when he turned his head there was Howard's kid, Benjy, in the chair where Howard had been sitting. The kid wore long-sleeved pajamas covered with red fish. His dark hair was messed up, like he'd been sleeping.

Benjy: Did it hurt?

Danny looked at him, letting his eyes adjust. The kid's pajamas confused him—was it big red fish eating little red fish, or were all the fish the same?

Danny: Did what hurt? Falling out a window?

Benjy: No. The shot.

Nah. That felt good.

Benjy frowned, like he couldn't tell if Danny was kidding. Finally he said: Actually, I'm not allowed to climb on windowsills because it's dangerous.

I'll keep that in mind.

Benjy: Did your mommy ever tell you that?

Probably.

Do you have to go home now?

Why would I go home? I just got here.

Benjy: Is your home in an apartment?

Yeah. I mean normally it is, but right now I don't have one. I'm in between places.

Why the hell was he explaining all this? Danny squirmed on the bed, looking for someone to rescue him from this kid. But as far as he could tell, they were alone in the room. Wind blew in through the window and shook the tapestries on the stone walls.

Benjy: Do you have a wife?

No.

My mommy is my daddy's wife.

Yeah, I picked up on that.

Do you have a dog?

No.

Do you have a cat?

I have no pets, okay?

What about a guinea pig?

Jesus Christ! It came out loud, and Benjy looked startled. Danny hoped that would shut him up.

Benjy: Do you have any children?

Danny gritted his teeth and stared at the ceiling beams. No, I don't have children. Thank God.

The kid went quiet for a long time. Finally he said: What *do* you have?

Danny opened his mouth to answer. What did he have?

Benjy: I said, what do you—

I heard, I heard.

What do you have?

I don't have anything, okay? Nothing. Now I'd like to shut my eyes.

Benjy leaned closer. In his face Danny saw sympathy mixed in with a kind of cold curiosity you never saw in adults. They'd learned how to hide it.

Benjy: Are you sad to have nothing?

No, I'm not sad.

But he was. The sadness came on Danny suddenly and buried him. He saw himself: flat on his back in the middle of nowhere, with a smashed-up head. A guy who had nothing.

Benjy: Are you crying?

Danny: You've got to be kidding.

I see tears.

That's just from the . . . my head hurts. You're making it hurt.

Grown-ups cry sometimes. I saw my mommy cry.

I need to sleep.

Benjy peered at him. Danny shut his eyes. He heard the kid breathing next to his ear.

Benjy: Are you a grown-up?

Bang. Bang. Bang.

Danny. Danny. Danny. Danny. Danny.

Howard again. Danny opened up his eyes. The kid was still there, in Howard's lap.

Howard: Okay. We're back in business. You've been—ah, out for quite a while there, Danny.

Benjy: He was awake.

Howard: Benjy says you woke up while I was talking to the doctor outside. But Nora was here, and she says no.

Danny looked at Nora, who looked at one of the tapestries. So she'd left the room when she wasn't supposed to, and she didn't want Howard to know. Normally Danny would find a way to let her know that not only was she busted, but she owed Danny something for covering her ass. He couldn't think how to do any of that now.

Danny: I thought the doctor didn't speak English.

Howard rolled his eyes. We have a translator: guess who? It involves a fair amount of yelling. But the main thing the doctor said, he really stressed this time, is how important it is for you to *stay awake.* Danny saw the strain in Howard's smile.

The kid's eyes were on Danny, and the sadness came back down on him all over again. How had he ended up with nothing? Did he always have nothing? Did he really have nothing, or was this head injury just making him think he had nothing?

The walkie-talkie sputtered on Howard's belt.

Danny: Can I have that, Howard? The . . . ah. . . . He was pointing.

Howard: This? Sure. He looked surprised, curious. He put

the walkie-talkie in Danny's hand. It felt the same as a phone or a BlackBerry or any of that stuff: compact, with a rubbery keypad, a heavy core to its small weight, which is where you felt its reach.

Danny pushed a button. Static. Such a beautiful sound! It shrank his sadness away in a matter of seconds, dried it up so fast that Danny knew it had never been real—nothing real could disappear that fast. At first all he felt was relief to be rid of the sadness, but within a minute or two that relief had tipped over into joy: he didn't have nothing, he had *everything*. He just needed to be reattached to the everything he had.

Howard: What do you hear?

Danny smiled. Just static.

Howard: I've got more faith in your brain than I do in that machine.

Danny glanced at him. The kid in Howard's lap was getting sleepy, his head resting on one of the chair's cushioned armrests.

Howard: It could almost *be* your brain, you know? The machines are so small now, and using them is so easy—we're a half step away from telepathy.

Danny: Except we're talking to people who are *there*. You can hear them.

Howard laughed. They're not *there*, Danny. Where's there? You have no idea where they are.

Danny turned to him. What's your point?

My point is, screw the machines. Throw them away. Put some faith in that brain of yours.

My brain can't make a phone call.

Sure it can. You can talk to anyone you want.

Was this guy for real? He couldn't be. Danny pushed himself into a sitting position, wide awake. You're telling me I should talk to people who aren't there? Like some loony tune in the street?

Howard leaned in close. He spoke softly, like he was letting Danny in on a secret. No one's ever there, Danny. You're alone. That's the reality.

I'm the opposite of alone. I know people all over the fucking world.

Benjy jolted in Howard's lap. He said a bad word, Daddy.

But Howard's eyes were fixed on Danny. He seemed wide awake, too. What are they giving you, the machines? Shadows, disembodied voices. Typed words and pictures if you're online. That's it, Danny. If you think you're surrounded by people, you're making them up.

This is absolute crap.

I'm saying you're the boss! Have some faith in the power of your mind. It's doing more work than you realize. And it's capable of so much more than that!

Danny knew what he was hearing: a Motivational Speech. Before his pop gave up on him completely, Danny used to get one of these every few months. The message of a Motivational Speech was always the same: Your life is ridiculous, it's shit, but there's still a way to turn things around—if you do what I say.

Danny leaned toward his cousin. He talked right into his face. Howard, listen to me. I like machines. I love them. I can't live without them, and I don't want to try to live without them. To be honest, I'd rather cut off my balls than stay in a hotel like yours for one frigging minute.

Howard: Fantastic! Better yet!

Why?

Because it'll mean that much more when you figure this out!

Fuck you, Howard.

Daddy—

Danny: You're really pissing me off. Are you doing that for a reason?

Howard: I'm trying to keep you awake. This is the longest you've gone yet.

Danny felt a surge of rage. It gathered low in him, somewhere around his groin, which he actually felt stirring under the sheets. His voice came from high in his throat: I'm not interested in my brain or my imagination. I like *real things,* okay? Things that're actually happening.

What's real, Danny? Is reality TV real? Are confessions you read on the Internet real? The words are real, *someone* wrote them, but beyond that the question doesn't even make sense. Who are you talking to on your cell phone? In the end you have no fucking idea. We're living in a supernatural world, Danny. We're surrounded by ghosts.

Speak for yourself.

I'm speaking for both of us. Old-fashioned "reality" is a thing of the past. It's gone, finito—all that technology you're so in love with has wiped it out. And I say, good riddance.

The rage plunged up through Danny. Fuck this guy. He'd cut Danny off from everything he had, but that wasn't enough—now he had to convince Danny that it didn't exist at all, that he was making it up! And he did it with a smile, like he was enjoying himself. *Fuck this guy!*

Danny couldn't take any more lying down, he had to stand. He dropped a foot off the side of the bed and was halfway onto his feet before Howard realized what was going on. He put a hand on Danny's chest and stopped him. Howard spoke very softly. Wait, wait, no, buddy. You're getting carried away. The kid was still in his lap.

Danny tried to push against Howard's hand, but being even halfway vertical made his head start to spin. It was almost a relief when Howard took one of Danny's shoulders in each of his hands and eased him gently back.

Howard: You can't stand up, buddy, no, no. You're not ready for that. And I—I went too far. I'm sorry, Danny. I was trying to engage you, but I went too far.

Danny thought he might be sick. He took long, shaky breaths. The room was dead quiet.

Howard: You okay? You hanging in there? He held two fingers to Danny's wrist like he was checking his pulse.

Howard? Benjy?

It was Ann. She stood in the doorway in a blue bathrobe, looking confused. Her voice was sleepy. I looked in Benjy's room and he wasn't there and I sort of freaked out.

Howard went over, carrying Benjy in one arm. The kid attached himself to his mother like a monkey glomming onto a tree trunk. Danny was glad to be rid of him.

Howard: He's been keeping me company. Haven't you, Big Guy?

Ann: It's—isn't it the middle of the night?

Yeah, we're trying to keep Danny awake. Then he spoke softly to Ann so Danny couldn't hear.

Ann's eyes refocused. She gave the kid back to Howard and came to where Danny lay. She looked the same straight out of bed as she did in bright sunlight, telling how a dip in a swimming pool was going to turn around some washed-up lady's life.

Ann: Oh, Danny. How're you doing?

Danny: Fending off the coma. So far.

Howard: Not coma, please don't say that word. Gripping sleep or—or grabbing sleep.

Danny and Ann looked at each other. She was scared too, but not the way Howard was. Ann wasn't scared Danny would die, she was scared he would tell.

And then it all came back: the whole reason he'd fallen out the window in the first place. Danny hadn't exactly forgotten it, but he'd been thinking backward, crooked, maybe because of the drugs. This whole time he'd had a fact inside his head that would blow a hole straight through the middle of Howard's life. And having that fact put Danny in charge.

His anger at Howard dried up instantly, like his sadness. He floated in a weird state of relief.

Howard: Nora, what's the time?

Nora: One fifty-four.

Howard: Wait—what? He turned to look at her.

Nora: More than two hours. Almost two and a half.

Howard let out a shout: Yes, yes! Danny, you did it! You did it, buddy!

He half fell on top of Danny and embraced him—the warmest envelope of a hug Danny could remember in his life. Howard's torso covered all of his, and the heat from it sank between Danny's ribs and pulled in around his heart. Confused, he reached up and clung to his cousin.

When Howard stood up again, his eyes were wet. He wiped them on his arm. Fuck, I was worried. I can say that now, Danny. I was so fucking worried about you.

Benjy: You said fuck! Fuck!

Ann: Benjy! Howard!

But she was laughing. All of them were, even a few graduate students who must've come in from the hall. There was crowing, hi-fiving, all that stuff. Only Ann was still afraid. Danny saw it in her eyes: a kind of squinting, like the sun was out.

Danny was tired, so tired. The old exhaustion rushed back in to fill up the place where his anger had been. He felt it wrapping around his eyeballs, rolling them back in his head. He shut his eyes and passed out.

CHAPTER TEN

My crew and I are digging up a plumbing line maybe twenty feet inside the perimeter fence when I notice a little tan Subaru coming up the road. This road connects the interstate to the prison. It runs parallel with the outer fence but at a distance, and what with the two layers of chain link in between plus all that razor wire, you've got no idea who's driving. I don't even know what makes me look. But that's bullshit. We always look.

There's no visiting on Thursdays, so the parking lot is empty except for staff. The Subaru pulls in and takes a spot. I've got no reason to be thinking about Holly—Thursday isn't her day. And I'm not thinking about her, but for some reason by the time the door opens on that Subaru I'm waiting for her to get out. And then she does.

She's smoking, that's the first shock I get. Usually I can smell it on a woman when she smokes, her hands and hair and breath, but with Holly I had no hint. It's a nasty habit, especially in a woman—too bad if that's sexist. But watching Holly take a long drag outside her car, shielding her eyes from the sun, I'm not disgusted. More impressed. That she was smoking all that time and I didn't even know.

Shock two is her outfit. Instead of the loose stuff she usually wears, she's got on a long dark skirt with some kind of pattern on it and a pale green blouse like you wear to an office. Her shoes have a little heel on them, enough to tip her forward onto her toes. And her hair is down, blowing around in the hot breeze. She takes one last drag and squashes the butt under her shoe.

By now my eyes hurt from the brightness of all that wire I've got to look through to see her, not to mention the white stone rubble they use to fill in the dead space between the inner and outer fences. It's white to set off any foreign object that happens to land there, for example any one of us who somehow manages to clear the first fence, which is thirty feet high, without nicking an artery on all the razor wire they've got spiraling along the top. The outer fence has a wall underneath it that reaches twenty feet into the ground. Nothing gets through but the pipes.

Someone you know, Ray? the CO says.

Someone he *wants* to know, Angel says.

She's my cousin, I say, and for a minute they all look at me like maybe it's true and then they all laugh, except for the CO.

Move or I'll start writing tickets, he says, and he means it. Jenkins writes more tickets than any other CO in this place, that's pure fact. We call him the Meter Maid.

We're digging out a rotten plumbing main, exposing a leaky, crusty system that smells like a corpse. Later on in the week we'll replace it all. I've got an eye on the admissions building, because with visiting closed I know Holly will get through there fast. Then she'll come out the other side and walk maybe thirty feet to the prison building, at which point I'll see her again with no fences in between us.

Sure enough, she's back out two minutes later. The path from admissions to the prison lobby has flower beds on one side from the horticultural program, and they're blooming like crazy.

Maybe that's why Holly slows down, to look at those flowers. But that can't be right—there must be flowers everywhere on the outside. More likely she slows down because she doesn't want to breathe in the smell that gags you when you first walk into the prison building. If I knew how to give you that smell in words I wouldn't need a writing class. All I can do is name some stuff that's in it—cigarettes, germ killer, sweat, chow, piss—but the mix is so much worse than those smells combined could ever be that at first you think you'd rather stop breathing than have it in you. And after an hour you can't even smell it anymore, which I guess is worse. So Holly goes slow past those flower beds and for a minute or two I'm just in awe of my good luck, happening to be in this spot right at the second when she walks through on an off day. What are the chances? It's like being high, like I'm somewhere else, like whatever thing it was that started up in me all those weeks ago in Holly's class was leading me to this: watching her walk up that path on a sunny day. I don't know how to say it.

The guys are muttering *tasty* and *sweet* and *wouldn't mind a little of that stuck to my face,* but so softly it's like rustling more than words. Not even Jenkins can hear it. Red and Pablo, the rapists, don't say anything, just follow her with their eyes. Holly glances our way and as soon as she does she speeds up and then boom—she's gone, into the lobby. And when I try to replay it in my head, to watch her walk through those flowers all over again, what I see is just us: seven prisoners in green khakis and vendor-approved work boots digging out a reeking hole. Guys without faces, except Red, maybe, who's a foot taller than the rest of us. And the good feeling drains out of me so fast I get woozy, like I nicked an artery. I sit on the edge of the hole we just dug.

On your feet, Meter Maid says. Fuck's the matter with you?

I stand up.

Take that shovel and dig. That's a direct order. He says it like that so if I don't move he can write me up. There's no way I'll give him the satisfaction.

My shovel goes in and comes back out. I need to think. If I think, I can make this feeling stop. But I can't think.

You sick? Jenkins says, and I read his mind: He's remembering Corvis, last month. Corvis conked out on his laminating machine after the CO wouldn't let him break. Died on the spot from a heart attack.

Yeah, CO, I say. I'm sick.

Me too, Red says.

We're all sick, CO, Angel says. Too sick to dig.

But we keep on digging.

You're a bunch of sickos is what you are, Jenkins says, and he laughs like mad at that one.

At the next class, Holly looks like she always looked before: loose clothes, hair pulled back. At break there's the usual crowd of guys trying to get her attention. Normally I go straight into the hall, but today I hang around. I wait.

Eventually it's just Hamsam and me waiting, and when Hamsam sees I'm behind him he gives up his spot and walks out. Hamsam and I were brothers in a past life.

Holly smiles at me. It's the first time we've really looked at each other since Mel threw me on the ground those weeks ago. It feels strange, naked.

What's on your mind, Ray? she asks.

Now that I'm here with her looking right at me, I don't know what the hell to say. Finally I tell her: I saw you. On Thursday. Coming in.

I saw you too, she says.

Liar, I tell her.

You were digging something.

That amazes me, floors me. And even though I'm standing right in front of Holly, close enough that if I put out my hand I could touch her, I still don't smell the smoke. Not a trace of it.

I say, How did you know it was me?

Your face, she says, and we both start to laugh, and the more we laugh the funnier it gets.

There's noise in the hall, someone raising his voice, and it makes this room with just us in it seem even more quiet. Every minute that door doesn't crash wide open is one more miracle.

I want to talk to you, I say.

Aren't we talking?

I mean get to know you. I want to hear your story.

For a second, the pain I saw one other time swims right up under Holly's face. No you don't, she says.

Why's that?

She thinks about it. Because it's complicated without being interesting.

I want to complicate it more.

I get that feeling, she says. You want to get me fired.

You've got another job. And that one you *dress* for.

No comment, she says, but the smile is back.

Are you married? I ask, and when she doesn't answer right away I say, Divorced. Or separated. And "complicated" means kids—two at least, but I'm guessing three.

Something peels off her face and for a second she looks raw, almost scared.

You're a con man, right? she says. That's what you're in here for, conning people?

Con men don't end up in here, I say. They go to nicer places.

And you?

I'm in for murder.

Liar.

I'm serious.

Holly gets quiet. When she finally answers, her smile is long gone. If you thought that was going to impress me, you were way off.

Just answering the question, I say. But my chest goes very tight. Did I think it would impress her? I don't even know.

She opens up a folder and looks inside. Holly, I say, but she keeps her face turned down. And then the door bangs open like it should've done all those seconds we were talking. Break is done.

I go to my desk and sit. My chest is tight.

For the first time ever, Tom-Tom's brought in something to read. It's handwritten and looks about eighty pages long. Holly tells him right off that there's no way he can read all that and Tom-Tom looks kind of deflated. Then he starts up in a nasal, whiny voice that sounds like it's making one long excuse for something. The voice is so bad, and the way he reads is so nervous and wired, and he has to stop so many times because he can't read his own writing, which is gigantic to the point where every couple of sentences he has to turn a page, that at first I can't even listen. None of us can. But finally some stuff starts to come through. Summer in the deep South. Poor family. Too many kids. A mom drops a pot of boiling water on her three-year-old boy and his arm stops growing. Sick as I am from the conversation with Holly, how wrong it went, I lose track of where I am. The boy grows up and starts doing crystal meth. The ending is right after his first robbery, when he twists an old man's arm and breaks it in three places.

Tom-Tom stops. Turns out he read us the whole thing. No one says a word, and finally Tom-Tom laughs in a nervous way and says, Guess you were too bored to stop me, huh?

Holly checks the clock, then her watch. Her eyes are funny, like she's been sleeping. Okay, she says. Let's talk about it.

Allan Beard starts off with the same comment he always

makes: he wants more context. Beard's a context freak, can't get enough of it. Or maybe he just wants Holly to know he knows what context means.

Cherry says, It's sad, Tom-Tom. Made me real, real sad.

Mel says, You got to get some humor in there, T-T. It's urgent, man, just maybe a joke or two, but something's gotta be funny.

And on it goes, Holly nudging them with questions like: Context for what? and Is "getting you down" necessarily a bad thing? and This really speaks to the question of why we read. And watching her, I know that Tom-Tom has managed to do the thing I meant to do, should've done, *needed* to do in that long, beautiful break I was given with Holly: he reached her.

Finally Holly says, I give up, and we all look at her. She comes right up to the first row of desks.

If I haven't taught you enough to know that what we just heard is good—powerful, honest, moving, all the things we hope for when we sit down to write—I must be the worst teacher out there. Seriously, I don't know what we're doing in here if you can't see that.

She stands there waiting. No one says a thing. And you might think one person at least would be happy, hearing all that, meaning Tom-Tom, but then you wouldn't understand him. When Holly's done talking he turns and looks at me. Why so quiet, Ray?

I don't know, I say. Do I need a reason?

I just poured out my frigging heart and soul on that paper. You'd think I could expect one frigging comment out of you.

I feel Holly's eyes on me. And I know that if I go ahead and say what no one else seems to get, that Tom-Tom is a fucking genius and he wrote something great—*great*—then the bad thing that happened between Holly and me will disappear. And I have the words, the exact words, right in my throat. But they're too far down.

Tom-Tom's watching me, too. He's around thirty, I'd guess, but like all meth freaks he's missing half his teeth, so his face caves in. Still, right now he looks about eight years old, his eyes jumpy, full of hope. Any little thing from me will make him melt, I don't know why. I don't know why I have that power over Tom-Tom. I don't even want it. But I can't give it up.

The seconds pass. I know what's going on because it's the same thing that always happens: give me something nice, something I love or want or need, and I'll find a way to grind it into dust.

Tom-Tom's eyes go flat. Fuck you, Ray, he says, and he turns back around. I see his bent spine through his shirt. Holly looks down.

And I'm fucked. I know that.

.   .   .

That night I lie on my tray and try to write. Holly left class without taking my pages, but I'm hoping next week she'll start up again. And maybe that way I can fix it. Maybe I can reach her like Tom-Tom did.

What I mostly do is lie there.

Davis is on the tray below, rustling and chuckling like he's watching TV. Except there's no TV, just the "radio."

Once in a while he pokes out his head and says, What's wrong with you?

Nothing's wrong, I say.

Then why are you lying there like a volcano belched you up?

No reason.

There has to be a reason. There's always a reason.

The words I didn't say to Tom-Tom are still in me, caught in my neck like a hook. I feel like I'll die if I don't get them out.

Davis stands up and looks at my face. You sick? Is that it? he asks, and I get the feeling he's trying to be nice. But any sign of weakness pisses Davis off.

That's it, I say. I'm sick.

Yeah, well. Let's hope you do some getting better fast.

At six the next morning, we walk to chow. Normally Davis won't go near it—he survives on seafood ramen noodles he stockpiles from the commissary. But even Davis will haul ass over to chow hall on pancake days. I mean, who doesn't like pancakes?

Chow hall is like a huge factory floor, with long windows on the top facing the sky where it's red from the sun coming up. The place has its own foul smell: steam from the steam trays mixed up with boiled vegetables and ammonia from the floor and today there's also the sweet of phony maple syrup.

Every table seats four, I guess the idea being that smaller groups are less likely to get in fights. Davis and I sit alone. The hall is full of men, but what you mostly hear is echoey scraping sounds of eating. Davis and I eat without talking. We're done in under five minutes.

I'm in line to dump my tray when I see Tom-Tom waiting for pancakes. He's got a gecko on each shoulder and another one climbing between the buttons of his shirt. Those little bright faces next to Tom-Tom's dried-out toothless head give me a pain in my chest. I wonder if I should go over and say it right now, tell him I liked what he wrote. Even if it's too late. Even if Holly won't ever know.

Before I can do anything, Tom-Tom starts coming my way. He's walking fast, but I'm too distracted to take that in. I stand there holding my tray and it's only when people start to make way that I get what's about to happen. And then time stretches out, it opens up and I'm looking into Tom-Tom's blank eyes thinking, *How did I miss it? Did the geckos trip me up?* And then something shifts and I feel like I already knew, like it all happened before. Like I've been waiting for it.

Tom-Tom throws an arm around my neck and puts a shank in my gut so fast I'm still holding the tray when he's done. Davis is on him a second later like a wild man, a man who does seven hundred push-ups a day. He lifts Tom-Tom into the air and chucks him onto a table ten feet away. But Tom-Tom's got backup: three guys from his lock who throw punches at Davis's arms and head until the COs pull them off. I'm watching all this with a hot pain in my gut. The shank is still in me, and when I try to pull it out it resists, so I leave it. I feel the blood pushing out in gasps, and I hold my hands there trying to stop it. Then I lie on the floor because I'm tired and the words are starting to come up and I want to hear them, I want to catch them. I shut my eyes: *redneck* and *juicehead* and *fuckwad* and *crapshoot* and *hothead*, words floating around me like leaves coming off a tree, like I'm a kid lying on my back in the grass watching them come down: *jive* and *joystick* and *jalopy* and *hollow* and *holy* and *Merry Christmas* and *Whose turn is it to put the star on the tree? It's Paulie this year. No Paulie went home, his folks came and took him home, lucky SOB, except it wasn't luck, he shaped up, that's what happened, he did what he was supposed to do and I don't know why that's so hard for you, Ray, why you can't seem to do that, maybe you're just bad. Yeah maybe I am or maybe I just don't want to go home, maybe home is worse than this. . . .* Voices, I'm hearing these old voices and wondering where the hell they're coming from because it can't be from here, can't be this place. And then I see Davis holding his radio up to the window, twisting the knobs, working the reception, and I think: It's true! He's right! The technology works! Davis winks at me and I wink back because sure I hear them, yes I do, it's been a long fucking time but I'd know those voices anywhere.

CHAPTER ELEVEN

Danny woke up sometime deep into the night. He was alone in his room and the castle was quiet. He had no idea what time it was or how long he'd been sleeping.

He got out of bed and went to the window. Big clouds were moving around, but every couple of minutes they'd free up the moon, bright and round as a spotlight. Underneath him the garden was black.

He'd been standing by the window awhile before he realized that the pain in his head was gone. Gone like he'd taken it off and left it back on his bed with the sweaty sheets. He touched his head, thinking maybe the bandages would be gone, too, but they were there, wrapped around the top half of his head and a little wet. Still, Danny felt good. Better than good—he felt strong and clear and completely awake for the first time since coming to the castle. How could he feel so good? Had all that sleeping finally wiped out his jet lag?

In fact, Danny felt too good to stay in this room. He needed to get outside, move around in that moony light.

He spent some time looking for his boots before he remembered he'd lost them. They were back at the keep, probably underneath that window he'd fallen out of. He put his sandals on instead. The air actually felt good on his bare toes.

He looked around his bed for the walkie-talkie, but it was gone. Howard must have taken it back.

The electric candles in the hall were still lit. Danny had no idea whose door was whose or which way was out, but he went left, and where the hall turned a corner he found a curved stairwell that looked a lot like the one he'd gone down with Howard that first day. There was a fluorescent bulb at the top, but the stair turns choked away the light as he went down. Luckily, Danny had his flashlight.

It turned out these weren't the same stairs. The ones Howard had taken him down were half renovated at the bottom, whereas these led straight into several feet of garbage: rotten sleeping bags, charred piles from fires, bent cans, cigarette butts. It reminded Danny of the crack dens he'd had to haul his friend Angus out of a few times. He picked his way through debris toward a door he was pretty sure led outside. He felt crawling on his bare feet and caught the oily flash of insect shells. Shit! Danny kicked, sending heavy bugs through the air as he pushed his way out the door into the garden.

Its coolness wrapped around him. He sucked in big lungfuls of air that smelled like flowers. The wind was picking up in a way that felt like rain, and the clouds were moving fast across that flashing moon. He'd been inside a tower: Danny tipped back his head and saw its curved top against the sky, those square indentations.

When he looked down, his feet were two white ghosts. Danny needed his boots, no question. He needed them now.

Above the canopy of twigs and leaves over his head, the keep made a long black rectangle against the sky. There was flickery orange light in a window near the top, a fire. Danny used this to navigate, but something always got in his way: bushes, branches, rocks, vines. The sandals made his limp worse, and stuff touching his feet drove him half nuts. How did he ever wear sandals before? It was like walking around naked.

But Danny felt good. Too good, almost. Not because he didn't like feeling good—who doesn't like feeling good? Because some little part of him didn't believe he *could* feel this good. It seemed too easy. And because of that, there was an anxious feeling in Danny's gut, a wobbly feeling, the kind of feeling that makes you worry (even though you feel *good*!) that something bad is about to happen.

When he finally got to the keep, Danny put his hands on the stone and felt his way around to the side facing away from the castle, where Mick and Ann had been. And damned if one of his lucky boots wasn't sitting right in the middle of bare ground like it was waiting for him! Too easy! Danny picked up the boot and stuck his nose inside and pulled in its sweet leather smell. When he'd first bought the boots all those years ago, he would keep them right by his bed so the last thing he smelled before he went to sleep and the first thing he smelled when he woke up was their leather. He'd figured the smell would fade, but it didn't fade. Even after eighteen years that leather smell was still strong, which amazed Danny to the point where he wondered sometimes if he was imagining it.

He took off his left sandal and pulled the boot on over his bare foot. This meant that his injured right leg was now maybe an inch and a half shorter than his booted left leg, forcing him to hobble while he looked around for the other boot. Danny searched every inch of ground between the base of the keep and the tree where Mick and Ann had been standing. He even groped around the corners of the keep, pointing his flashlight into places where there was no way the boot could have fallen. Nothing. He kept looking up at the window he'd fallen out of, trying to see where else the boot could have landed, and the fifth or sixth time he looked up he noticed something: a dark shape, like a hook, hanging off the window's edge. He aimed his puny flashlight up and squinted into the dark.

Unbelievable. The right boot was still hanging there.

Danny chucked a rock at the boot, but he was way off. He tried again, then lobbed a bigger rock and this time it made a hollow sound like it was actually hitting the leather, but the boot stuck. He took a big stick and whaled it up there and it whacked the glass and Danny froze, expecting to hear shattered pieces falling, the baroness's angry squawk. But nothing happened. She must have closed up that window and left his boot hanging there out of spite. Or maybe she was too short to see it. Anyway, a rock big enough to bring the boot down could easily break the glass, and that would bring on the baroness. No thanks. He'd have to come back in daylight with a ladder and a long stick.

Danny kept his left boot on and carried his extra sandal away from the keep. Walking with a limp plus a big gap between his legs was not a lot of fun, but if he gave up on trying to walk normally, just let himself gimp along, it was sort of manageable. He would never have done it in front of people.

He headed back into the overgrown garden. The moon was all covered up and the air had the heavy feel of a storm. The ground was soft. When Danny shined his flashlight, the branches tunneled themselves around his beam. He felt the weight and mass of the garden around him, crowded with so much live stuff but at the same time empty, dead.

After a few minutes of hobbling, Danny slowed down. Was he heading back to the castle? He felt like he'd been there for months. To the keep? Not with the baroness holed up inside it.

An outside wall? But they all seemed far away, inaccessible, and how the hell would he climb one wearing a boot and a sandal, on top of his fucked-up knee?

Danny stopped walking. There was no place he wanted to be. And realizing this made his good feeling start to leak away.

In the sudden quiet of not walking, Danny heard a snap in the bushes near him. He froze and listened: wind creaked the branches, and there were little sounds that could be birds or mice. And behind all that, around it, something else. When Danny moved again he heard it move, too. Something in the garden.

He got a coldness in his chest, like condensation. Fear.

Danny's heart kicked awake, and adrenaline washed his sinuses clear. He started walking again, hobbling as quickly as he could, wondering if he should take off his left boot and put his sandal back on. But he didn't want to stop. Didn't want to part with his lucky boot.

He thought of the pool. The space around it was open, and in that clearing he'd be able to see what was near him, *who* was near him. He could face them head-on. And another thing made Danny want to get to the pool: the satellite dish was somewhere inside it, deep down. He wanted to be nearby.

Just having a destination helped Danny hold himself together. He walked, limping, in what he guessed was the general direction of the pool. He tried to make noise as he went, to block out the sound of the other thing, but he could still hear it, sense it moving through the garden behind him. Danny had a creepy feeling of watching himself: a gimping, head-injured guy with a right foot full of big white toes anyone could reach out and grab, stumbling through a rotten garden outside a castle full of strangers in a country he didn't know the name of. A guy at the end of the line is what Danny saw, with no options left. A guy with nothing, or why would he be here?

Another squirt of cold. Danny talked to himself: Get it together. Get. It. Together.

This was how the worm got in. You opened yourself to that kind of thinking and the worm crawled inside you and started to eat and didn't stop until nothing was left. You saw yourself as a weak powerless guy and it was only a matter of time before everyone agreed you *were* that guy. Danny had seen it happen. The worm ate people up the way years had eaten away this castle: caving in ceilings, chewing through walls, tunneling under floorboards until even a perfectly renovated hallway with varnished doors and fake candles on the walls had a thousand bugs crawling around a few floors underneath it.

Danny smelled the pool before he got there. A wind caught its foul odor and brought it through the cypress wall, tickling Danny's face with it, ruffling up his hair, and he stopped walking, it was automatic. Stopped and felt that unclean wind on his face and heard something moving inside the cypress, a scratchy leathery sound that made the skin on his head shrink to the point of tugging under his bandages where the scalp was numb. Danny's heart rammed his ribs. He stood still, scalp tightening and crawling. Only his eyes moved. He wasn't going to run. *This is all in my head. This is all the worm trying to get in.*

Danny reached in his pocket for the phone. The urge to make contact was so deep it cut through the facts (such as: he didn't *have* a phone). It was a brain need, a reaching out from inside Danny's skull that had nowhere to go, nothing to fasten itself to. He jabbed his fingers so deep in his pockets that they tore through the fabric. But there was no phone. And so that reaching urge reversed itself and bored straight back into Danny. It woke up the pain in his head.

Danny found an opening in the cypress and pushed his way through. There was the pool: round, quiet, black. The Imagination Pool. In the dark you couldn't tell its blackness came from inside. The wind was strong, leaves cartwheeling over the marble paving. That white marble was holding on to light from somewhere, maybe the sky, so there was a glow around the pool like you get just after it snows. Danny turned carefully in the open space, looking in every direction. No one else was there. He felt his heart calm down.

The slowing of his blood made Danny dizzy, the relief of not being afraid and even more than that, knowing he'd been afraid of nothing. Not that Danny was safe—the worm was trying to get inside him, that was clear. He knew the signs. When you were vulnerable to the worm you had to take precautions, put a few key facts in a strong place where the worm couldn't touch them if it somehow did get in. Danny used to think of his heart as that strong place, but now he had a better word: the keep. His own keep, inside him, where his treasures would be hidden in case the castle was invaded. What should go in Danny's keep? A lot of stuff went through his head, a whole storm of stuff from eighteen years of friendships, girlfriends, triumphant moments, powerful people whose number two he'd been, but when it came down to what he couldn't live without, there was only one thing: Martha Mueller. That she loved him. Danny pictured himself holding that fact in his hands like it was alive, putting it in a box inside his ribs and sealing up the box. And then the fear left him. He felt safe. Weak, wiped out, but safe. As long as Martha was in the keep, the worm couldn't win.

Danny had to sit. It wasn't jet lag anymore, it was—what? The head injury, maybe. The hobbling. He went to the pool and kind of collapsed on the bench where he'd sat before. He looked at the water. The clear parts had a silver light from the sky or the stone, and the foul parts had the silver too, but in a texture like a greasy rug. Danny watched the water, taking long deep breaths. There was a pulse of light in the sky, faraway thunder. And then the water moved.

It rippled, not small ripples that could come from a stone dropping in or a fish swimming around—these were ripples made by something big.

A wave rolled under the sludge and washed up against the white marble edge of the pool with a little slap that sent a puff of bad smell into the air. Danny's scalp tightened, pulling on his stitches, or staples, whatever they were. He felt the hair lift up from his head.

The place had gone quiet. No insects, no wind, no rustling leaves. Quiet like a pause between things. Like someone holding their breath.

Then Danny saw the shapes. Maybe they'd been there all along, but the water had him too distracted to notice. Two of them. It was hard to say if they were light or dark; they seemed a little of both, like he was looking at a negative. They started out apart and then came together at the edge of the pool and merged, so you couldn't separate them. And then the water rippled in a long stinky wave.

Danny wanted to stand. He actually said it out loud: Stand the fuck up. But he couldn't move. His heart was beating so hard he thought he might puke.

Was he seeing the twins? Was he watching them die? It seemed violent, whatever this was, like one person shoving another person. Or someone shoving both of them.

Apart. Together. Push. A long ripple under the water and then a splash against the marble. Each splash a little bigger than the last one.

Run, said a voice in Danny. *Get out of here!*

Danny: I don't run. I never run. I'm not afraid. But his heart was grinding, and there was ice in his chest.

The water in the pool was starting to shake. It trembled, vibrated in tiny ripples like something huge was coming up from underneath.

Danny stood up. *This can't be real. This isn't real. I don't believe this is happening.* What he saw was the water opening up, a hole coming open in the water like a mouth or a tunnel or a grave, some dark cavity that made a little thread of puke jump up in Danny's throat. *It's not real, I'm hallucinating. It's all in my head so there's nothing to be scared of.* And below that, another voice, raw and terrified: *I don't want to see. Run, run!*

The hole in the water caved in, spreading wider and wider until the pool *was* the hole, a round black opening that looked like it led straight down to the center of the earth, its molten core. A sound came out of the hole—Danny barely heard it at first because it was one of those hums that could just be your own ears ringing, but the hum got louder every second until it was a roar, a howl, a scream—some horrible noise that filled up Danny's ears and then shorted them out so all he heard was buzzing. That was when the words *gripping sleep* and *grabbing sleep* popped into Danny's head, and all of a sudden he understood, his body jolted from the impact of figuring it out. *I'm not awake! This is all a dream; I've been dreaming this whole time. The gripping sleep has got hold of me and it's showing me all kinds of shit that looks real but it's all just a dream, it's all inside my head.*

Yeah, but what's real? came a familiar voice close to Danny's ear but somehow outside him, outside the pool, all of it. You're having an experience, right? said the voice. You're going through it, right?

Danny smelled mint. It filled the air around the pool, zinging and pricking Danny's eyes. And he realized that the new voice was Howard's voice. Howard was here! He was nearby, inches away, which meant that Danny *wasn't* here—he was lying in bed, and Howard was in the chair next to the bed, just like before. Danny hadn't ever come outside, hadn't even moved. He was dreaming.

He shut his eyes to close out the roaring pool, which wasn't real. He set his mind on Howard's voice and minty breath outside the skin of the grabbing sleep. He felt like he was about to cry.

Danny: Howard, help. I'm all fucked up.

You're doing fine, buddy. Just hang in there.

Danny: I'm scared.

No shame in that. We all get scared.

Please wake me up. Please.

I can't, Danny.

Danny heard something that sounded like laughing, or at least other people. Was it the graduate students? Were they all in the room together?

Danny: Please, Howard. There's got to be a way. Belt me, kick me across the fucking room. I don't care, just wake me up.

More noise. Definitely it was laughing, Howard too. Missed that one, Danny. Come again?

Danny's teeth were clamped together. Please. Wake me up.

Oh, I can't, buddy. This is too much fun.

What?

I'm enjoying this. Tell me what it's like, Danny. Tell me everything. How does it feel to be scared out of your mind with no one to help you?

The cold hit Danny in a body shock, a squirt of fear that was the same as what he'd felt in the garden—something bad around him, nearby him. And Danny knew what it was: Howard.

It was all Howard.

Please, Danny whispered, his eyes shut tight. Help.

You want help? More laughter. C'mon, buddy. I'm nice, but not that nice.

Please.

The mint was strong in Danny's face—Howard must be leaning close. Danny felt the heat coming off his cousin's skin. Drops of someone's sweat fell on his cheeks and eyelids. Howard's voice seemed to come from inside Danny's ear.

You're scared? You want my help? That's a lot to ask, you cold fucker. You vicious sonofabitch.

Danny shrieked and opened his eyes. He was standing by the pool. It was a pool again, thousands of raindrops tapping on its surface. Rain ran from Danny's hair down over his face. And having things back to normal brought back the rational part of him that had been on ice for a while now, erased by his fear: *It was all a dream, even Howard was part of the dream. This is real. This rain, this pool. Nothing but this.*

Then thunder exploded and lightning broke the sky, and the terror clamped on Danny again. He started to run, bolted blind through the cypress and dove into the underbrush, stumbling through twigs that snapped back, scratching his face, raking his skin. He tripped over a root and landed face-first, a brassy taste of dirt filling up his mouth. Now the rain was pounding Danny, soaking his bandages until they were heavy on his head, gushing into his eyes and nose so he choked on it. But Danny kept running even if running made no sense. That was the one thing every part of him agreed on—running made no sense—but he was too scared to stop. There was a riot inside Danny's head, the spooked and rational parts of him fighting it out in a way most of us would recognize, except it didn't happen like I'm going to write it, piece by piece like a conversation. It was a knot, a confusion, a chaos in Danny's head:

He brought me here to torture me. To punish me.

Don't believe it. This is the worm.

He's hated me all his life.

You're letting in the worm. Don't!

He wants me to die.

Shut it out—if you push it back you can still keep it out.

He wants me to lose my mind. This whole thing is a setup to make me lose my mind.

Bullshit. Bullshit. You're losing it on your own, you're making all this happen on your own.

From the very beginning it was him. Maybe even falling out the window—maybe that was him.

Impossible crap and you know it.

Now my brain is damaged, there's something wrong with my brain. It's the gripping sleep, the grabbing sleep.

It's the worm.

The graduate students are in on it, too.

The worm.

And Mick and Ann—they all want to wipe me out.

You're pulling that worm inside you. You're sucking it in. It's a choice. You're making this happen.

I need to get away from here. Away from the castle.

That's not going to solve a thing.

I'll run away. I'll get a plane back to New York. All I can do now is try to get out alive.

There's no place to go. The worm is inside you, Danny. It's *in* you.

Help!

Help yourself.

Help! Help! Danny hollered this out, screamed it into the night, as he stumbled toward the castle through the rain.

main intros—

Danny got out by climbing over a broken wall—the same one he'd climbed from the outside to look at the view on his first night. Obviously there were better ways to exit the castle, but finding one of those would mean asking someone, and no way did Danny want Howard to know he was leaving.

He left behind most of his stuff. Taking it with him would be slow, not to mention obvious. When he walked out the door of his room the next day his clothes were still in the big medieval dresser and the Samsonite was empty in the closet. All Danny brought along was a shoulder bag stuffed with three pairs of underwear, two extra shirts, deodorant, toothbrush, toothpaste, hair mousse (optimistic, since his head was still bandaged), and socks. In his jacket pocket he had his passport, three hundred bucks, and one working credit card with about five hundred left on it. Somehow, that combination was going to have to get him back to New York.

Now I should back up here, because quite a few hours have passed since Danny was getting rained on out in the garden, and someone's got to be wondering: (1) Was he ever really outside, or was it all just a dream? (2) Has he seen Howard since he got back (or dreamed he got back) to the castle? (3) Which part of Danny won the argument, the part that blamed everything on Howard or the part that blamed the worm? And I wish I knew how to sprinkle these answers around so you'd get the information without even noticing how you got it, but I don't. So I'll just stick them in when the time seems right.

Danny headed down the hall between the rows of electric candles. He was careful to walk, not hobble [*Answer number 1:* It wasn't all a dream, because the only footwear Danny had to his name was one left boot and one right sandal (he must've dropped the other sandal while he was running), which meant he *had* been outside, not in his bed. Which also meant Howard hadn't really been sitting by Danny's bed making nasty comments into his ear. But to Danny, finding this out didn't change much of anything. It was like dreaming you've fucked someone and not being able to look at them the next day: Danny saw Howard a different way. It made him get what he should have gotten from the very start: that Howard's niceness, his reasons for bringing Danny over here, were too good to be true—were bullshit. A cover-up for something else.], in case someone saw him, although it was noon, and pretty soon everyone would be heading into the great hall to eat some tomatoey thing with plenty of garlic that Howard had been cooking all morning. It smelled unbelievably good.

Danny passed a big gold mirror, but he avoided looking in it. He was wearing a sock under his sandal to keep stuff from touching his toes, but he had a hatred of how sandals looked with socks and some pretty strong beliefs about the kind of loser who *wore* sandals with socks, so he wasn't especially keen to see he'd become that kind of loser himself. Not to mention the way he must look from the neck up. Danny knew it was bad from the expression on Howard's face. [*Answer number 2:* Howard came into his room that morning at around six with the bearded guy who'd given Danny the injection. Howard smiled at Danny (who was lying in bed wide awake) from the doorway and then the smile froze on his face and he charged over.

Howard: What the fuck happened in here?

Danny: Nothing happened.

Howard: Your face is all cut up.

If Danny didn't know what he knew—that Howard had brought him over here to mess with his head—he would have bought this act completely because it was fantastic. A virtuoso performance of being worried. (*Answer number 3,* sorry to stick this one smack in the middle of number 2 but that's where it fits: The voices in Danny's brain went back and forth on who his real enemy was, Howard or the worm. The debate came down to this:

Howard.

The worm.

Howard.

The worm.

until Danny reached a kind of frenzy and it all started running together: Howard The worm Howard The worm Howard The worm and finally: HowardthewormHowardthewormHowardtheworm. And that glob of words gave Danny his answer. The loop collapsed: it wasn't Howard *or* the worm, Howard *was* the worm. They weren't opposites, they were one thing, one evil terrifying thing that had waited years to catch up with him. And Danny had felt it there. All that time he'd sensed it waiting—even named it—without ever knowing who it was.)

Danny: I couldn't sleep, so I went outside to get some air.

Howard: You went *outside*? Are you crazy, Danny? Did I not explain what kind of—

He stopped. He took a long breath and ran his hands through his hair. His voice got quiet and angry: I knew I should have slept in here. I knew it. Doc, look at this. He went outside last night and look what happened to him.

Danny: Relax, Howard. It's a few scrapes.

Howard stared at him wild-eyed. You don't get it, Danny. I must not've explained this right. You have a—ah, fuck it. He sat down heavily on the chair by Danny's bed.

The doctor came over and took Danny's head between his small cool hands.

Howard: He's here to change your bandages. Which look like shit, by the way.

Danny: They got rained on.

Howard shook his head. The doctor went straight to work, unwrapping the bandages from Danny's head and lifting them away, scattering water and blood and pus, with a pair of tongs. Howard stood close, watching every move. Judging from his expression, it wasn't pretty.

Howard: Is he . . . okay?

The doctor said something Danny couldn't understand. Howard gestured at Danny's head and spoke louder. Is he okay, Doctor? Should it—should it look like that?

Doctor: Ya, ya. Is okay.

The doctor squeezed some ointment from a tube over the top of Danny's head and tapped it down with his bare fingers. Danny felt the pressure of the doctor's hands on his skull, but not his scalp. It was too numb. The doctor wrapped a fresh white bandage around the top half of Danny's head. For some reason, it hurt less after that.]

One of the graduate students was supposed to bring Danny lunch, which gave him an hour, maybe more, before anyone would notice he was gone, and another hour at least before they figured out he'd left the castle. It was more than enough time, but Danny walked as fast as he could without stumbling. The only advantage he had was that Howard didn't know he'd seen through his act, and Danny had to hold that lead. He went to the garden and followed the inside of the wall to the broken part he'd climbed before, clawed his way over, then tracked the wall back to the front of the castle and turned down a path he figured had to lead into town. This escape energized Danny. His mind was sharp and his fear was under control. The worm had gotten inside him, no question, but Martha was safe in the keep. When Danny thought of her, he felt a glow near his heart.

The climb down was longer and steeper than he remembered. Danny did it in a kind of trance, and eventually there were cobblestones under his feet. When he looked back at the castle it was two or three miles away. He had no idea he'd walked that far.

He remembered this town as a place with no color, but as he headed toward the central square the brightness of everything hurt his eyes: red roofs, leafy trees, kids dashing around in stripes, dogs that looked like they'd just climbed out of a bubble bath. Crisp hills, blue sky. The castle was on the tallest hill, gold in the sunlight.

Danny had one goal: a ticket back to Prague on the same mountain train he'd taken to get here. And a secondary, optional goal (if he happened to see a travel agency): a plane ticket back to New York. He tried not to think about how insane he'd been to accept a one-way ticket from Howard. That alone should have tipped him off.

There were red benches around the square, and an older guy with a monkey in his arms was sitting on one. Danny sat next to him. The monkey was small, covered with soft pale fur. His pink-brown face looked somewhere between an ancient man and a newborn baby. The monkey's owner offered Danny a hazelnut. Danny smiled and shook his head, but the guy kept smiling back at him and offering Danny the nut until he realized the guy wanted him to feed the *monkey.* Embarrassed, Danny took the nut and handed it over. The monkey took it in his long dry fingers and turned it slowly. Finally he cocked his head and started taking small bites, keeping his round dark eyes on Danny. The monkey's face had more emotions than a human's: curiosity, pity, exhaustion, like he'd already seen too much. Danny had to look away.

Eight or nine boys were kicking a ball through the square. They were excellent players, even the littlest ones. Danny didn't think much about his own soccer days anymore, but once in a while he'd remember something from that time: the smell of crushed-up grass or how the sky looked when he would walk home after practice, a strip of rust above the houses, then neon blue edging into black. Coming home in the almost dark made him feel grown up—a taste of grown-up life. Looking back, that seemed like one of the best parts of being a kid.

Danny felt a kind of heaviness coming on him. He said goodbye to the monkey man and hauled himself off the bench. He followed one of the narrow streets that tilted up the hill. Every shop had something nice laid out in its window: fish, bread, wine. It all looked cleaned up and polished to a point that seemed abnormal, like today was a holiday. Danny asked a lady selling flowers where the train station was, but she smiled and shook her head. She didn't understand. She pointed up the street to a store with a wood clock hanging outside it on a hook. *Inglee, inglee,* she said, still smiling.

Danny smiled too. Good. Perfect. Thank you.

The shop was cool and dusty and smelled like clocks. There was a faint sound of ticking, not one tick but a thousand different ticks overlapping. A guy with pale greased hair combed back over his head smiled up at Danny from a table covered with little parts of clocks. Danny smiled back. His face was starting to hurt from so much smiling.

Danny: Do you speak English?

Clock man: A little bit.

Fantastic. I'm trying to find the train station.

No train here. Next town. And he said some mouthful of a name that sounded like *Scree-chow-hump.*

Danny: Whoa, wait a minute. I took a train here, to this town, a few days ago. So there's got to be a train station here.

The man smiled: No train here. Train in Scree-chow-hump.

Danny stared at the guy. Was this a different town from the one he'd arrived in? Were there *two* towns near the castle?

Danny: Can I walk to Scree-chow-hump?

The man's eyes moved over Danny. Walk? Is too far, I think.

Okay, Danny said. So he was in a different town. Which made sense, because nothing about this town was *like* the town where he'd waited for the bus. He'd ended up in the nice town instead of the shitty town, but the problem was that the train only stopped in the shitty one.

Danny: Bus? Can I take a bus to Scree-chow-hump? Or a bus to Prague? That would be the best.

Prague, no. Bus for Scree-chow-hump, of course. The man went to one of maybe fifty clocks stuck to the wall and moved the hands to 8:00.

Danny: Tonight?

No. The man made a rolling motion.

Tomorrow? One bus, all day?

One bus only.

At eight in the morning.

Yes. Eight.

Not eight at night. . . .

No.

That's absolutely ridiculous! What the fuck is the matter with you people? His voice slammed the walls of the tiny shop, and Danny shut up. He sounded like a maniac. But the clock guy had no reaction, the smile was still on his face. In the quiet Danny heard that crazy ticking and it made him desperate, like a bomb was about to go off.

Man: The people of Scree-chow-hump, we don't like them. And they don't . . . he gestured at his own chest.

Danny: They don't like you. The people in the towns don't like each other?

Yes! Heh-heh! We don't—yes!

Okay. Danny shut his eyes. All right. And what about . . . is there a travel agent around here? You know, travel agent? *Travel . . . agent!* He was getting loud again, he couldn't help it. The clock guy kept smiling, but Danny picked up a vibration of anxiety under the smile. The guy was scared of him. Scared of Danny! What the fuck.

Suddenly the man nodded like he understood. He got up and led Danny to the door by one arm, gesturing up the street. Danny headed off in that direction, but there was nothing like a travel agency. The guy must've been trying to get rid of him. The street ended in a turn, and Danny lurched around it and found himself heading back toward the square. He took another street and followed it away from the square, but a few minutes later— boom—he was back again. This happened no matter where he went.

Danny saw a wooden globe hanging on a hook outside a shop, and he rushed over there thinking Bingo, a travel agent. But it was antiques. He didn't even bother to go in, just looked through the window at a huge wooden arrow thing that must have been a longbow. And while he looked, light hit the window in a way that made his reflection jump out at him from the shiny glass: bandaged head, mismatched feet, a face that looked like someone had whacked it with a baseball bat and then raked it with a fork. It was a godawful sight, painful to look at, but Danny couldn't take his eyes away. Who *was* this guy? He looked disturbed, like a person who shouldn't be out in the world, a guy Danny would avoid on the street. It was only when he focused on what was behind the glass (big antique hunting knives with ivory handles) that the picture disappeared.

Some kind of afternoon siesta was starting up, and the streets were thinning out. Danny followed the road back to the square. The monkey man was gone. He sat on the empty bench and looked up at the castle, which made a black shadow over the hill below it. He felt confused, pissed off: he'd expected to be heading out of town by now, or at least waiting at the train station with a ticket in his hand. Instead he was looking up at Howard's castle with no frigging idea what to do next. He remembered what the baroness said: *The town and the castle have served each other for hundreds of years.* As long as Danny was still in this town, he was under Howard's thumb. And wouldn't you know, he couldn't seem to get out.

Something moved in Danny's gut: the worm, eating. How powerful was that telescope in the castle's kitchen window? Could Howard be using it right now to watch Danny struggle and come up short? The idea made his heart pitch. Danny looked around at the square lined with perfect shops, the sausages hanging in windows, the café with its blue umbrellas open, and wondered if any of it was real. Could it all be a setup made by Howard to distract him, to complicate the game of watching Danny flail around and get nowhere?

And as soon as Danny had this thought, the fakeness of the town seemed obvious to the point of stupidity: The too-bright soda bottles on a vendor's cart. The flowers in boxes. The way everyone smiled. Danny stood up. Fear had its cold tongs on him again. But unlike last night, his brain was calm this time, it was making a plan. Because Danny was a fighter. That's what no one

The fake down? steal knife
drop map

(his pop especially) ever seemed to realize. He wouldn't go down without a fight.

Danny went back up the street he'd just come down. Knowing the town was a fake made it seem alive to him for the first time. Finally, all those perfect details made some sense.

A lady was pulling down an awning over the antique shop with the globe outside it when Danny got back there.

Danny: Are you closed? I wanted to buy something.

The lady smiled and opened her door. She had buckteeth and red lipstick and shiny black hair. Danny smiled right back at her. So she did speak English, or at least she understood it. Maybe they all did. Hell, maybe they were all Americans putting on accents.

Inside the shop, Danny stepped around the crossbow he'd seen through the window and pointed at a framed map hanging high on a wall, too high to reach. Bingo: the lady went into another room, leaving Danny alone. He glided straight over to the window and swiped one of the hunting knives he'd noticed behind his horrible reflection. It was done in a second. Danny dropped the knife into the inside pocket of his jacket.

It was heavy. He felt the knife pulling at the fabric on his left shoulder and it steadied him the way hearing his own pulse could steady him sometimes. The blade hung directly over his heart.

The lady came back with a ladder and climbed to the top. Her skinny legs wobbled in her high-heeled shoes when she reached for the map. And even though Danny knew she was putting on an act, that she worked for Howard, he held the ladder for her.

The lady lifted the framed map off the wall and handed it down. It was too wide to tuck under an arm; Danny had to spread his arms just to hold it. As soon as he saw it, he recognized the keep—this was a map of Howard's castle and the hills around it. There were two towns on the map, one of which seemed to be this one; at least the church looked the same. The other town must be Scree-chow-hump.

Danny paid for the map with a hundred cash. A plane ticket was probably out of the question now. Except it always had been—he was trapped here. He was Howard's prisoner. It felt almost good to admit it.

When Danny left the shop, the town was quiet. He walked slowly back to the square, holding his framed map out in front of him like a shield. The only person left in the square was one of the older soccer boys, still practicing his footwork. The kid glanced at Danny, then looked away—the first person in town to look at him and not smile.

That was the thing about kids. They couldn't fake it.

Danny shut his eyes, listening to the kid work the ball. He could actually picture the kid's moves just from the sounds the ball made in the square. That's what a great player Danny had been, back in the day.

When he opened his eyes, hours had passed. Danny knew from the light, the way it slanted in over the hills, orange and thick as paint. The town was even more crowded now than when he first came. The café chairs were packed with old ladies holding tiny dogs in their laps. There were girls in bright dresses, a guy selling balloons attached to sticks. Everything had that same colorful look, like a picture in a kids' book that your mom would point to and say, See the dog? See the policeman? See the apples?

Someone was sharing Danny's bench. He looked over, then pulled himself straight. It was Mick.

Mick (smiling): Good morning.

Danny: Jesus.

Mick: Howard asked me to come down and look for you.

It surprised Danny that Mick would admit this. Was he worried I couldn't find my way back? It came out snide, mocking.

Mick: I think he doesn't know what to expect. You're turning out to be kind of a wild card, you have to admit. Then he laughed. Ah, it's good for Howard. Keeps him on his toes.

Danny: Yeah, well. He's keeping me on mine, too.

There was a silence. Danny wasn't giving anything away. Mick was his enemy's number two, which meant he was even more dangerous than Howard. Danny should know.

Mick: So, what do you think of this town?

Danny: Very nice.

I always like coming down here. Clears out my head.

Danny waited a minute, then asked: How long have you known my cousin?

Since we were fourteen. Reform school.

This made so much sense that Danny felt like he'd known it before and forgotten.

Danny: Why were you in there?

Mick glanced at him. We were bad. Why else do you go to reform school?

But you got better.

Mick grinned. Howard got better. I got older. He seemed more relaxed now, sitting next to Danny in this fake town, than he had at any other time so far. Danny wondered why.

Mick: I owe your cousin a lot, is the bottom line.

He must owe you, too.

Mick: I keep trying to even things up, but I just get in deeper.

He glanced at Danny, and it was all on the table: everything Danny had heard between Mick and Ann. For some reason, Mick wasn't holding it against him. The opposite.

Mick: So. You feel like heading back up?

Not really.

Mick took a long breath. Me either.

They sat looking at the square. An old guy was playing a harmonica. Kids chased pigeons around. Danny felt something open up between him and Mick, even without talking. They were alike: two number twos.

Danny: I want to get back to New York. He said this without really deciding to.

Mick: Howard doesn't like people leaving.

Yeah, I get that feeling.

Makes him feel like he hasn't done a good enough job. Like he's been a bad host. Especially now, with your head all busted up. He'll want you to get better first.

Danny: I feel fine.

Mick turned to him. You looked in a mirror lately?

Danny: Not if I can help it. They started to laugh, and then Mick looked at Danny and laughed again. What did you *do* to yourself?

Beyond falling head first out a window?

More laughing. Danny felt like he might not be able to stop.

Mick: That would be enough for most people.

Not me. I like to finish a job. Danny fought the laughter. It felt unhealthy, somehow.

Mick: Hey, you want to use this before we go back up?

He was holding out something Danny recognized, but the news of what it was seemed to take a while to reach him. He gaped at the hunk of precious metal in Mick's hand. A cell phone.

Danny: Where—where did you get this?

Mick laughed. They're around. It's not like *no one* has cell phones, it's just Howard's . . . idea right now. Things come and go with him. Anyway, go ahead and call someone. It's programmed for the U.S., so you can just dial.

He gave the phone to Danny and crossed the square to the

soda cart. When he turned back around, Danny hadn't moved. He was staring at the phone. It seemed alien, unfamiliar. Mick held up a bright green bottle and waved.

Danny opened the phone. The whole thing felt dreamlike. With a shaking finger, he pushed in Martha's number at work. A second later he heard her voice in his ear.

Mr. Jacobson's office.

Danny was too surprised to react. How did he get to Martha so quickly? It seemed impossible.

Martha: Hello? . . . Hello? I'm not hearing any—

Danny: Martha.

Her whole voice changed. It dropped and seemed to get even closer. Danny, is that you? Are you . . . oh my God, I've been worried out of my mind!

Martha?

Oh, honey. Are you—what the fuck is going on over there?

I'm not sure.

You sound funny.

Danny couldn't believe it was Martha. It seemed too sudden, too much in denial of how far away he felt.

Martha?

Danny, it's Martha. Why do you keep asking?

Tell me something so I'll know for sure.

There was a pause. Is this a joke? You just called me at my desk and I answered the phone—who the hell else would I be?

Danny wanted to believe her, but it seemed too easy, an impossible wish. You thought of someone and then there they were, talking right into your ear? He said, Tell me something that'll prove it's you.

There was a long silence. Finally Martha said, Danny?

Yeah.

You sound different.

I feel different.

You sound . . . not like you.

Danny: I just need some identifying information.

Martha: Information! Who is this? What kind of information are you trying to get?

It wasn't Martha, now Danny was sure. It was someone else.

Danny: Anything you feel like telling me.

Where's Danny? How did you get this number?

I'm Danny. What the fuck are you talking about?

Martha: I don't believe you're Danny.

Danny: I don't believe you're Martha.

The person on the phone sounded scared. More proof—Martha never got scared. Her voice dropped almost to a whisper. You've done something to him, haven't you?

Danny just listened. The voice was familiar, no question. But it wasn't Martha. Martha was far away, back in New York.

Martha: Are you still there, you asshole? Is this all about that fucking restaurant? Oh God, did he even get out of New York?

Danny stared at the phone in his hand. How could he tell where the voice was coming from? He looked up at the castle. The sun had moved behind it and it wasn't gold anymore, it was almost black. Its shadow covered the whole hill and was creeping toward the square. Danny wondered if the voice could be coming from inside it.

Whoever was on the phone had started to cry, or pretend to cry. All right, you fucker, I'm hanging up. But if you have one decent cell in your miserable body, you tell Danny I love him. *Martha loves him,* you got that? Tell him, you bastard. Now go fuck yourself.

The line went dead. Danny was shaking. He looked across the square without seeing much. Mick was coming back.

Mick: Everything okay?

Danny: Yeah, fine. He almost dropped the phone handing it over.

Mick stood in front of Danny, looking worried. It worked okay? You reached someone?

Danny: Yeah. He felt like he had to say something else, so he added: Girl trouble.

Ah. Okay. Well, I wrote the book on that.

Mick handed Danny a bottle of green soda and Danny took a long slug. The drink was too sweet, but nice and cold. Danny could have drunk forty of them. He felt a sudden coolness. The castle's shadow had reached the square and was slowly covering it up.

Danny: Are we going back?

Mick: Yeah, I think it's time. Don't forget your . . . whatever that is. He was pointing to the framed map propped against the bench. Danny had forgotten it.

Danny: I don't care about that. I'll just leave it here. But he could see from Mick's expression that that was a weird thing to do, so he hefted up the map. It was incredibly awkward to carry.

Mick: What is this thing? He took the map from Danny and looked it over. Oh, boy. Howard's gonna love this.

Danny: We aim to please.

Mick looked surprised, then he laughed. Here, I'll take it. His arms were long enough that he could wedge the whole frame underneath one of them. Danny carried his shoulder bag.

They headed back up the hill. Danny was limping worse than ever, maybe from sitting down for so long.

Mick: By the way, I got your other boot off that windowsill on the keep. It's in your room.

Danny didn't understand what Mick was saying at first. He had to think: Boot. Window. Keep. Then he was too over-whelmed to answer. It was a while before he said, Thanks.

No problem.

They walked a long time without talking. It was an easy silence. Gradually the trees started closing in around them, cutting out the light. The air got cold. Danny remembered the knife in his pocket. It tugged his coat with every step he took.

Danny: You were a junkie, right?

Mick turned to him, still walking. He looked surprised, and Danny wondered if he shouldn't have said it.

Mick: Am.

Still?

It's forever. Like love. And then he laughed.

You miss it?

Every fucking minute.

Which part?

Mick: That's a good question. He thought a while. I miss the . . . *equations,* I guess you'd say. This many dollars buys you this, which gets you this many hours of high before you need another hit, which'll cost you this. The counting, you know? I like to count.

Danny: You could count other stuff.

Mick: I count everything. I'm counting our words. I'm counting my steps. I'm counting the trees.

What do you do with all the numbers?

Mick laughed. Do with them? Nothing. I forget them. It's all just a way of not going nuts.

Danny felt the castle before they got there—a low vibrating hum coming up through his feet. Then the gate loomed over them, the same one he'd tried to find a way through that first night. Mick went around the side of it and opened a door Danny hadn't seen. So there it was, finally. The way in.

Before he went through, Danny stopped. Mick?

Mick turned around.

Danny: Why can't you leave?

Why can't I . . . ?

Leave. The castle.

Ah. You picked that up.

Big-time.

Well. I resent it.

Sure, but why can't you?

Mick left the doorway and came to where Danny was standing. The branches hung low over their heads, and Danny smelled pine.

Mick: I'm on parole. I did five years for trafficking, and I got released four months ago into Howard's custody so I could come here and work. I can't go anywhere unless Howard goes with me. See, I owe him again.

I don't know. Sounds like he owes you.

No. No, it's not like that. I resent it, so I'm putting a spin on it, but Howard's doing me the favor. It's a huge responsibility. If I violate my parole, he has to deal with bringing me back and notifying the board. And from my point of view, you can't get a job as a felon. Like, *can't*. Period. It's—it's a lot more than I deserve, what he's doing.

Danny: Okay.

He followed Mick through the doorway into a shady passage paved with cobblestones. Inside the castle walls it was almost dark. Danny felt the beginning of fear, that ice in his chest. He touched the knife through his coat.

At the end of the passage was a second door leading into the castle itself. Mick put down the map and dug in his pocket for the key. He was sweating. Danny looked at his cashed-out face and felt an ache. All that struggle, all that failure. And now Mick was under Howard's thumb. You poor shit, Danny thought.

Mick found the key and opened the door. There was a short, strange time when he and Danny just stood there, waiting to go in.

Mick: Okay. Home sweet home.

CHAPTER THIRTEEN

Day on Morphine

There's a tube coming out of my gut, that much I know. When I ask why it's there, I get: Complications from the second surgery.

Second surgery? What about the first one?

The first one was just to get the knife out. They did that right away the day you came in, from the ER.

It's my favorite nurse talking, Hannah. There are rules about talking to convicts, but Hannah wrote her own rulebook and that's the one she follows. To hear her tell it, the doctors and nurses are all under her direct command. If she doesn't know them, it's because they're too far down on the totem pole.

I love you, Hannah, I tell her. I say this a lot, but I'm not sure exactly how much I say it. My memory is shot from all the drugs.

She rolls her eyes, but you can tell she likes it. She calls me LB for Lover Boy. You love the morphine, she says, that's what you love.

She's right. But they never give you enough morphine, and there's plenty of Hannah. You can't ask a lady what she weighs, but I'm guessing three-fifty. And all that fat looks fantastic on her, like some thick gorgeous robe that only the queen can wear.

Hannah, I say. Why did they have to operate just to pull out a shank?

And right then I get a feeling I have a lot, something nudging me from inside my brain, and I wonder if we've had this whole conversation before, Hannah and I. Maybe a few times, or more than a few. But she never lets on.

It was one of those nasty shanks, she says, which I know means a Christmas tree. Christmas trees have prongs angled along the sides so when you pull one out it brings a good chunk of your guts out with it. But Tom-Tom never got a chance to pull it out—Davis took him down first. Which means buggy Davis saved my life.

So they what, they cut it out? I ask Hannah.

That's what surgeons do: they cut. It's not rocket science. It's not even complicated, like what we do up here. But it has to be done right.

This whole time, she's working. Changing bags of stuff, adjusting monitors, responding to a lot of boings and beeps. The room is dingy. The walls are the color of skin. Dustballs crowd up the corners. But Hannah brings it up a notch just by being here.

And what did they do in the second operation?

They were supposed to refine what the first team did. Smooth out some of those rough edges that got left behind because the situation was urgent.

So why the tube?

Her mouth flattens out. Hannah's mad about the tube. It's a lot of work for her: cleaning it, monitoring it, doing whatever needs to be done to whatever comes out of it. I'm not sure what that is, exactly. There's so much stuff coming out of me I've lost track.

Let's just say that particular surgeon has some tough love coming his way, she says.

Five minutes later, when that particular surgeon comes into the room, Hannah goes quiet. He's a young guy with prematurely gray hair that stands up a little on his head like he's moving fast. And you get the feeling he'd rather keep moving than stand in here looking down at the likes of me.

He fingers the tube, moving it around. You can tell he doesn't like it either. At the beginning I asked a lot of questions, but half the time I didn't understand the answers the doctors gave me, and even when I did I still didn't know what they meant. And then I forgot it all anyway.

The doctor talks to Hannah and she answers *Yes, Doctor* and *No, Doctor* in a voice almost like a whisper. The first time this happened I was too embarrassed to look at her, but when I finally did her expression made it good again: she had a look on her face like she was testing the doc, waiting and watching, not getting in the way, giving him a chance to prove himself or hang himself, whatever it was going to be.

When the doctor leaves I ask, You gonna fire him, Hannah?

Depends if he can learn to do his job better than he's doing it now, she says. I believe in giving folks a chance to turn themselves around.

Right about there, she starts to fade. This happens a lot: a gray almost mist comes in and then I feel my eyes start to roll back. I'm thinking, a Christmas tree means Tom-Tom really wanted to kill me. And I never saw it.

I keep writing stuff down, but there's no way I'll be back in time to finish out the class. It's a habit by now, I guess. One minute I don't know what the fuck's going on, and the next minute I start noticing things, collecting them in my head like a list. And I feel what Hannah must feel, watching that doctor: organized. Back in control.

No Hannah for three days, and I'm losing my mind. The

nurse I've got instead is called Angela, but she's no angel. She hates convicts, you can tell, she's just doing it for the hazard pay. Those nurses are usually scared or mad or both. This one's just mad.

Where's Hannah? I ask on day three. Not that I didn't also ask on days one and two.

She's off.

Why so many days in a row?

That's not my concern.

Meaning you don't care or you don't know?

She doesn't answer.

Is she sick? Is something wrong? Did she go on vacation?

I can pass along your questions to the supervisor.

Right as she says that, I look at my gut and I get a shock: the tube is gone.

Where's the tube? I ask.

Dr. Arthur removed it this morning while you were sleeping.

Does that mean it's getting better?

It means you're going back into surgery.

When?

Today sometime.

Is there any chance Hannah will be back today? It's crazy, but even though I know Hannah is just an ordinary nurse with no power, and the rest of it is pure fantasy, I don't want to go into surgery without her. There's no telling what could go wrong.

I'll tell the doctor you'd like to speak to him when he has time.

Great, I say. Maybe the president will show up, too. Can't you just give me the lowdown? Does the fact that they're operating mean things are better or worse? Is it a reward or a punishment is what I'm saying.

She turns to me, and I swear to God her eyes are bugging

half out of her head. Are you aware, she says, that every question you ask is costing the taxpayer money? Those two guards outside the door, how much you think they're getting paid? We're turning people away downstairs because they don't have insurance, and you robbers and rapists and murderers are lying around here being treated like kings. I don't get it.

I try again. But the operation—

They should have a meter running right next to your bed, she says. Just so you can see the burden you are. Then maybe you'd give me a peaceful minute to do my work.

Is it the same as the last oper—

That's fifteen dollars.

Or is it something—

Another fifteen. You're up to thirty.

I stare at her. My head is starting to fog up. I say, Are you seriously asking me for money?

Angela looks behind her, realizing all of a sudden that this doesn't look too good. I don't hear you, she says, and starts to hum. She hums and hums. I try to talk, but all she does is hum.

The gray's coming on, a nice morphine gray. I welcome it.

Don't ever leave me again, I tell Hannah when she finally comes back.

I'm sorry, LB. I had some personal business. Now they went and gave you another operation behind my back.

How does it look? I ask her.

She lifts back the covers and glances at my gut. It's been a long time since I've seen it.

Not bad, she says. No muss, no fuss.

No tube.

Exactly my point, LB. That tube was a sign of trouble, I can tell you that, now it's safely out. People downstairs do their jobs right, you shouldn't need a tube.

My head is thick. More drugs. Why? I wonder. Not that I'm complaining.

How long have I been in here, Hannah? Total.

She picks up my chart. Twenty-three days.

So the class is almost over. There were only four more left when I got cut.

Any chance I'll be out next week?

No chance, LB.

So that's it. No more Holly. But I keep on writing anyhow.

Hey, Hannah, I say. How come you're so nice to criminals?

That's got nothing to do with me, LB, she says. That's between you and God.

I have dreams, oh shit. Drug dreams, those ones where the past slops all over the place like a backed-up line. Sometimes I'm at school. The other boys would steal your food if you didn't steal theirs first. Howie couldn't do it. When he first came in he says, I don't want their food. I can't eat that much. I just want my own food. And I tell him, Take it, man, or they'll take yours and then you'll starve. I've seen it happen. They bring in fat kids like you and the next thing you know they're skeletons. They take 'em out in coffins and bury them in unmarked graves. And then I start to laugh. He's so new, that sweet scared face. Everyone's like that at first. But you stay in here long enough, you can laugh about anything.

There's a blank where my mother should be, a hole like when you cut someone out of a picture. My dad I remember, not really his face but his legs. He was tall. Strong calves and thighs with delicate knees, like a horse. How I had to jump to try and reach his hand. And then my own hands on the TV screen when he's watching. I must be really small, standing there with my hands on the screen to balance me. And all of a sudden I notice them there, surrounded by light: two hands. Fat baby hands. And that's me.

I open my eyes and Holly's next to my bed. Or more like: a person is sitting there in a yellow paper outfit and mask like they all wear around me now, and her face is Holly's face. The drugs, it's got to be. I shut my eyes and try again.

Hi there, she says.

That can't be you.

Then I'm in trouble, Holly says.

I would laugh, except you need muscles to laugh that I think I lost in one of those surgeries. How did you get in here?

I have my ways. She's smiling, I can tell from her eyes, even though the mask covers up her mouth. And under that smile she's scared to death.

Hannah must've let her in. But Hannah hasn't been my nurse since they moved me down to the ICU. And anyway, how could she get Holly past the guards? Then I think: Hannah could do it. Hannah can do anything.

I'm glad, I say. I'm glad you came.

We missed you in class.

Come on.

Really. It felt . . . small.

Yeah. I guess Tom-Tom's gone too.

I heard they moved him to the supermax.

There's some kind of distress, or despair, something, pushing out from her face. Even with just her eyes to go on, I see it. *Anguish*. It's not a word I use, but that's it.

Ray, I feel sick, she says. About what happened to you.

Relax, it goes on all the time. You'll get used to it.

Bullshit.

She's looking at me, not my face but the rest of me. The tube is back in, which is why they moved me down here. Does it hurt? she says.

It must, or I wouldn't be this high.

The room seems quieter than usual. Even the buzzers have piped down. I'm thinking, Am I making this up? It's like that day in Holly's class when I was alone with her on the break and no one came in for so long. Like God had decided.

I look at Holly. In this strange place, in our weird costumes, all the stuff that's in between us disappears. Holly T. Farrell, I say, who are you?

I'm no one special, she says, and I can see she believes it.

Was I right? Three kids?

Just two.

Who left, him or you?

There's a pause that tells me whatever she says next probably won't be true.

I left.

Good girl.

She's wearing what she wears for her other job. Something with a pattern, I see it above the yellow paper collar. A little chain around her neck. I can't see her hair inside the cap.

You look nice, I say.

That's my job, she says, and then she laughs. Not really. I work at the college, in admissions. They let me get my BA and now I'm doing a master's in writing. Slowly.

The kids?

Two girls. Ten and thirteen.

Each fact is like a sweet nugget landing near my heart. I don't even mind how hot I am. I've got a fever they can't get rid of.

Ray, she says, and leans closer to me. I—I keep wondering about what happened.

You mean with Tom-Tom?

No. Before. Why you went to prison.

Oh. That.

I want to understand it.

I don't understand it.

Then the facts, if you can talk about it. It—it would help me, I think.

I wait awhile before I answer. Finally I say: The facts are, I shot a guy through the head.

She swallows. Did you know him?

We were friends.

She looks down at her hands. I keep my eyes on her, not because I want to see her reaction, I don't want that, but even more I don't want to miss a second of her time in here next to me. I want to memorize it.

I'm assuming you had a reason, she says.

I had plenty of reasons. Too many reasons. I could make up a lot of shit so it would sound better, but I'm too sick. It's just something I did.

Holly chews that over for quite a while. Finally she says, I don't like thinking things can happen that way. It makes the world seem too dangerous.

Love those kids, I tell her.

She looks up. I've caught her by surprise. Her face opens up and all of a sudden it's like that paper mask is transparent. I'm looking right through it, and I get a flash of some kind of life we could've had—barbecues, dogs, kids flopping over us in bed—it rolls through me fast but strong and clear, like one of those cooking smells that blows in the window so sharp you can pick out the ingredients. And then it's gone. It's gone, and Holly's holding my hand. Finally, after that long long wait, her hand is back on mine. Dry cool fingers, slim. The rings loose. I close my eyes. My hand is so hot, I feel my pulse in every finger. I'm afraid she'll let go but she doesn't let go. She keeps her hand around mine and it's like she's holding all of me in her cool sweetness, calming my fever back down.

When I open up my eyes, Holly's crying. The paper mask is all wet. Something bad happened to you, I say. Didn't it?

She nods. The tears keep coming.

It takes me about as much energy to lift up my head as it took Davis to do his seven hundred push-ups, but I force myself. I want to see our hands. And there they are, intertwined on my chest like two people lying down. Beyond them is the tube: brown plastic. My neck is shaking.

I let my head fall back. The gray is coming on—all that head lifting has close to knocked me out. I hear Holly sob, and I hold her hand tighter, afraid she'll move it away. But she uses the other hand to wipe her face. And I know why they let her in here.

CHAPTER FOURTEEN

Howard: I give up, Danny. What's your secret?

Danny: Secret? The knife was still in his jacket pocket. He forced himself not to touch it. What are you talking about?

Howard was hunched at the long table in the great hall, using the light from a candelabra to study the framed map Danny had bought in town. They'd just finished dinner, Danny's first meal in twenty-four hours: chicken stew with olives and silver leaves, cooked by Howard. Danny was pretty sure it was the tastiest chicken stew he'd had in his life.

Howard: You kind of . . . don't take this the wrong way, but you kind of bumble around, and you seem like you're just barely hanging on, much less getting anything done, and then you turn up something like this.

Danny: You like it.

Howard looked up. *Like* isn't really the word. It's unbelievable, Danny. It's—it's the thing we've been looking for every one of the how many days have we been here?

Forty. Mick's voice. The only light in the room came from the candles on the table, so Danny couldn't see him.

Howard: It's huge, Danny—it's *it*. The missing piece. And you stumbled on this with your head in a sling, for fuck's sake!

Danny smiled as naturally as he could, which was not all that naturally. Howard was freaking him out. Danny was almost sure his cousin was mocking him, laying it on extra-thick to make Danny squirm. Or it could be the worm, eating its way deeper into Danny. But Howard *was* the worm. He was going in circles. It all came down to whether Howard knew about the knife. If he did, Danny's advantage was gone and this was open war. And even though Danny kept telling himself there was no way Howard could know, and there was no exact *reason* to think he knew, Danny had the feeling he did.

Howard: Have you looked at this map, Danny?

Not for too long.

Howard: So what made you buy it?

I'm not sure.

Danny felt the weight of the knife in his pocket, and suddenly the pressure of being watched by Howard was almost physical. Danny couldn't meet his cousin's eyes.

Howard: Think back. I'm genuinely curious. Why buy something you'd barely looked at?

It was just an impulse.

Howard left his chair and came over to Danny. *Where* did you get it?

Little antique shop near the square.

So what caught your eye? What made you even go in?

The food tumbled in Danny's gut. He wondered if the knife was making his jacket hang funny. It took all his willpower not to touch the pocket.

Howard was behind Danny's chair now. I'm asking you all these questions, I hope you don't mind, Danny, but I'm starting to think you have a—people call it all different things—I want to say a nose. For picking out things other people can't see.

Danny: Thanks. Howard was pulling on the posts of his chair. Danny wondered if his cousin was going to tip him backward.

Howard: Anyway, let's look at it now. Everyone, come on over and look at this map Danny found. He called this out into the dark room, where some graduate students were still milling around after dinner. No one seemed especially interested.

Howard moved a few candelabra together around the map. Graduate students began to trickle over. The kid, Benjy, came too.

Benjy (to Danny): Hi.

Danny: Hi.

How's your head?

Just fine. How's yours?

My head is fine, of course! He laughed at Danny and waited, but Danny didn't smile. Are you still sad?

I was never sad.

Yes you were, I saw—

Danny walked away.

Howard: Danny, come on back. Let's look at this map.

Eventually, a group gathered at the table. Light from the candles swished over the map. Look, Howard said softly, and there was a long pause while everyone did.

Ann: Incredible.

Isn't it? Mick, you seeing this?

Yep.

Mick was in back. Danny hadn't made eye contact with him since they'd come back inside the castle, but it was different now. There was an understanding between them. And part of the understanding was to hide it.

Howard: That tunnel? Under the keep?

Ann: And then that connects to all these other tunnels. . . .

It was true. When Danny looked at the map in town he'd assumed those dark squiggles were paths on top of the hills. But they were tunnels *underneath* the hills. They started out below the keep and fanned out every which way, exactly like the baroness said.

A mutter of excitement went through the graduate students.

Howard: It's something, eh? I mean, obviously the whole thing could be a fantasy—

Danny: I don't think so. The baroness told me there were tunnels.

Howard turned to look at Danny. So did everyone else.

Howard (to the group): Check this guy out! Danny, this is what I'm talking about! What else've you got up your sleeve? Don't hold out on us!

The mockery was right out in the open: Howard knew. He had to know. Danny's face went hot.

Danny: You've got it all, Howard. There's nothing left.

There was a pause. Howard and Danny looked at each other.

Howard: The problem is, I don't believe you anymore.

So there it was: war. Danny let himself touch the knife through his coat for the first time in front of Howard. He'd given it a careful once-over when he first got back to the castle, after he finally took a long bath and the doctor changed his bandages. A ceremonial knife, it looked like, with an ivory handle carved with scenes of guys hunting a deer. The blade was long and curved and sharp. Did Howard have a weapon? In a T-shirt and shorts, it seemed unlikely. Where would he keep it?

Benjy: When can we go in the tunnels, Daddy?

Howard: Good question. The smart answer is probably later, after we've gone through a lot of rigmarole. But I'd do it right now.

Ann: In the dark?

Doesn't matter when you're underground.

Not with the kids, obviously.

Yes with the kids, Mommy! Yes with the kids.

Benjy could come, couldn't he?

I can come! I can definitely come.

Ann (softly): Howard, think. We have no idea what's down there, if the tunnels are even stable. Look how old this map is!

But Howard couldn't think. He could hardly hear, he was too high on his own excitement. He wanted to go, he wanted to go! There was something desperate in his wanting, Danny thought, like if he waited too long it might all disappear or become impossible.

Howard pointed to the map. He said softly: You see what this is, Ann. Don't you?

Ann: I do, but I—

It's the thing we've been waiting for. Do you feel that too?

Possibly, but—

With something like this I just want to jump in there. I can't wait!

Fine. Jump. But leave the four-year-old out of it.

Benjy: Four-and-a-quarter!

Howard: We'll go slow. Just give him a taste. And if things seem even the slightest bit unsafe, you'll pull him right back out.

Please Mommy please Mommy pleasepleasepleaseplease-*please*! Benjy threw himself onto the floor and lay rigid. Everyone laughed, even Mick. Danny could pick out his laugh, separate from all the others.

He felt the battle in Ann: how much she wanted to please Howard to make up for the stuff with Mick and keep this castle adventure a fun thing for everyone, but also how she knew it was a shitty, stupid idea to go in the tunnels and didn't want to go or let her kid go. But if she stood in the way, Howard would go ahead and have the adventure without her. And she'd be the one who stayed behind.

Ann: Okay.

It was pushing midnight by the time they left the castle. Most of the graduate students carried flashlights, and those twenty-odd beams electrified the dark as the group bored through the garden. The overhang of trees turned into a ceiling, and things Danny hadn't seen before started jumping out of the gloom underneath: stone frogs and rabbits and dwarves. A horse on wheels. A table set for two swallowed up by vines.

Howard couldn't stand to leave anyone behind. He'd combed the halls and worked his walkie-talkie, tracking down stray graduate students. There was a manic excitement to him now that made everything before look like snoozing. This filled Danny with dread. Even the baby girl was along for the ride so that Nora, the so-called Child Care Specialist, wouldn't have to miss out. Ann carried the baby in the pouch around her neck. She gave in easily that time—she'd crossed some kind of line, and now she seemed half giddy with the adventure. They all were, snickering and whispering like a bunch of kids on a school trip as they blazed their way toward the keep.

Except Danny. The meaning of what he was doing—going underground with his cousin—tightened around him with each step. Every ten paces or so he fought the urge to slip away from the group and make a break, climb the castle walls and *run*! But he'd tried running, he'd tried all of it. There was no getting away. And a part of Danny craved that coolness of being underground. The web of secret tunnels: in a way, he wanted it, too.

The knife thumped Danny's chest as he walked. He knew Mick was behind him, bringing up the rear with the map under his arm, and Danny had a feeling he could count on Mick if something started to go down. Thanks to Mick, he had boots on both feet and legs the same length for the first time in twenty-four hours. This felt so good it made his knee injury fade into nothing. Danny was walking without a limp for the first time in weeks.

Near the bottom of the keep they stopped. All its windows were dark.

Howard (softly): Okay, a couple of things before we go in. One: stick together. I don't know what we're going to find down there, but let's find it as a group. No solo expeditions, deal? And second, we're not trespassing, obviously, but there's a person in there who thinks we are. She's probably asleep, so let's not talk for a while unless we really have to.

Danny looked up at the keep. The baroness asleep? He didn't buy it. It was easier to believe she was dead.

Slowly the group began climbing the outside staircase that wound around the keep, Howard first, holding Benjy's hand, then Ann with the baby, then everyone else. Danny stayed in the middle. One by one, they rose above the trees into the starry night.

The door was wide open when Danny got there, and he heard shoes scuffing on the stairs. No one was talking. More people were coming in behind him, and Danny took his place in the downward flow. As he followed those scooped-out stairs, down, down, he felt his brain relax, give up the work of thinking for itself. All those feet made a sound like whispering, like the keep was whispering into Danny's ears. Or the keep was a giant antenna picking up whispers from some other place.

They passed the window he'd fallen out of and continued down into the windowless part of the keep, where he'd wanted to go that other day but stopped himself. The farther Danny went, the louder the whispering got, like words in a language he couldn't understand.

Thanowa . . . shisela . . . hortenfashing . . .

Himmuffer . . . soubitane . . . laningshowingwisham . . .

The stairs snaked through a horizontal iron door held open by an ancient hook. Danny hesitated, figuring this must be the point where they passed underground, but he was a link in a chain whose back part was moving forward behind him, pushing him through that door, so Danny kept walking. It was easy.

Down another level of curling stairs. The air changed; it got thick and cold and smelled like clay. Danny sensed something happening in front of him, a slowing down or a breaking up. Sure enough, after another couple of turns the stairs fed into a hallway, and he followed the human chain through an arch cut out of a wall. Beyond it was a room full of dust. It was fine dust, like what covers up your windshield after you drive down a dirt road. It filled Danny's lungs like little claws. And rising out of the dust were rows of wood shelves stacked with hundreds of bottles of wine.

The group was spreading out, hacking and wheezing, holding bottles under flashlight beams. Danny went to a shelf and blew dust off a bottle. The label was written by hand in some kind of calligraphy. He picked up another one. They were rounder than wine bottles today. Some were dry inside, the corks crumbling or missing. Others still had liquid in them, colored wax holding the corks in.

Through the sniffing and sneezing Danny picked up murmurs of the graduate students: *Are these real? . . . can't be real . . . seems totally real . . . don't believe it's real. . . .*

Howard: Hey. Hey, everyone.

He was standing on top of something so they could see him above the shelves. He held a flashlight under his chin that made gouges around his eyes and lit up his hair. He looked like a spirit rising up out of the dust. Danny's heart lurched. He touched the knife in his pocket.

Howard: A reminder, folks. The whole mission of this hotel

we're putting together is to help people shed the real/unreal binary that's become so meaningless now, with telecommunications yada yada. So this is our chance to walk the walk. Let's not analyze. Let's just have the experience and see where it takes us.

Ann stood just below Howard, holding Benjy's hand and using her other sleeve to cover the baby's nose and mouth from the dust. Howard caught her eye and stopped. Enough said. Let's keep moving. And it's okay to talk. I think we're deep enough.

He led the way back out of the wine cellar into a narrow hall with a curved ceiling made of thin yellow bricks. The flashlight beams turned it bright, and Danny saw words in some other language carved into the stuccoed walls, even pictures: A hand. A horse. A fish. Ann and the kids had fallen behind, closer to Danny. Everyone stayed pretty quiet.

They were still in the hall when they heard a thud—felt it, too—a big vibration under their feet. Everyone stopped walking, bumping each other in the narrow space.

Benjy: Daddy, what was that? His little kid's voice cut the quiet.

Howard: I'm not sure.

They stood, listening. There was no other sound. The whispering pushed at Danny's ears—*shorahassa . . . wishaforshing . . . lashatishing*—so close that he could almost feel the breath that came with the sounds.

Howard: Mick, you back there?

Mick: Yep.

Howard: No stragglers?

Mick: Not a one. I've been counting.

Howard: Huh. Okay, let's keep moving.

They walked down the hallway. Danny noticed himself starting to zone out, maybe from the voices in his head or how little sleep he'd had. Whatever it was, he kept having to remind himself of his war with Howard, the knife, all that, because it was slipping out of his head, fading away like the pain in his head had faded, he didn't know when. He just noticed at a certain point that it was gone.

The front of the chain made a right. Excited rumbles and murmurs chased the whispering out of Danny's ears. Something big was coming up.

A thick wood door stood open. The space inside was gigantic compared to the wine cellar. It swallowed up the flashlight beams, so at first Danny wasn't sure what he was seeing: auto chassis? gym equipment? But when everyone was finally inside filling the space with light, he realized he was looking at instruments of torture. He recognized a rack, and one of those boards with metal cuffs where a person's wrists and ankles would go. Then a man-shaped suit made of spiked metal strips. And other stuff he couldn't ID but it made his skin hurt to look at it.

Howard: Benjy, where are you, son? An echo warped his voice. The kid clung to his mother's hand.

Howard: Benjy, c'mon over. Look at this stuff. This is like—talk about King Arthur! No one's going to believe this!

The kid wanted to please his dad, you could feel it. He let go of Ann's hand and bumped his way through the crowd. Howard lifted him onto his shoulders and led the way deeper into the room. Flashlights woke up the space as they moved. A far wall came into sight with three curved openings in it, sealed off with vertical bars.

Howard: What've we got here?

Everyone moved toward the arches, taking Danny with them. Beams of light poured between the bars into some kind of pit. For a second the darkness just sucked them up. Then Benjy screamed.

What a scream. It ripped through the space, stabbing Danny's eardrums. Ann flinched so hard she woke up the baby,

skeleton

who started wailing, too. But the bigger kid drowned the baby out. He was shrieking from his perch on Howard's shoulders, his head pushed up against the bars. Maybe being that high up was what let him see it first.

And now the whole group saw what he was seeing: skeletons, lots of them—on the floor, piled against the walls, some with bits of stuff around them that might have been clothing. They lay in the positions they'd died in, arms stretched out, yellow skulls angled up toward the bars as if they were still hoping someone would show up and let them out. Their eye sockets were huge, like flies' eyes, and their grimacing jaws were jammed with teeth. Danny knew what a skeleton looked like, but that was no preparation. His mind went numb, not believing it. It had to be fake. He wanted it to be fake. The whispering in his ears reached a kind of crescendo—he could hear it even through the screams of the two kids.

Ann pushed her way along the bars to Howard. In a flat voice she said: I've got to get Benjy out.

Howard seemed too stunned to speak. He'd taken Benjy off his shoulders, and the kid lunged for his mother's legs and clung to them, sobbing. Panic flickered through the group like electricity, but something kept it in check—peer pressure, maybe.

Howard looked down into the pit and swallowed. Yeah. Go. You know where? Tell Mick to go with you.

Ann: No, no. We're fine, Mick can stay. She didn't want to be alone with him.

Danny: I'll go. He was frantic to get out.

Howard: You know where?

Mick had come over quietly. Danny turned to him. It's just a straight shot back down that hall, right?

Mick: Yeah. He was looking at Danny hard, trying to get something across.

Danny: I should take a flashlight. Ann, too.

A couple of graduate students handed theirs over. Mick held the map under his arm, looking at Danny in that searching way.

Danny (softly): They'll be fine, Mick. I promise.

Mick nodded. Ann took Benjy's hand, and she and Danny started threading their way back through the torture machines. The kid's head hung as he walked. He was moaning, a low whine that didn't show any signs of letting up. The baby was still awake, looking around with big eyes like she was waiting to see a thing she recognized.

They passed out of the torture room and back into the hall. There was relief in just getting out of there, although the hall seemed a lot darker with only their two beams lighting it. They were inside the earth, with no light from any direction. Danny wondered why there was even air in these tunnels—were there vents of some kind? Or did you have to go deeper before the oxygen ran out?

Danny: We'll be out of here fast.

Ann: We should never have come in.

Danny: Nope.

Ann: I had a brain lapse.

Danny: You went with Howard. We all did.

Ann: My judgment is shot.

The kid kept moaning, but he moved his legs. After a while they passed a curved doorway on the left, and Danny's beam picked out the rows of wine bottles. They were right on track.

His heart galloped when they hit the bottom of the steps. God, he was desperate to be aboveground. He felt a second of delayed amazement at the fact that Howard had let him get away so easily.

They'd barely started climbing when the kid's legs went liquid. He flopped down on the stone and lay still.

Ann: Benjy, you have to walk. Please, honey, I can't carry you with Sarah on my chest.

The kid just lay there. Danny had an impulse of pure rage—
if there had been a cliff, he would've kicked Benjy over it.
Instead, he leaned down and tried to lift the kid off the ground.
He'd never held a kid in his life, not even a baby. He told
Ann: I've got him. But he didn't have him—the kid's head and
legs and arms dangled heavily. Danny couldn't get a secure grip
and thought he might drop him. Fuck! But when he finally got
his arms under the skinny butt and the boy's head on his shoulder, things improved. Benjy fastened himself onto Danny, arms
tight around his neck, knees clamped at his waist.

They started up the stairs again, Danny first with the kid
suctioned to his chest, then Ann with the baby. Now that the kid
had stopped moaning, Danny noticed the whispering again.
It came back like water filling up a hole—*hershashasha* . . .
wassafrassa—almost words, but not quite. They took one turn
up the stairs, then another.

Danny: We're getting close, I think.

Ann: Let's hope.

A second or two later, something smashed Danny's head
from above. The kid flailed in his arms and Danny dropped his
flashlight. It tumbled down the stairs and Ann shouted, scared.

What happened? Is Benjy okay?

Danny stood there, bewildered. He tasted blood—he'd bitten his tongue. He thought someone had hit him over the head
with something heavy, but when he reached up, he found a hard
surface cutting off the stairs.

Danny: He's fine. There's—can you point your light?

Ann aimed her flashlight up. The horizontal door that the
stairs twisted through had been shut. Danny shoved at it with
both arms but it didn't budge. It was locked.

The baroness.

He swallowed. For a minute he didn't feel anything, and

then a tidal wave of panic came up in him, a panic like he'd never felt before, even running alone in those woods. This had nothing to do with his mind or the worm—it was deeper. Skeletons stretched out in a cage. Danny had a physical need to scream, flail, something, but the kid in his arms kept him still. And for some reason, not moving seemed to hold the panic back.

Danny looked at Ann. There was absolute alto between them.

Ann: We have to go back.

She gave him his flashlight, which he hung on the fingers of one hand. Ann headed down the stairs, but Danny hesitated. Finally she stopped too.

Danny (whispering): Wait.

They were quiet, and in the quiet Danny heard something shift. A sound on the other side of that door.

He said: Liesl?

Until that second, he'd had no idea he knew the baroness's name. She must have told him that night.

A rustle above the door. She was there, listening. Danny's whole body broke out in goose bumps.

Liesl. Please let us out. It sounded wobbly, desperate.

There was a stirring, a scrape of pointed heels on the iron door. I'll do nothing of the kind. The iron muffled her voice, took away its shrillness.

Danny: We've got little kids down here. All kinds of other people. Just open the door.

The baroness laughed. It was a terrible sound, wet and raucous. You think I care what happens to you? To any of you?

Come on, Liesl. Open the door.

You don't believe me. You can't believe I won't do what you want me to do. You're children, you Americans, every one of you. And the world is very, very old.

Danny: You're right, I don't believe it. I think you're a better person than that. Christ, what was he talking about? *A better person?* Danny wasn't sure she was a person at all.

The baroness howled with laughter. She was having the time of her life. The sound of her laugh made Danny sweat.

Danny: Just tell us what you want. Anything. It's yours: money? Howard's rolling in it.

I have exactly what I want. I set a trap and you've fallen in it like the idiots you are. There's no way out of those tunnels except through this keep. You'll die, all of you, the children too. And as your screams grow weak and faint, I and the eighty generations who made me, the twenty-eight Liesl von Ausblinkers who lived and died before I was born, will rejoice. We'll laugh! The Tartars couldn't take this keep and neither can the Americans, with all their power and all their money.

She was bonkers. Sick—how had Danny not seen it?

He'd already turned and was heading back down the stairs. The kid was jerking in his arms, and Danny couldn't let him hear any more. As he rounded a curve, he heard the baroness laugh.

Going so soon? Too bad! We had such fun the last time, Danny . . . you especially, I think!

Danny's legs shook so spastically that he worried he'd collapse trying to get down the rest of the stairs. He was cold and soaked with sweat. When they got back to the hall, Ann stopped. She pushed the hair out of her face and held the baby's head in her hands. Danny saw the terror in her. She kissed the soft hair on her baby's scalp.

Benjy was moaning. The baroness's words were caught in his ears, Danny could tell. He needed to erase them, keep them from tunneling into the boy's brain. He started whispering into his hair as they followed the endless hall: It'll be fine, you'll see, you'll grow up and you won't even remember this stuff, it'll all be so long ago, just a funny thing you'll tell your friends and they'll say: What? No way! And you'll say: Yeah, it's true, I promise, that stuff really happened but I was a brave kid and I got through it, I kept my cool because that's the kind of kid I am. . . .

Where was this shit coming from? Danny had no idea. He whispered to the kid and meanwhile the whispering voices kept piping their weird language into Danny's ears until he wondered if he was translating, if the voices were actually telling him what to say. And it worked. Or at least Benjy stopped moaning. They passed the wine cellar, and a while later Danny saw a patch of light and heard Howard's voice and the graduate students', a back-and-forth of breathless sound that shook Danny. They were happy. They had no idea what was coming. The panic rose back up in him like bile.

He followed Ann into the torture room. Howard was standing on one of the machines. When he saw Ann and Danny he dropped to the ground. What? What happened?

Ann was moving toward him. Danny followed behind her.

Ann: We can't get out that way. The stairs are blocked off.

She didn't scream or cry, none of the things Danny would've expected. She said it gently.

Howard: *Blocked off?*

Ann: That door? In the stairs? It's shut now. So we'll have to find another way out.

She took Howard's hand. It was incredible—like she'd forgiven him for getting them into this thing, when they weren't even out yet. Might never *get* out. Danny was still holding the kid. Benjy's weight had gone very solid in the last few minutes, and Danny thought he might be asleep.

Howard: I—I don't understand. Say that again.

Ann: The door. We can't go that way. We have to go another way.

Who says there *is* another way?

Danny watched the panic he'd felt in himself roar over Howard and swallow him whole. The guy didn't have a chance.

Howard: The door—no! It has to—

It'll be fine, honey. We just have to find another way.

No! There's—no! Oh my God!

Relax, sweetheart. Ann put her hand on Howard's head, but he twisted away.

No. No! We have to—oh my God, please!

His voice raked the walls. Everyone stared at him. Howard shut his eyes and jackknifed over so his head was near the floor. Ann leaned over him, trying to straighten him up without letting the baby slide out of the pouch on her chest. She must have seen this coming, known how he'd react. But she couldn't pull Howard back up. He'd started to scream, and every scream tore through Danny and seemed to take some of his blood away with it. He felt on the verge of passing out. That current of panic moved through the group again: there were cries and flashlights swung around, making the room wild with light. A bunch of people ran back into the hall and headed for the stairs. Danny thought of the baroness waiting there.

Howard had left his body completely—he was somewhere else. No, no, please! Please! Oh my God, I can't breathe. Help!

The room was starting to spin. Danny felt like all the oxygen had run out. The harder he tried to breathe the dizzier he got. The kid stirred in his arms and he thought, I can't pass out while I'm holding this kid.

Ann: Howard, stop. You've got to stop. Stop! We've got the kids here and a lot of other people who need to get out.

But Howard couldn't stop. His body went suddenly rigid, his eyes wide and blind. He clawed at the air and then, in a terrible guttural voice, he screamed Danny's name, dragging it out so it filled the torture space with one long howl.

Howard: Danny! Danny! Danny help me, please let me out.

Danny please, I'll do anything—please let me out. I'll give you anything you want. Wait, Danny, don't go! Don't leave me here!

He wasn't looking at Danny, but everyone else was. Mick and Ann and the graduate students who were still in the room gaped at him in confusion. Each time Howard screamed his name seemed to push Danny's skull one step closer to exploding. Unbelievably, the kid in his arms was still asleep. Danny noticed himself squeezing Benjy, clutching onto him like the kid was holding *him* up.

Howard: Danny! Don't do this to me, please. Please come back! Ple—ee—ee—Big gasping sobs broke up his screams. Howard was crying like a little kid cries, his face slick with snot and tears. It was something no one should see.

The graduate students who had run to the stairs stampeded back in, frantic. *It's locked, the door's locked, we're trapped down here, we're going to die.* Now the room seized up with real hysteria for the first time. At the beginning it was aimless, swerving terror, but when Howard shouted Danny's name again the group pulled in around it in desperation. A panicked mass of people closed in on Danny, crazed and wailing: *Danny, help!*

If I pass out I'll drop the kid.

Danny, Danny, please let us out please help us please. . . .

Danny: Okay. Okay!

But no one heard him. He couldn't hear himself. Their cries ricocheted off the stone walls: Danny please. Please help us please help us please. . . .

Danny: Okay. Shut *up*.

He said it loudly, and the people closest to him piped down. Pretty soon the other ones did, too. Everyone stood there, waiting for Danny to do something. What should he do? He had no idea what to do. Howard had crumpled to the ground and was hunched there, sobbing. Ann knelt next to him, her arms around his neck, the sleeping baby still hanging from her chest.

Danny: Okay. I—uh . . . Nora, where are you? He was stalling.

Nora came forward with wet, jumpy eyes.

Danny: Take this kid. When Nora didn't move, he said, Do your fucking job for once and take this kid.

Nora jumped like he'd slapped her. Fuck you.

Fuck you, too.

She lifted Benjy gently from Danny's arms, then elbowed him away.

Danny: Mick, where are you? Mick? He was buying time, trying to make the cringing feeling he had go away. Danny was a follower, not a leader. You could even say that as a follower, Danny *was* a leader. But not on his own.

Mick came forward. He was still holding the map. Danny reached for it now, putting off by another minute or two the time when they would all find out he had no plan, no solution of any kind.

Danny: Let's look at that map.

Mick lifted up the map and Danny pointed his flashlight at it, but the glass bounced the light right into his eyes. Mick broke the map over his knee and the glass dropped away. He was holding parchment. Danny stared at the map, his eyes not even focused. He was faking it—stealing one second, then another second, then one more second before the crying would start up again.

Mick: It looks like . . .

Danny: If you go down . . .

Mick: Or maybe that way?

In the background Howard sobbed: the saddest, most hopeless sound Danny had ever heard. He'd never cried that way, never in his life.

Danny: All right, let's just go. We'll figure it out.

He waited while Ann helped Howard off the ground. The guy was shivering, his wet face covered with dirt.

Danny: Mick, can you go last and make sure we don't lose anyone?

Mick: Sure thing. He seemed glad to get away.

Danny led them out of the torture room, following his flashlight beam into the dark. It was like walking on the bottom of the sea. Danny had no impulses, no hunches about what to do. He had one goal: to protect these people from the fact that he couldn't help them, pretend to lead them so they'd believe they were going somewhere and not cry and call out his name. Danny couldn't take any more of that. He thought it would kill him.

So he led the way through nowhere, into nothing, grateful for the quiet, the sounds of all those shoes behind him. He led them down, at an angle, deeper into the earth. Then left, then up a little, then down again. Danny moved fast—the fact that he was pretending, leading them nowhere, was waiting to jump him if he hesitated. As they all walked deeper, a kind of rhythm set in. They were moving, and after they'd been moving for a long enough time there was a feeling that they must be moving *toward* something. Danny felt it, too. Like faking it for long enough had made it true.

No one had spoken since they'd left the torture room. Even Howard was finally quiet, and the sound of just their footsteps in the tunnels brought back the whispering voices to Danny. He wondered if the voices were telling him where to go. Sometimes he caught himself muttering: Right or left, I don't know. Down, I think. Over there looks better than straight. Nope, I don't like this—gotta go back. The tunnels were endless, a world of tunnels under the earth. The air went from dusty to dank. Eventually there was the sound of water dripping. Danny had no idea how much time had passed.

They came to a stairway. They'd passed other stairs along the way, but those had all led down. This one went straight up, and the stairs were tiny, too small to hold even half of one of Danny's boots. Tiny and wet—impossible to climb! But something to try, to keep the group distracted. The tunnel went on past the steps, but Danny stopped.

The sound of a voice—his own voice—was strange after so much silent walking.

Danny: Okay, look. I'm going to climb these stairs and see where they go. Don't follow me, because if I slip and fall I'll knock everyone down. Point your beams up so I can see the way.

He felt the jump of their hope, their panic, barely under control. But Danny was calm. Weirdly calm, like he was having a dream.

Slowly, carefully, he started to climb. There were iron rings every few feet along the sides of the stairwell, which was what made climbing possible. Danny held a flashlight in his mouth, half gagging on it, grabbed an iron ring with one hand and used the other hand to claw at the slippery steps. It was the longest flight of stairs he'd ever climbed. At one point they shifted direction, and then he was beyond the reach of all the beams. He was starting to smell earth, not the gut of it where they'd been but the part that touches air: trees, grass, all those smells of life. And those smells kicked something alive in Danny—desire, an appetite. He started scrambling like a spider, throwing back his head every few feet to point his flashlight up and see what was above him. More stairs. More stairs. And finally he saw something flat: the underside of a door. Danny's arms and legs were shaking when he got there. He pushed the door with his hand: sealed, of course. He hunched there, the flashlight in his mouth, panting and sweating, thinking he might puke.

Danny yelled down around the flashlight: There's a door,

okay? I'm going to try to open it, and I'll make some noise.
Stand away, in case I fall.

A dim sound came back up.

There was an iron ring on each side of the door. Danny
grabbed one ring in each hand and walked his feet over his head
until they were braced against the underside of the door. He was
upside down, scrunched to the size of a tire, his head full of
blood. He tapped the door with the heel of his boot: stone, it felt
like.

Then he started to kick. He kicked and pushed like a mad-
man, like it was the one thing he was made to do on earth. He
kicked until he had nothing left in him, until he was gasping,
gagging, veins pounding in his temples and neck. But the door
didn't move.

He called out: *Mick!* and the flashlight slipped out of his
mouth and whacked its way down the stairs. Watch out, Danny
yelled. Stand back, something's falling. He couldn't even hear
the thing land. Then he called, Mick, can you come up? He was
absolutely spent. He clutched the rings and hung there, breathing hard in the total dark.

It wasn't long before he saw a light. By the time Mick was
fully in view, flashlight between his teeth, Danny had recovered
a little. Mick's shirt was off, and sweat poured down his torso
and ropy arms with their scarred-up hash of old track marks.

Danny: We've gotta kick open this door.

Mick: Let's do it.

They coiled side by side like Danny did before, each holding
an iron ring and bracing his loose arm around the other one's
neck. They started to kick. It made a lot of noise, but that was it.

Mick: Wait, wait. We've got to count. One, two . . . *three.*

They pushed and groaned.

Mick: Again. One, two . . . *three!*

They pushed together. Again. Again. Again. Danny thought the door gave just a little. Again. No, nothing. Again. Again. And then Danny felt a jerk under his feet. The door was starting to move. It's moving, they both muttered. Again. Again. And even after being so long upside down, veins popping, eyes running, lips hanging, sweat making his hand slip on the ring, Danny felt a jolt of strength rock through him from his head to his boots. His lucky boots.

Mick was panting almost too hard to speak: One more time. This is it, *one, two, three!* They pushed, groaning, and the door moved—it slid up just a little. *One, two, three!* Danny assaulted the thing with his boots, mashed and thrust and pounded, Mick doing the same until the door lifted away like the top coming off a grave.

They crawled through the opening and collapsed. It was a while before Danny looked up and saw stars. Trees. He knew where he was: by the pool. He could smell it. And the smell was so welcome to Danny it almost seemed sweet.

They'd lifted off one of the marble panels around the pool. A perfect square. Heavy as hell. Who knew when the thing had last moved.

When he could breathe again, Danny leaned over the hole and yelled down: Okay, we're out. I'll come back down. It's gonna take awhile, but we're done. It's all fine.

There was a second of silence. Then a cheer came up.

CHAPTER FIFTEEN

Danny helped Ann get up that long flight of stairs with the baby girl on her chest. She hooked one arm around Danny's neck so if she slipped (which she did, twice) he'd be holding her, and the baby would be safe.

He carried Benjy one-armed, climbing the stairs on two legs and a hand. As far as Danny knew, the kid slept through all of it.

He and Mick hauled Howard up between them, one of Howard's arms around each of their necks. Near the top, Howard started coming back a little. By the end he was doing some of the climbing himself.

Each one of these climbs took at least fifteen minutes, so getting everyone out of the ground was a project of hours. By the time it was finally done and they were all outside, every last graduate student lying on the marble around the pool sucking in that fresh air, the sun was up.

That was Phase One.

Phase Two was a lot of hugging. Everyone started hugging Danny, sometimes more than one person at a time, most of them laughing or crying or else laughing *and* crying. The only thing like it Danny could remember was high school graduation. He'd almost forgotten it, but the feeling came back: *We've been through something huge and now the rest of our lives are about to start up but we don't want to leave this behind, we can't, it's too big.*

Ann hugged Danny so hard that the baby on her chest let out a cry. Danny felt how physically strong Ann was, and it gave him an idea of what Mick must feel for her—how after all that strength had pulled in around you even just once, you'd feel stripped down to nothing without it.

Nora hugged Danny lightly, then kissed his cheek. And since Nora wasn't the kissy type, plus her lips were unbelievably soft, it was a sensual thing. Danny smelled her for the first time, and the smell surprised him: it wasn't like cigarettes or patchouli or BO, which is what he expected from a heavily pierced girl with dreads. She smelled like—what? Danny asked himself that while Nora walked away. And then she turned back and Danny saw her smile for the first time, saw the pretty girl Nora never wanted to be again. And then he knew what she smelled like—that fresh, delicate, complicated smell: lawn.

Nora: Thanks.

Danny: She said. . . .

Nora didn't get it at first. Then she laughed: Actually, that sentence was adverb-free.

Danny: Just, *thanks*?

Nora: That's it. Thanks. Or maybe, Thanks, Danny. Are you disappointed?

Danny: Not at all. You're welcome.

They looked at each other and started to laugh.

Benjy put his arms around Danny's legs. And this was the hug that walloped Danny, because the kid's arms were so small, and he was short enough that Danny couldn't even really hug him back, he just put his hands on the kid's head and felt the warm round skull under the thick hair. Howard's son.

The graduate students hugged Danny with shaking arms and wet cheeks, sometimes a few at once so it was a hug pileup with Danny in the middle like some kind of hero. A couple of times they almost knocked him down, everyone calling *Whoa—oh—oh—oh* while they stabilized. And Danny would've thought these hugs would be his favorites because they reminded him of scoring in the last seconds of a game, everyone rushing the field. But they actually made him feel shaky, guilty. Like he was getting credit for something he hadn't done.

In Phase Three it got quiet. Ann and Nora headed back to the castle with the kids, who were hungry. They waved, then slipped out through the cypress. Everyone else stayed behind, sticking close to the pool like they were waiting. Danny felt it too, a wanting to stay near the experience and the people he'd had it with. Because the closer he was to the time when he'd thought he would die, the more impossibly sweet it felt to be out here breathing in air, feeling sun on his face, all that stuff you never really think about.

Howard sat on the ground, leaning against the Medusa head spigot where Danny had seen the moving figures back when he was wigging out. His elbows were on his knees, his head on his fists. Something had gone out of Howard. Maybe Howard had gone out of Howard.

Mick was standing near him. Danny couldn't catch his eye.

Phase Four was when Danny realized that the power was his. Howard was done, Mick was out, which left Danny in the position he'd spent sixteen years waiting for, wishing for, scheming for, groveling for, grabbing and even (when he was really desperate) praying for. The force of getting this reward after so long overwhelmed Danny at first: the pure thrill of it. That lasted maybe thirty seconds, and then the thrill quieted down and Danny realized something he couldn't quite put a name to. It wasn't that he didn't *want* Howard's power—more that the whole power thing seemed phony, beside the point, or maybe just old, like it couldn't help Danny see this world he was looking at.

An invisible clock had started to tick. Danny didn't know about the clock, but he knew that some crucial minute had passed when suddenly people began to drift like someone had cut a cord that was holding them all in one place. They floated away, some back toward the castle, some into the woods, some up that broken wall Danny and Howard had climbed, and a couple (unbelievably) back down the stairs into the tunnels. And as they went their ways alone or in pairs or little clusters, white morning light poured down from the sky and began its work of wiping out what had happened underground, so that already it seemed incredible to Danny that any of these graduate students had ever panicked or called out his name, or that Howard had sobbed: a joke, a fantasy too exaggerated to be true.

That was Phase Five.

Danny sat down next to Howard. He hadn't really seen his cousin's face since they came outside. Mick he could see, and the guy looked wrecked. The euphoria, the relief that Ann and Nora and the graduate students felt—Danny too—all of that had passed Mick by.

The clock was still ticking, but Danny couldn't hear it.

Eventually Howard lifted up his head. His face looked gray, old. His voice was flat: You did good, Danny. Under there.

Funny answers, stupid answers, answers that are a way of not answering—all these went through Danny's head: *Hey, I needed the exercise* or *Falling out a window was a tough act to follow but I gave it my best,* or *It must've been those injections the doc gave me,* or *Thank God for that trail of bread crumbs,* or *Tell my dad, wouldja?*

But what he finally said was: I left you to die.

Howard looked up, squinting at Danny in the sun. But I didn't die. I got out.

Danny: They found you.

Before that. I escaped with my mind. I got out of there because I wasn't going to make it otherwise.

How?

I don't know. I left. I went into a game. Rooms in my head. We can all do it, you know—we're just out of practice.

It was weirdly easy to have this conversation, like they'd talked about all of it before. Like it was something they agreed on.

Danny: What the fuck am I doing here, Howard?

I don't know, buddy. You tell me.

Danny turned his face into the sun. It was weak morning sun, but still so bright. He said: I don't know. I thought I knew, but there was another layer.

Howard: Ditto. I wanted to—I don't know what. Impress you, maybe.

Well, you did that.

Howard: I felt a connection. I can't explain it.

Danny: It wasn't payback?

Howard looked at him, surprised. How?

I got a little flipped out the past day or two. Maybe the jet lag. Started thinking you had it in for me.

Howard: Come on, it's late for that. Bygones, right? Anyway, now I owe *you*.

Please. Don't say that.

The birds were suddenly loud, jabbering in the trees. Sun, birds, sky—it was like a band starting up.

Howard: You know, what I said before, Danny. I meant that.

Which?

Your help. How you get things done. To be honest, I wasn't expecting much.

My reputation preceded me.

Yeah, a bit.

Danny laughed. You got lucky, I guess.

Howard: But I feel like—we could work together on something.

Danny: I'd love that.

It came automatically. Work with Howard? The longer the idea sat in Danny's head, the more it felt like something he'd been waiting to do. Wanting to do. You mean . . . work *for* you?

No, no. Partners. The real thing. Howard was sitting up straight. He looked better, more like himself. There was life in his face. I've had this idea for years about a restaurant.

Danny: You're an unbelievable cook.

Howard: I say restaurant, but it's a whole—I've got this theory about food. About diet, really. It's a longer conversation.

Danny: I've been working in restaurants for years.

Howard: No shit?

That's what I do! I've been in restaurants for . . . Christ, it seems like forever.

I don't know squat about running one.

Well, they almost never make money.

Howard grinned. Come on, Danny, it's not about money. You know me well enough by now.

Danny: Yeah, I guess I do.

That was Phase Six.

Something made Danny look up at Mick. He'd completely forgotten him, talking to Howard like it was just the two of them by the pool. And Howard was doing the same. But Mick hadn't gone anywhere—in fact, he hadn't moved. He looked frozen, inches away from Howard, listening. When Danny looked up, their eyes locked (Phase Seven) and he was hit with the

absolute coldness in Mick's face—a blankness, like a machine. And right then, alto swamped Danny's mind like he was standing on top of the keep, looking down at every detail of the landscape: Howard was all Mick had. Mick was Howard's number two. And a number two will do anything.

Mick took a step in Danny's direction. One step, but Danny felt a jerk of adrenaline. And all that fear, the gnawing worm, the trapped, hunted feeling he'd had—it jumped up in Danny like it had never gone away. He was on his feet a second later, the knife in his hand. Its long curved blade caught the sun.

Mick: Drop it, Danny.

Howard: What the f—?

Howard scrambled onto his feet, stunned and confused like he'd been asleep or still *was* asleep. They were standing in the place where the moving shapes had been, which is maybe why it all felt so familiar to Danny. Like it had already happened. Or maybe that was the alto. Because Danny saw everything, now, and knew his place in it.

Mick: Watch it, Howard!

The gun came from somewhere on Mick's ankle. He was unbelievably fast.

Danny tried to lunge with his knife, but he was too late. He'd hardly moved when I fired at his forehead. He was looking at me when the bullet tore through, and I watched the light go out.

Why? That's a reasonable question. You shoot someone in the head, you should have a reason. And what I'd like to do right now is make you a list, pile up the evidence piece by piece (things like: *I actually thought for a second that he was going at Howard with the knife* and *I knew he'd tell Howard about Ann and me eventually* and *After fucking up Howard like he did when they were kids, I didn't think he should get off so easy*), so at the end of the list you'd say, Well of course he shot that asshole, and good thing—look at all these reasons! But I don't have a list. I liked Danny. He reminded me of me.

But I was getting erased. With Danny there it was all going to end, this little bit that I had: Howard and Benjy and Ann. Like for all those years I'd been holding his place.

And of course, after I shot him, it ended anyway.

Danny fell backward (Phase Eight), arms spread out like he was trying to catch something huge falling out of the sky. He fell into the black pool and it folded up around him. Howard jumped in too, groping for Danny in the thick water. But dead things are heavier than anything alive, and Danny sank. For a while they went down together, Howard holding on to Danny with both arms, trying to dredge him back up, but in the end he had to let him go or go with him.

Danny's eyes were still open. At first he couldn't see. It was dark and thick and he was falling, sinking, but then he felt something under his feet and realized there were steps beginning at the inside edge of the pool and leading down. He found his footing and started to walk, and maybe the water cleared up or maybe his eyes adjusted as he went deeper, because he started seeing stuff he remembered: the blue hose he'd used to help his dad water the bushes along the driveway, the nook by the living room window where he read his comic books, his artwork taped to the kitchen wall, the pink john with the rose soaps in a clamshell behind it, the shower curtain with the bumblebee, the soccer coach who blew his nose without Kleenex, the crab-apple salad his Aunt Corkie used to make, a sublet on Elizabeth Street full of Persian rugs and Persian cat hair, a girl on Rollerblades he'd chased through the Lower East Side, watching a guy pump fake butter onto a bucket of movie popcorn, New York all fuzzy with snow, a pigeon who built a nest on his air conditioner, getting a haircut, whistling for a cab, noticing a sunset between buildings—on and on, a tunnel of memories, stuff, information, and Danny was connected to all of it, he was floating through it, touching it. It was all still there. *Nothing disappears.* And Danny saw himself, too, in a way you only can if you're dead or so high you can leave your body behind: a grown man, sinking through black water.

The stairs went on and on. The water pushed its way into Danny's ears, his eyes, his lungs. But finally, near the earth's molten core, the stairs ran out. When Danny looked up, the top of the pool was the size of a dime, a dime of blue sky. And then Danny saw a door (Phase Nine) and opened it. He was in a white hall. The water was gone. The walls were smooth, no windows or doors or decorations. All Danny saw was a gray-blue end-point that looked like another door, and he walked down the hall toward that. It was a long walk, but when he finally got close to the door he realized it wasn't a door, it was a window. Danny couldn't see through it—the glass was foggy or dusty or maybe just warped. But when he got to the window and put his hand against it, the glass suddenly cleared (Phase Ten). I saw him standing there. And he saw me.

Where the fuck did you come from? I said.

Danny smiled. He said: You didn't really think I was going to leave you alone?

He said: Haven't you learned that the thing you want to forget most is the one that'll never leave you?

He said: Let the haunting begin. And then he laughed.

He said: We're twins. There's no separating us.

He said: I hope you like to write.

And then he started to talk, whispering in my ear.

Underneath me, Davis lay on his tray with the orange radio pushed up against his head. His eyes were shut. He turned the knobs, listening.

PART III

CHAPTER SIXTEEN

Hule

Ray's manuscript comes to me in a big brown envelope with a local postmark and no return address. Inside I find the castle story, some of which I've read, and then about forty pages of handwritten diary entries I've never seen before. Reading it takes me all night. I hear traffic in the background. You hear it everywhere around here, louder at night because that's when the big trucks make their hauls. It's echoey, like the sea, or like I think the sea would sound if there were a sea nearby, and I wish there was.

If I were a crier I'd cry, reading all that, but I'm not. There was a time when all I did was cry, but since then almost nothing. I'm dry.

When I finish reading, the sky is getting light. The house is quiet. The girls are still asleep, and who knows where Seth is.

Then I have an idea. I go to the kitchen and get a big green garbage bag and a metal spoon. I slip out of the house and quietly tap the chunk of pages on our two concrete steps to straighten them out. I put the chunk in the bottom of the garbage bag and twist the bag and wrap it back around the chunk and twist and wrap it again until there's no more bag to twist. Then I count my steps away from the house, like Ray would: thirty-five left. I start digging with the spoon. On top the ground is tightly packed, but underneath it's powdery. I go fast, because I know any minute the girls will wake up. I dig a hole and put the bag inside and then I cover it up with dirt. Not all the dirt goes back on. I stomp it with my foot. My hands look like I've been digging graves. And then it's done and the sun is coming up over the hill and oh, I'm so relieved to know it's safe, it's all safe, the whole story and me in the story, that teacher who left her husband, that pretty princess—she's buried down there like treasure.

I've buried the evidence, too. I know it's illegal to hold on to something sent to you by a convict who's just escaped.

I let the dogs out of their pen. They pound right over the buried pages. I throw the red ball, and that makes them run harder.

I go back to the house and sit on the steps to smoke a cigarette and enjoy the sunrise. I notice something moving up the road. My eyes see it before my brain does, and then I realize it's Seth and my stomach knots up because where's the truck? What has he done with the truck?

Seth gets to the door and I can see he's still tweaking but slowing down. He's been gone two days, which is usually what happens after he finishes a job. For a construction worker he's emaciated, and without his dentures in there's not a tooth in his head. And this was a rock star, not just locally but in other states. Onstage he'd take off his shirt and girls would throw their beer to see it run down his chest.

He looks at me with empty eyes.

"Where's the truck?" I ask.

"Had a flat on Eighty-five." He looks ready to crash, which is a lot like looking ready to die.

"They're asleep, get inside," I say, and he does, because the one thing we have, Seth and I, the only thing, is we both love those girls. It's not like loving each other, but it's more than nothing.

That same afternoon, two state police officers visit me at the college. One of them is Pete Konig. I've known him since fourth grade, but he's gotten fat since I French-kissed him at junior prom, and he's sweating in that heavy uniform. The other guy, Sergeant Rufus, looks like he needs an antacid. Everyone in the office stares when I go out to meet them.

"Pete," I say, "I have lunch in twenty minutes, can you wait?"

"Can we wait?" the other guy bursts out, like I've asked him to do my laundry. But Pete says okay, they'll be in the cafeteria.

I find them outside at my favorite picnic table. It's a nice spring day, everything full and light green. You can hear the traffic swatting by in the background. Someone with a good pitching arm could throw a ball and hit the interstate.

"Don't you want to get your lunch?" Pete asks me.

"I don't like to be the only one eating."

I sit down and light a cigarette. Pete says: "I understand you knew one of the inmates who escaped. Raymond Michael Dobbs."

"He was in my writing class."

"So I understand. Got stabbed by someone else in your class."

"Yes. Thomas Harrington. I guess they moved him over to the supermax."

There's a silence, but with all that traffic there's always something to listen to.

"You heard anything from him, Holly?" Pete asks. "Dobbs, I mean?"

"No," I say. "Nothing." And right as I say it I realize I'm breaking the law, and I feel sweat opening my pores.

"Any way he might know where you live?"

"I hope not."

Pete's seen me at my best: the girl who won the school essay contest and wrote a play that the whole class performed in eighth grade. And he's seen me at my worst: sores all over my face, waiting in the hospital while my baby boy, Corey, hung on to his life. There's so much sympathy in his eyes I have to look away.

Now the other guy steps in, Sergeant Rufus. "We understand you had a personal relationship with inmate Dobbs," he says.

"What do you mean by that?"

"You visited him in the hospital."

"That's true," I say. "They said he was going to die."

"And what was the nature of that visit?"

"Mostly I sat there. He was hardly conscious."

"Or maybe he's just a really good fake."

"I don't know how you fake a raging intestinal infection," I say, and get a warning look from Pete.

"You visited Dobbs again," Rufus says, "after he returned to the prison."

"Yes."

"You drove up like any visitor."

"Yes, I did."

"And what was the reason for that visit?"

"I wanted to make sure he was well."

"Beg pardon?"

"I just—I couldn't believe it. I couldn't believe he recovered."

That answer doesn't make anyone happy. Pete adjusts his weight on the picnic bench.

"On that second visit, what transpired between you and the prisoner?" Rufus asks.

"We just talked."

"You talked about *what*?"

"I can't remember. I wasn't there very long."

"You were there an hour and fifteen minutes, ma'am."

It's bad, I know. It looks very bad. I don't know what else to say.

"Did he mention any plans to escape or ask for your help?"

"Absolutely not," I say, and I think my volume catches them both by surprise. "Nothing. Nothing like that. I would have reported it immediately."

That shuts Rufus up—I'm speaking his language now. But for Pete, it may have worked the other way. "The break came as a total surprise to you, Holly?" he asks, tilting his head to look at me.

"Complete."

"You've heard nothing from this guy? Not a whisper?"

Those sweet eyes on mine. Pete's got four kids, his oldest girl just a year older than Megan. I look right back at him. "Nothing."

"Good, Holly," he says. "Because—well, you know this. It's a federal crime to aid a fugitive."

"I do know."

"And it's just—it wouldn't be worth it."

"No way."

"Not after all you've been through. Not when you're back on track and doing so well."

It was Ray and his roommate, Davis, who escaped. Ray diverted water from a plumbing main, and he and Davis dug their way down to the pipe, opened it up with a blowtorch, got inside, crawled under both perimeter fences, opened up another hole, and dug their way back out.

This may sound easy, but it was next to impossible. It

involved Ray and Davis digging that first hole under a tower with a sharpshooter in it, and even more unbelievably, it involved their not being missed until standing count at 4 p.m. People were in shock over that. *Not missed until standing count?* How? The answer was right in the newspaper: phony work orders, clearances, passes, all made by Davis, who was a forger on top of a murderer. He'd been peaceful and crazy for years, and they'd stopped watching him. Over at the prison, heads started to roll.

The last break was seventeen years ago, when I was a senior in high school. People still talk about that one: three guys used homemade stilts to scale both fences, then hid in the home of a family that was out of town. They sewed up their gashes with sewing needles and blue thread. I always remembered that, how the thread was blue. By the time they were caught they'd taken two hostages, shot a horse, and burned a barn to the ground.

The night I heard about Ray, I moved into my girls' room, dragging in the foldaway cot and opening it between their beds. Megan was away at a soccer game, but Gabrielle, my little one, was my accomplice. A slumber party with Mom! We were popping popcorn when Megan got home. When she heard about the plan she kicked off her soccer cleats and hurled them out the front door so they disappeared into the dark. Megan's too neat to get mud on the floor, even in a rage. She screamed, "I have no privacy in this house! Ever. Ever. Ever. Ever. Ever." She's thirteen.

"I understand," I told her, which is one of the things Dr. Riordan, the online psychologist I've been writing to about Megan, told me to say.

"You don't understand," she bellowed, "or you wouldn't have that cot next to my bed!"

"Megan, two prisoners escaped—"

"Oh, right. Like *you're* going to protect us?" She stood there with a hand on her skinny hip and it was my own face looking back at me, my young face, green-eyed and pretty. The venom and hatred I saw there was frightening, but I didn't react. Dr. Riordan says I need to let Megan express anger and show that I can take it.

When I heard Gabby sob, I snapped. "You've terrified your sister, you little bitch," I told Megan, then felt sick hearing myself.

I leaned over Gabby and put my face in her long, heavy hair, which is jet black and smells like apples. There's a sweetness still in Gabby that Megan lost years ago. Every day I feel like I'm holding myself around that sweetness, trying to protect it.

"I thought it would be fun," she sobbed.

"It will be fun," I said.

Megan had stormed into their bedroom. Through the walls I heard her burrowing into her private corner, which is a folding screen she bought and curled around one window. On the outside the screen is plain white, but inside it's a whole collage of her life: pictures of her friends, straw wrappers woven into a braid, a purple feather, a troll doll with green hair, a sparkling mask, some dried-out daisies. Gabby's under strict orders not to go into Megan's corner, but the person Megan really wants to keep out is me; she's shielding her life from me because she thinks if I touch it, it will shrivel and die like mine did.

Megan was still in her corner, elbows on the windowsill, when Gabby and I got into bed. Gabby sleeps with Measles, the bear Seth gave her when she had the measles long ago. We forgot to have her vaccinated.

I lay awake a long time. Eventually Seth came home. He was working double shifts, which meant he was clean for the moment. I heard a beer pop, the TV come on. Megan crept out of the dark bedroom and went to him. I heard them talking, and the anger came up in me. Why him? What had he ever done for her? And then I thought about Dr. Riordan, whose e-mails I've read so many times I've memorized them: "Megan has many things to be angry about. It may seem unfair that she feels more intimacy with her father, but the betrayal she felt as a result of your drug use was probably much greater." And that was true. Lying there, I told myself: What I feel is meaningless. My job, my only job, is to keep these girls safe and healthy so their lives can mean something. It helped me to think that way. I imagined myself dissolving into nothing, or not nothing but a kind of liquid sap that would fill up my girls and give them a chance and also the focus and confidence to take that chance, unlike me. If I can do that, really do that, I told myself, I can die without regrets. I'm thirty-three.

Our baby, Corey, was red and very small, about the size of a hand. He looked scalded. You could see he shouldn't be out in the world. Can't we put him back? I asked that question several times. Isn't there a way to put him back? No one even answered me.

He had a tight little face, a shrunken face like a mummy dug up after centuries. The pain of thousands of years was in it.

I would sit there, watching him through the glass. He moved like a boiled hand, opening and closing weakly. "We need to turn him," the nurses would tell me, and I'd move away.

I only took a bump when I couldn't move or care for the other two without it. I'd think, Just a little one, just enough to get them to school, and I'd take the bump and feel the baby clench up in me.

After Corey died, I was in a psychiatric hospital for months. I just want to die, I'd say, and they'd tell me, You have two girls who need you. And you're clean, you've kicked your habit and your whole life is still ahead of you.

I told my mother, "The doctors say I have to forgive myself

or I can't go on. So I'm trying to do that." And my mother said, "Forgiving yourself is one thing. Getting God to forgive you is something else."

The prison-teaching gig came to me through the college. It was a huge opportunity because I'd only just started my master's and I wasn't qualified to teach yet, but they fudged that to give me the chance, because they needed someone. The money was great—hazard pay, they called it. And I thought, If I can teach someone else how to write, maybe that will mean I can do it myself.

When I got my list of students I showed it to my cousin Calgary, who's been a CO at the prison for years. He started to tell me about them. Melvin Williams: "Big, stupid guy," he said. "Found religion and all that." Thomas Harrington: "Smart. Works with reptiles. A meth freak like you." Hamad Samid: "Keep an eye on that one. He's a Muslim." Samuel Lawd: "They turned him gay. The big black guys pass him around." Allan Beard: "Oh yeah, the professor. They caught him with an airplane hangar full of pot." But I stopped him there. I didn't want to know their crimes. It would prejudice me against them.

When he got to Raymond Michael Dobbs, Cal said, "He's nothing. Trash."

"What do you mean, trash?"

"He's just—trash. That's all he is."

This pissed me off, I don't know why. "Trash is something sitting in a trash can," I said.

"That's where you're gonna be teaching, darling, in a great big trash can." And maybe Cal was thinking it or maybe it was just me: *Then I'll fit right in.*

I got to my class the first night and there they were: the trash. Looking huge at their desks. Most of them seemed edgy, curious, but not Ray Dobbs. He was lean, with thick dark hair. Handsome. But his blue eyes were dead.

I gave him an assignment: Write a story three pages long. And he came back the next week and read out the vilest shit about fucking his teacher. All of them were howling and I was really scared, knowing if I lost control of the class there'd be no getting it back. And that gave me an adrenaline surge that was the tiniest bit like getting high.

So I started to talk. And as Ray Dobbs listened to me I saw something open up behind his eyes like a camera shutter when the picture shoots. It made goose bumps rise up all over me because *I'd* done that; I'd made that happen just by talking. It felt intimate, like something physical between us.

After that I could feel Ray watching me. It made me alert, like someone had scrubbed mint all over my skin. I'd walk into that stinking, miserable prison and for the next three hours, a wise and beautiful woman would float out of the wreckage of my life, and her words and thoughts and tiniest movements were precious.

I tried not to look at him. I was afraid he'd see I wasn't a teacher or a writer; I had no credentials to be standing there. And I didn't want him to know. It would ruin everything.

I bought new clothes. People noticed at work. Before I started at the prison, Calgary had told me clearly: "Piece of advice: don't go in there looking like anything. It isn't even the prisoners, they know better, but if you get all dolled up the staff will hate you." So I never wore any of it to class. But I was doing it for him.

One day, I invented a reason to meet Calgary at the end of his shift and take him to Home Depot to help me look for shelves. It was crazy—I actually took a half day off work to do this, knowing my chance of seeing Ray was infinitesimal and that even if I did somehow glimpse him, we couldn't speak.

And when the day came there was Ray, right by the entrance. Months of planning couldn't have made it turn out any better. And even though I never looked at him directly, just walked through the sun into the prison to meet Calgary, that encounter was the equivalent, in the real world, of going to a movie, holding hands through dinner, coming home, making love, waking up, and doing it all over again. I'd forgotten what that kind of love felt like. Right then was when I knew how deep this thing with Ray had gone, how there was no getting out.

Gabby and I are eating supper and she's telling me about the pregnant guinea pig in her science class when I look out the window and see the state police car come up the road. Gabby hears it and jumps onto her feet and runs to the screen door, and then the joy just falls right out of her. "Mommy," she says.

Pete gets to the door first. "We didn't want to bother you at work again," he says. He's acting formal in a way that tells me something is about to happen that I'm not going to like. Gabby stands so close to me I can hear her breathing. Thank God, Megan's at soccer practice.

They come in, squeaking in their uniforms or boots or whatever it is about cops that always squeaks. "Sergeant Rufus has some information we wanted to run by you," Pete says.

"Okay." The coffeemaker grumbles and spits behind me. I feel Gabby's cheek on my arm and my heart speeds up, but what am I scared of? I don't even know.

Rufus starts in, standing right in the middle of the room. "The visitor's log shows you made a visit to the prison on a day when you weren't teaching, a day when visiting isn't even allowed."

"It wasn't a visit. I was picking up my cousin Calgary. He's a CO there."

"He has a vehicle of his own, doesn't he?" Rufus says.

"So?"

"So why pick him up?"

"Because that's the plan we made, okay? Is that against the law?"

Pete's pink skin is wincing up around his eyes. Gabby holds my arm.

"Did you see inmate Dobbs at any time during your visit?"

I hesitate. And once I've done that I know I have to answer yes. "He was working outside with some other prisoners when I came in."

I think Rufus is disappointed I've answered honestly, and that calms me down. Keep it together. They don't know anything—there's nothing to know! I keep wanting to glance out the window at the place where Ray's manuscript is buried, but I stop myself. It's not what they're looking for, but they'd take it.

"Did you greet the prisoner?" Rufus asks.

"No."

"Did you acknowledge at any later point that you'd seen him?"

"Yes. I told him I'd seen him."

"He tell you what kind of work he was doing out there?"

"No."

"Well, I'll tell you right now: he was working on *the exact pipe he and Davis would later escape through*," Rufus says. "That's what he was doing." He drains the coffee I've poured him and sets down the cup.

"I didn't know that."

"Of all days you choose to come to the prison outside of work," Rufus says, "it happens to be that day, when he's paving the way for his escape. And you come to the prison for a reason that doesn't sound like much of a reason to me."

"I told you why." My mouth is dry. I look at Pete. "Please tell me what you want."

"We'd like to look around the house," Pete says. "With your permission. We don't have a search warrant—"

"But we can get one." Rufus jumps in. "We have probable cause."

"We *may* be able to get it. And you know, Holly, those types of searches aren't too respectful of personal property."

Oh yes, I know. As in: breaking, smashing, slitting open pillows and mattresses. As in, your home will never be the same.

"Okay," I say. "But please, be careful in the girls' room."

Rufus is already making a beeline down the hall to our bedroom, where the door is closed. That's when I realize they think that Ray is actually in my house. Which makes it seem possible for a second, and just thinking of that fills me with longing. I hug Gabby to me.

When they get to the girls' room, I dash in after them. "That little screen over by the window," I say, "be careful over there, okay?" I look at my watch. Megan will be back in forty-five minutes.

In the front room, Gabby's kneeling on the couch, looking out the window. I sit down next to her and say, "Hey."

She doesn't answer. There's a blankness to her face that reminds me of Megan.

Rufus sticks his head out of the girls' room. "What's this bed between the other beds?"

"That's where I sleep," I say. I almost add, *Since the break-out,* but I stop myself, thank God.

They come back out and start looking around where Gabby and I are sitting. We move to stools by the countertop where we eat. Our dinner plates are still there, the food half eaten. I wonder if giving Pete and Rufus the manuscript I've buried will stop all this, but I don't think so. I think it'll make things worse.

Gabby leans forward and rests her head on the counter between the two plates. I rub her back. Rufus is going through

Seth's tool kit, which he keeps on a shelf above the TV. He pulls something out and says, "Pete." Just the tone of his voice makes me turn and look. And even when I see what Rufus found—a bag of crystal—even when I feel the sick horror of what's about to happen because Seth broke our ironclad rule: never in the house, keep it on your body but never in the house, or we'll all be liable (but what do rules mean to junkies?), even with all that going on in my head, I keep rubbing Gabby's back because she's peaceful, and the longer that peace lasts for her the better. Even if all I can buy her is one more minute.

I look at Pete, my barometer of how things are going. He looks like he's about to puke. Rufus comes over to me, holding the bag. "Do you know what this is?" he booms out, and Gabby jerks upright, terrified.

"It looks like a bag of crystal," I say.

"Looks like? You're saying this isn't yours?"

"It's my husband's, I think. He still has a habit."

"We're going to have to take you in."

"Whoa, whoa," Pete says. "There's no reason to take *her* in."

Rufus looks at Pete in disbelief. "We just found a bag of crystal on the premises and you don't want to make an arrest?"

"It's not hers," Pete says. "It's Seth's. I know these people."

"Yeah, I know you do. You've been bending the rules from minute one trying to protect this lady. But we're officers of the law, Pete. You don't look the other way when you find a bag of crystal just because you're pals with the lady who lives there, unless you're looking to get into trouble. Which I'm not."

"Please," I say. "Please."

Pete looks like he wants to die on the spot. And then I know it's going to happen, because Pete has four kids and he can't afford trouble of any kind.

Gabby's clinging to me, begging, "Don't go, Mommy, please don't go," but something has gone dead inside me. "It'll be fine, sweetheart," I say, and I pry her arms off me. "I have to call Grandma."

I pick up the phone and dial my mother's number, praying she'll be home. It's been a long time since I've had to make a call like this.

The phone rings. Gabby starts to cry. Pete looks at Rufus and says, "You find this kind of thing fun?"

Rufus looks down at his shoes. He doesn't look like he's having any fun at all.

My mother answers.

As we're winding down the drive, I see Megan coming up from where the soccer bus lets her off. She looks thin and narrow in her red uniform. The headlights hit her and she covers her eyes and steps to the side of the road, and I watch it all move over her face: curiosity about this car driving away from our house, anxiety when she sees it's a police car. Pete rolls the window down.

"Hey, Meggie," he says.

"Hi, Mr. Konig."

"How'd you and Amy do out there tonight?"

"I'm not on Amy's team. She's varsity."

"Listen, your mom's coming in to help us with something. Shouldn't take but an hour or two."

"What about Gabby?"

"Here, talk to your mom." He rolls my window down and Megan comes over and leans in. I hide the cuffs between my legs.

"Honey, it's nothing," I say. "I just have to go in and talk to them." It feels strange not to reach up to her, but I can't let her see those cuffs.

"Okay." When she isn't being sarcastic, Megan sounds very young.

"Grandma's up there. Can you go up and meet her?"

"Okay." She turns and keeps walking.

Pete and Rufus take me to the county jail and hand me over to corrections. At that point I'm officially out of their hands. It's evening, and no judge is on duty, so I'll have to spend the night in jail and go to court in the morning. I'll be late to work, if I get there at all.

I've been to this jail before, but always high, so this feels like the first time. A female CO takes me into a little room and leaves the door open. She makes me strip and toss my clothes on a bench. Naked, I have to bend over and spread my cheeks. At that point I sort of leave my body the way I did in the kitchen with Gabby; I think, this isn't me. This ass isn't mine, and all these parts of me spread out in front of this lady don't belong to me. I hear a new sound and when I drop my head and look between my legs I see two male COs standing behind the lady, taking in the view. This isn't me, I think. We're all just looking at each other through a window.

"Now squat and hop up and down," the lady says.

"What?"

"You heard me. I asked you to squat and hop."

"Why?"

"Are you refusing?"

"I'm asking why."

"I'm not here to answer your questions."

As soon as I start squat-hopping, I know why: so any contraband I might have hidden inside me will pop out. My breasts are flopping and I can feel sweat dripping from my underarms onto the floor. I'm terrified that something bad will come out of me, some awful thing I don't even know is there. I want to stop so it won't come out, but the lady keeps telling me to hop, maybe because she feels my worry, maybe to punish me for asking a question, maybe to keep the guys behind her entertained. So I keep hopping.

As a little kid I made up stories; they bubbled up in me like something that couldn't be stopped. There was a voice in my head all the time, whispering. We had a secret, the voice and I: I was one of the ones who would go away and do things that everyone back home would know about. There weren't many of those around here, but there were a few—an ice skater, a comedian—and when they came home to visit, everyone buzzed about what bar or church party they were supposedly going to. My teachers thought I was special. And my mother. My green-eyed girl, she called me.

My first mistake was being in a hurry. I grabbed for what was in front of me: marrying Seth the rock star, having a child—I'd always been special and I thought the specialness would still be there no matter what, but this other stuff might not.

And by the time I saw how really bad things were—Seth fighting with his band, disappearing for days while I scrambled to take care of two kids—by the time I realized what a pit I'd fallen into, it was too late. I had two little girls, a husband who was smoking meth, and one year of community college. I still lived twenty minutes from where I grew up.

I smoked my first pipe with Seth. I knew the stuff was bad, but I was so tired of being the cop, begging and raging at him, throwing Pampers in his face when he walked in the door. I wanted to be on the same side again. So I smoked with Seth one afternoon when the girls were napping, and oh my God, I can only think about this for a minute or every part of me will turn into a mouth wanting more: the sexiness of it, fucking Seth like wild for the first time in months, going on even when the girls started to whimper and bang on the door. Then looking out the window and seeing the world shake itself to life: the heavy trees, the sky. And I was back on top. We were going to make it, Seth and I. The voice in my head was back again, telling me stories, too many to write down or even tell one from another.

And after all the horrors, the searches and arrests, after losing Corey and those dark blank months in the hospital, after all that I was just relieved to be alive and clean and have my children back, the two that were left to me. I moved carefully, like the world was made of glass. I got the job at the college and finished my BA and started a master's in writing. But even with all that, which I was grateful for and knew full well I didn't deserve, I can't exactly say I was happy. Relieved, yes. Lucky, God yes. All that. But I thought happiness only came from getting high, and I was never doing that again, never, even if it meant not being happy one more day in my life.

And then Ray brought it back. The excitement that rocks through your body when you're a kid like lust does when you're grown up: just pure excitement—for Christmas, for grape Kool-Aid, for playing in a treehouse—I felt that all week long as my teaching night got close. I started reading again, finishing a novel every few days. On my lunch break I'd sit outside at my picnic bench and listen to the traffic, those big loops of sound, and behind it I'd hear something else, barely there, so shadowy I tried not to scare it away by paying too much attention, but I knew the voice was back.

The next morning I'm arraigned before the judge with my court-appointed lawyer. Pete is there. He tells the prosecutor that the meth isn't mine, that they found it in Seth's toolbox and that it's only an eighth of an ounce. The judge dismisses the case and I go home to shower and change before work.

That night, I fold up the cot and roll it out of the girls' room. It's been a month since Ray escaped, and I know he's gone. If he were still around, they would have caught him.

A depression comes on me suddenly, like a blanket I can't get out from underneath. It's summer now, and I barely can get the girls to camp. At work I lay my head on my desk if no one's around. I hear my computer clicking, the shouts of summer school students, distant phones. I lie very still and watch the colors behind my eyes. When footsteps come near my cubicle, I sit up and put my hands on the keyboard.

On weekends I can't get out of bed. My face puffs out and the girls are scared to look at me. I lie on the cot in the room I share with Seth. Sometimes Gabby comes in and lies next to me. I know I'm doing damage just by lying there, bringing more unhappiness on her. But I can't move.

"I want you to feel better," Gabby says.

I hold her in my arms. The effort of it makes me breathe hard. I want to say I'm sorry, but I know that's pure selfishness— asking her to forgive me.

"I love you so much, my little girl," I say. "Do you know?"

She nods.

"Do you really know?"

"Yeah, I know."

Which is something, I guess. Megan doesn't come in, and I don't blame her.

Finally my mother shows up—the girls must have called her. I'm dreading what she'll say, but she puts a hand on my forehead and holds it there. Her cool fingers feel so good, I close my eyes. "You need to get away," she says.

"Away?"

She takes her hand off my forehead to adjust one of the ivory combs she always wears in her wild gray hair. "To replenish yourself for a few days," she says. "I'll be happy to take the girls if you can think of a place you'd like to go."

"I can't leave them," I say. "I've already done that enough."

One day at work, while I'm eating lunch at my desk (no energy to walk into the heat), I google *hotel* and *castle* and *Europe* and start looking at the little pictures that come up on the screen. One site leads to another site like you're falling through trap-doors. I'm thinking, How can there be so many castles? They always say Europe is small, so I guess in my mind there wouldn't be enough room for all of them.

Somewhere along the way I notice a hotel called the Keep. The picture shows a castle with towers. I click on its website and a little slide show starts up: a castle with gold sunlight on it, then a long square tower, then an ancient-looking map showing a maze of underground tunnels. Then a big round swimming pool.

I push my chair away from my desk and put my head between my knees. I'm afraid I've gotten high without realizing it. I go back through my day to make sure I haven't smoked a pipe.

When I sit back up, the slide show is still playing: castle, tower, map, pool. It's Howard's castle—Ray's castle. The same place. And then I start to laugh. It's a weak laugh, full of relief. Because all the time I was reading Ray's story, week after week, I never believed that the castle existed.

Map, pool, castle, tower.

I found him. Or he found me.

I didn't think a hotel could be so expensive—to pay for two nights plus airfare, I have to cash in part of my 401K. I make the arrangements without ever believing I'll actually go. I have vacation days left at work, and my mother makes good on her promise to take the girls. When the plans are all in place and I'm supposed to leave in a week, the truth of it hits me. The whole thing seems wild, self-indulgent, not allowed. I can still get back my deposit on the hotel, although the plane ticket is nonrefundable. When I call my mother, she won't even listen. "You're going," she says. "That's it. Now go." I get the feeling traveling overseas to foreign countries is the sort of life she used to imagine for me.

When I drop off the girls at my mother's house, Gabby hugs and kisses me and Megan leaves the car without a word. Then, as I'm driving away, she runs back out of the house. I stop, but already Megan's slowing down, and it takes her a while to get to the car. "Did you forget something?" I ask.

She doesn't answer. There's a tiny gold locket around her neck, but who gave it to her is anyone's guess. It's high summer now, cicadas chattering in the trees. Finally Megan says, "You're coming back, right?"

"Megan!" I say, and she starts to cry. It's been a long time since I've seen her cry. She's like me in that way: dry.

I lift up my arms and kiss her through the window.

I take a commuter plane to New York and catch an overnight flight to Paris. A feeling of unreality sets in at the John F. Kennedy Airport. It's been years since I got on an airplane. I had to buy a suitcase; all we had were the old canvas bags we used to pile everything into when Seth was touring with the band.

I have a window seat. When we take off, the city lights look like embers. I have a feeling of shock; if I'd only realized that all this was going on—planes taking off and landing, cities looking like embers—I would never have fallen so deep inside my life.

The hotel sent me a packet of stuff I haven't had time to open in the rush of getting out. Or maybe I'm saving it. The envelope is really a flat shallow box made of creamy paper. When I break the seal I smell vanilla, spice. Inside the box are a few square cards printed with brown ink on that same creamy paper. The first one says:

> Anticipation: You are almost here. Which means you're on the verge of an experience that will send you home a slightly different person than the one you are right now.

I laugh out loud, but I'm intrigued. What the hell do they mean?

Another card:

> The Keep is an electronics- and telecommunications-free environment. Close your eyes, breathe deeply: you can do it. We have a secure vault, where all your gadgetry may be stored when you arrive. This ritual of renunciation is important. If you feel the urge to thwart it, pay attention. You may not be ready.

And another:

> Apart from the live medieval music at dinnertime in the Great Hall, we provide no formal entertainment at the Keep. That's your job. We trust you. Now trust yourself.

I find myself turning to the guy next to me, who's already cocooned inside his blue airline blanket with a sleep mask over his eyes. There has to be someone to share this joke with me! I scan the airplane, row after row, and wait for a set of eyes to look back at me with knowing, with understanding. Because I'm not alone. I know that. I've felt it ever since I saw the Keep on my computer screen.

We land at 5:30 a.m. in a smoky sunrise. I haven't slept. My view of Paris is mostly baggage handlers pulling suitcases off our plane and babbling in their wonderful language.

Another plane to Prague, then a train. We pull out through a poor section of the city, children waving to us as we pass. Finally I go to sleep.

I wake up in a different world. Mountains, trees. Little cottages with wood beams on the outside. Where am I? Where are my girls? I freeze in my seat, feeling I've done something horribly wrong, abandoned them, risked their lives. It takes some minutes to calm myself down. And then I have an odd thought: that none of this is real, that I'm still back home with my girls. Everything is exactly the same as always, but in some other dimension a part of me has broken off and is having this dream.

Later, the conductor taps me on the shoulder. I've nodded off again. The train groans and sighs pulling into the station. When I get off, I'm surprised by how cold the air is. A thin blond guy named Jasper is there to meet me, and he takes my suitcase. We come out of the train station into a valley surrounded by narrow pointed hills. The castle looks down from the one directly ahead of us, gold-brown and majestic in the sun, and maybe it's exactly the way I imagined or maybe it erased whatever was in my mind before I saw it. But looking up at it, I think: *yes!*

We take a gondola from the valley. As we glide over thick cables, I look down and see that a lot of the trees are already bare. When I look back up we're swooping toward the mountain as if we're about to smash right into it. I shut my eyes.

Jasper says, "Is scary, yes?"

"It is," I say.

A big iron gate, two towers. A side door leading inside. All of it so familiar it's like I'm coming back for the second time. Did Ray do such a perfect job of describing it? I'm not really sure. I loved what he wrote because he wrote it, because he'd touched the pages, because it gave us a way to have a conversation. I tried not to ask if it was any good.

The lobby is fancy, hushed, its craggy stone walls exaggerated by tiny bright lights pointing up from the floor. The couple checking in ahead of me is wealthy; even their skin looks expensive. The woman glances at me for a second, and I'm relieved when she looks away.

I put my electronics in a silver box, which I lock and keep the key. In my case, it was only a hair dryer.

Jasper walks me up a curved staircase to my room. He tells me about this castle: how the keep was built first, in the twelfth century. Then the rest of the castle in the thirteenth and fourteenth centuries. In the eighteenth century, it was converted into a family estate.

A fluttering in my chest. It feels like soap bubbles. I can't concentrate.

My room might as well have been Danny's room: high ceiling, a bed with a velvet curtain, fireplace with a burning log in it, little pointed windows. Outside I see the keep, square and narrow, rising above the trees.

I lie down and feel the mattress give under me. I open up a second envelope box they gave me downstairs and find more of those creamy vanilla cards.

> Forget about getting dressed. We've provided loose, comfortable clothing that looks the same rain or shine, day or night, no matter who wears it, so you can look at other things.

Our premises are absolutely secure. You may go wherever you wish, day or night. If you need light (especially important in the tunnels) just ask. Our staff is plentiful and, we hope, unobtrusive.

Be mindful of the fact that other guests may be using a space at the same time you are. Remember—you're here to talk to yourself, not each other. There is no need for greetings or even eye contact. You have the rest of your life for that.

I fall asleep. When I wake up the fire's gone out, leaving the room cold, and my clothes feel sweaty and foul.

I take a long hot shower. I comb out my hair and let it hang. I put on the outfit they've left for me, which is like a sweatsuit except it's made out of cashmere, which means it's unbelievably soft. There's a pair of puffy rubber-soled boots. I notice my chest fluttering again. The soap bubbles. I picture them overflowing the tight little pot of my heart.

There has to be a word for the feeling that comes from seeing a place you've imagined and having it fulfill your expectations. But I don't know it. I follow a hall lined with electric candles to a curved stairwell that winds down to a set of glass doors opening onto the garden. White shell paths gleam out through the dense green. There are small signs pointing the way to various places, but I don't really need them. The keep is straight ahead of me.

Around the bottom of the keep, the bushes and trees have been cleared away. A woman sits cross-legged on bright green grass and a man stands near her, shielding his eyes from the sun. Neither one looks at me, and for a second I feel insulted, invisible. Then the feeling passes. They're dressed exactly like me.

Walking up the outdoor stairs, I have another impulse to use that unknown word. The rubbery soles of my boots grip the stone like suckers, and I rise up over the trees.

The door to the keep is heavy. My heart pounds as I push it open. There's a second door, just like I expected, and beyond that is the room where Danny met the baroness: gold, shiny, heavy draperies next to tiny windows, a purple-orange sunset pouring in from outside. The lack of a word to describe the matching up of this place with my expectations is starting to hurt. So I pick one. I pick Danny's word, *alto,* and I give it my own definition. *Alto:* when things are exactly the way you imagine they'll be.

There's a fireplace with a burning log, a brocaded couch, a shiny wood table in the shape of an oval. Alto, alto, alto. I go to the windows and look out, my back to the door. My hands shake on the windowsill. I don't tell myself what I'm waiting for, but of course I know.

I stand there and wait. The anticipation is so intense I feel I can't sustain it. That it will break me. *Now* and *now* and *now.*

Now!

I hear a sound and turn. The room is empty but the air quivers against my arms. Like a ghost has come in.

"Ray," I whisper.

No sound. The logs shift in the fireplace.

"Ray."

I go to the door and open it, then the second door. I look down the outdoor stairs and over the trees at the horizon. "Ray," I call, but the wind has come up and it blows my voice to pieces.

"Ray! Ray! Ray!" Suddenly I'm hollering, because he has to be here. He must be; otherwise I've spent all that money and left my girls and come all this way for nothing.

I call his name until my voice gets weak. I go back inside the keep and lie down on the brocade couch. I'm overwhelmed by the purest sadness I can remember in my life—not like Corey, where the sadness was mixed up with guilt, responsibility—this is just loss. Pure loss. I know Ray is gone, and I'll never see him again.

I start to cry. I lie there, sobbing into the cushions. A couple of times I hear the door open, but I don't look up. I know it's not Ray. It's other people in cashmere sweatsuits who leave as soon as they see me.

Eventually I stop. I lie there while darkness fills up the room. The only light is from the fireplace. And then I hear a bell. It ripples in through the windows, a clear beautiful sound. It rings five times, each one like a silver wave rolling onto a dark beach.

After the bell stops ringing I hear movement, as though the keep has suddenly come to life. I even feel it: a rustling behind the walls, doors pushing open, the whispery sound of feet as people move down from the top of the keep through all those internal stairwells and begin passing outside through the doors on the floor where I am.

Dinnertime.

I lie there, empty from crying, and listen to the movements of people walking. And even though I don't want to eat or listen to live medieval music, I find myself getting up off my couch and leaving the room. I join the stream of people in beige cashmere sweats and move with them back down the outdoor staircase.

At the base of the keep, the group follows a white shell path toward the castle. I go a different way. The air is sharply cold on my hands and face, but the cashmere keeps the rest of me warm. The sunset is an orange tear at the bottom of a solid gray sky.

Hotel employees are lighting candles along the paths, each one inside a glass globe. *Alto.* I know where I'm going as if I remember it.

The wall of cypress. An opening lit by a lantern. I squeeze

through, and the beauty of the pool rocks through me like the
bell did—it's huge and round, lit from under the surface. The
water is pale green. The white marble around it turns the whole
area bright, as though it's earlier in the day. A few people sit
along the edge of the pool in thick beige bathrobes. Some are in
the water. I've stopped looking at faces, so I don't know how old
they are, if they're male or female. Off to one side is a cloth tent.

The air hurts my fingers, and I pull my hands inside the
sleeves of my sweater. Cold skims steam off the top of the pool,
and it whirls and dissolves like dozens of mini-twisters. It's getting darker by the second, but that globe of light around the pool
lasts and lasts, like a bubble you know will break, can't believe
hasn't already broken, but there it is, intact.

The last time I saw Ray, it was a formal prison visit. I wasn't
teaching anymore, which made it easier to drive up, park, go in,
and give my name. The guard knew me.

Because I wasn't on Ray's list of preapproved visitors, I'd
had to arrange things ahead of time through Calgary, getting an
earful every step of the way: "Look, Holly, I don't know and I
don't want to know, know what I'm saying?" and "It's got nothing to do with me, but people are talking, okay?"

I told him, "He almost died. I want to see him again."

"Like I said, it's your life, know what I'm saying?"

And so on.

I sat in a yellow chair and waited in the noisy visiting room,
which was full of tired dolled-up little kids and the smell of
vending-machine nachos heating in the microwave. Twenty minutes later, Ray came in. His hair was longer and he looked tan,
but maybe that was just compared to how pale he'd been in the
hospital. I saw him and it was all still there between us, without
a word being spoken. He sat down on a chair across from me
and said, "You look beautiful."

"I can't believe you're alive," I said.

"Me either," he said, and laughed. "Wasn't my turn, I guess."

"I'm glad," I said. "I'm so glad."

We were quiet. It wasn't uncomfortable, exactly. It felt like we were in the real world, on the outside or as close to it as we'd ever been. I could imagine us getting up and walking out of there together.

Ray moved and sat next to me. "You took a risk," he said, "coming here like this."

"I had to."

It went on like that, little comments with a lot of silence in between, and the silence seemed more powerful than all the rest.

A half hour, I'd told myself. I let it drag to forty-five minutes. "I should go," I said.

"One thing."

I leaned back in my chair.

"That stuff I wrote," Ray said. "I know it was shit."

And when I tried to protest that it wasn't shit, it was just rough, it needed work like everything does, it was a beginning, *blah blah blah,* he pushed a finger to my lips. It was the first time he'd touched me.

"I want to give it to you," he said. "Not that it's good, we've covered that. But maybe you can make something out of it."

In his eyes and face I saw that hope, that belief in me that had filled up my life all those months. But class was over now.

He was watching my face. "Or not. It doesn't matter. But I wrote it for you."

"Keep it," I said.

He looked startled. "Why?"

"I can't write," I said. "You're better off holding on to it."

"I don't believe you."

"I'm sorry," I said, because the need to confess was welling up in me, I couldn't stop it. "I was your teacher under false pretenses. I'm not even qualified."

"Crap." He sounded angry.

"I'm telling you this so you don't do anything stupid," I said. "I'm not a writer. Or a teacher."

"I know who you are," Ray said.

I looked down at my hands. They were shaking, and the nails were bitten. I should have given myself a manicure. There was a long pause, and then Ray took my bitten-up hands in his hands. It was hard to believe they were the same hands I'd held in the hospital—those had been hot and damp and swollen. Now his hands were strong, cool. Healthy hands. He got well, I thought.

"Holly," he said, and when I looked up he was smiling again. He's happy, I thought. I've never seen him happy before. "Don't you get it?" he said. "You're free."

We watched each other. I thought, It sounds like he's saying goodbye. Why, when I'm the one leaving?

In the cabana, an older lady gives me a black one-piece swimming suit and a thick terry-cloth robe. There are private changing cubicles with canvas walls and full-length mirrors. I watch myself change into the swimsuit. Thirty-three years of wear and tear, but there I am.

When I come back out, it's dark except for the big green circle of swimming pool. The cold bites at my fingers and calves and feet. I stand there listening, because a new sound has started up, like thousands of tiny glass pieces breaking above and below and all around me. I turn my face to the sky and then I feel it, bits of cold on my face: snow. In the total quiet of this place, I can hear snow falling through the air and landing on the marble. A trillion invisible clicks.

The steam on the pool is thicker now, like spinning bales of white hay. I can barely see the people underneath it.

And I don't know if it's the snow, or the night, or that pale green water, or something else that's separate from all that, but as I walk to the edge of the pool I'm filled with an old, childish excitement. I wait, letting the snow fall and melt on my hair and face and feet. I let the excitement build until it floods my chest.

I close my eyes and dive in.

Acknowledgments

My massive thanks to those who have listened, read, calmed, housed, inspired, informed, and otherwise aided me while I worked on *The Keep:* David Herskovits, Amanda Urban, Jennifer Smith, Jordan Pavlin, Lisa Fugurd, Kay Kimpton, Don Lee, Monica Adler, David Rosenstock, Genevieve Field, Ruth Danon, Elizabeth Tippens, Peggy Reed, Julie Mars, David Hogan, Alexander Busansky, and the Dorothy and Lewis B. Cullman Center for Scholars and Writers at the New York Public Library.

"*Egan goes deeper, surprising us again and again. [She] limns the mysteries of human identity and the strangle-hold our image-obsessed culture has on us all in this complicated and wildly ambitious novel.*"
—Newsweek

LOOK AT ME

At the start of this edgy and ambitiously multilayered novel, a fashion model named Charlotte Swenson emerges from a car accident in her Illinois hometown with her face so badly shattered that it takes eighty titanium screws to reassemble it. She returns to New York still beautiful but oddly unrecognizable, a virtual stranger in the world she once effortlessly occupied. With the surreal authority of a David Lynch film, Jennifer Egan threads Charlotte's narrative with those of other casualties of our infatuation with the image. There's a deceptively plain teenaged girl embarking on a dangerous secret life, an alcoholic private eye, and an enigmatic stranger who changes names and accents as he prepares an apocalyptic blow against American society. As these narratives inexorably converge, Look at Me becomes a coolly mesmerizing intellectual thriller of identity and imposture.

Fiction/978-0-385-72135-6

ANCHOR BOOKS
Available at your local bookstore, or visit www.randomhouse.com.